Acclaim for Nicole Seitz

"*The Inheritance of Beauty* is an illuminating story that juxtaposes youth and old age, innocence and guilt and the murky depths of memory brightened by the piercing light of truth. Nicole Seitz is a fresh voice in fiction."

—MARY ALICE MONROE, *NEW YORK TIMES*
BEST-SELLING AUTHOR OF *THE BUTTERFLY'S DAUGHTER*

"[*The Inheritance of Beauty* is a] tender tale of childhood secrets and lifelong ties, from a skilled writer who understands the beauty of enduring love. George and Maggie will make you want to learn your own family stories!"

—LISA WINGATE, NATIONAL BESTSELLING AUTHOR
OF *LARKSPUR COVE* AND *THE SUMMER KITCHEN*

"In *The Inheritance of Beauty*, Seitz has skillfully brought life, depth, and beauty to an often forgotten part of society, reminding readers of the power in strong bonds of love and friendship, the weight of memory and childhood, and the significance of reckoning with the past. Through the voices of an intimate group of individuals brought together in an elderly center, a haunting story unfolds with striking fluidity and the underlying presence of spirituality. Seitz has weaved into the lines of this moving page-turner a mysterious tale of healing, wrought with a sweet touch of southern warmness that truly speaks to the soul."

—NONI CARTER, AUTHOR OF *GOOD FORTUNE*

"Nicole Seitz joins a long line of distinguished novelists who celebrate the rich culture of the Lowcountry of South Carolina . . . She joins Josephine Humphries, Anne Rivers Siddons, Sue Monk Kidd, and Dorothea Benton Frank in her fascination with the Gullah culture. Her character, Essie Mae Laveau Jenkins, is worth the price of admission to *The Spirit of Sweetgrass*."

—PAT CONROY, BESTSELLING AUTHOR OF
THE PRINCE OF TIDES AND *SOUTH OF BROAD*

"This beautifully written, imaginative story of love and redemption is the must-read book of the year. The ending is so surprising and powerful that it will linger long after the last page is turned."

—CASSANDRA KING, BESTSELLING AUTHOR OF
THE SAME SWEET GIRLS, REGARDING *A HUNDRED YEARS OF HAPPINESS*

"An unforgettable novel about sisterhood, salvation, and miracles."

—KARIN GILLESPIE, AUTHOR OF *DOLLAR DAZE*, REGARDING *TROUBLE THE WATER*

"Seitz has a gift for creating wonderful characters . . . marvelously memorable."

—*PUBLISHERS WEEKLY* REVIEW OF *SAVING CICADAS*

"Nicole Seitz takes the loose threads of her characters' lives and ties them together in a vibrant pattern of love, forgiveness and truth. In words that resonate with emotion, Seitz writes of things that are only understood with the heart."

—PATTI CALLAHAN HENRY,
BESTSELLING AUTHOR OF *DRIFTWOOD SUMMER*

". . . A surprisingly creative tale that will leave readers guessing until the end."

—RIVER JORDAN, AUTHOR OF *SAINTS IN LIMBO*, REGARDING *SAVING CICADAS*

"Her words are magic. Pure magic."

—TIM CALLAHAN, AUTHOR OF *KENTUCKY SUMMERS:*
THE CAVE, THE CABIN, AND THE TATTOO MAN

The INHERITANCE *of* BEAUTY

Other novels by Nicole Seitz include

The Spirit of Sweetgrass
Trouble the Water
A Hundred Years of Happiness
Saving Cicadas

The
INHERITANCE
of BEAUTY

A Novel

NICOLE
SEITZ

THOMAS NELSON

Since 1798

NASHVILLE DALLAS MEXICO CITY RIO DE JANEIRO

Published in Nashville, Tennessee, by Thomas Nelson. Thomas Nelson is a registered trademark of Thomas Nelson, Inc.

Thomas Nelson, Inc., titles may be purchased in bulk for educational, business, fund-raising, or sales promotional use. For information, please e-mail SpecialMarkets@ThomasNelson.com.

Scripture quotations are taken from HOLY BIBLE: NEW INTERNATIONAL VERSION®. © 1973, 1978, 1984 by International Bible Society. Used by permission of Zondervan Publishing House. All rights reserved.

Publisher's Note: This novel is a work of fiction. Names, characters, places, and incidents are either products of the author's imagination or used fictitiously. All characters are fictional, and any similarity to people living or dead is purely coincidental.

Library of Congress Cataloging-in-Publication Data

Seitz, Nicole A.
    The inheritance of beauty : a novel / Nicole Seitz.
        p. cm.
    ISBN 978-1-59554-504-6 (pbk.)
    1. Older people—Fiction. 2. Family secrets—Fiction. 3. Beauty, Personal—Fiction. 4. Life change events—Fiction. I. Title.
    PS3619.E426I54 2011
    813'.6—dc22

                                        2010043998

Printed in the United States of America

11 12 13 14 15 16 RRD 6 5 4 3 2 1

For my grandmother,
Miriam Alice Coulter Furr, and friends:

Richard Jacobus
Robert "Bob" Flanagan
Andreas "Red" Evans
Fred M. Robinson
Irene Nuite Lofton

As we grow old, the beauty steals inward.

—RALPH WALDO EMERSON

Author's Note

My grandmother was a beautiful woman, so beautiful that her candid photograph—taken at a municipal pool—adorned the front page of a 1937 *Charlotte Observer,* and eventually made its way in life-sized form to the 1939 New York World's Fair. I've always wondered whose eyes might have seen that photograph, who may have been inspired by her beauty. I have the original, but the life-sized portrait, to my knowledge, has never been found.

I went to visit my grandmother in her nursing home a couple weeks before she passed away in 2009 at the age of ninety-one. She was still beautiful, and although she could no longer speak to me and could not open her eyes, I perched on my knees at the foot of her wheelchair and told her how much I loved her, thanked her for all the incredible things she'd done for me and my family over the years. All the sacrifices. All the prayers. After a while, my grandmother leaned forward, eyes still closed, smelling so sweet, so clean, so beautiful, and she pressed her forehead against my own and rubbed it back and forth ever so slightly. She was communicating with me the only way she could. She was loving me till the very last moment, me and every one of her children, grandchildren, and great grandchildren.

Author's Note

This is a book about beauty and age, about the blessings and curses of each, and how the true beauty of a person—on the inside—never fades.

May you know a love, a beauty, like this in your lifetime.

PROLOGUE

Her

LEVY, 1929

I am seven years old, holding the magician's wand, cool and silver in my hands. My breath is hot against the canvas bust of Mama's dressmaker's dummy. I'm inside of it, hiding.

There is green gingham wrapped around me, around the dummy. My brother, Ash, and I play here sometimes, hide-and-seek. I can feel the metal skirt hoop and smell the musty canvas. I can hear her screaming, begging him to leave us be. There is a thump and a cry at the same time.

Then silence, nothing but the sound of my own breathing.

I don't know who's still standing, but I can feel trouble—it fills the room. Someone's looking my way. *Can he hear me breathing? Can he see my feet? Does he know I'm here?* I pull my toes in and try hard not to exhale.

I close my eyes. *Go away, go away.* Footsteps move across

1

the room, and I hear shuffling around. They come closer, painfully slow. I'm about to lose my breath. I'm seeing stars. My knees are shaking.

It's dark. I'm afraid in the dark.

I hear a sound, a short, quick scratch.

Then another, and another.

Finally, there's a *whoosh* and the footsteps are running away. I wait to be sure they're gone. I wait, I wait, but I'm getting hot. I might pass out. I open my eyes and look down at my bare feet. Orange fire is on the hem of the green gingham dress. There's fire, and all I can think is I've got to get out of here. I stand up straight and hit my head on the metal. The dummy falls over with me in it.

I wake up, looking into my brother's eyes with the blue sky and white smoke above us. He's saying to me, whimpering, "Please, Maggie, talk to me!"

I try but the words won't come.

Him

The fire dances, a great orange jack-o'-lantern high above the trees, well into the night. Every man in town is here, buckets of water in hand, sweat on their brows. The heat is nothing I've ever felt and nothing I ever hope to feel again.

The watering hole must be empty by now. I think of the fish. I think if they're frying on the burning embers of the house. I think there might not be any more fish to catch and worry how to restock Togoodoo Creek. Funny what the mind goes to at a time like this. I should be thinking about more serious matters. About the stranger and if he's dead in that fire. About her, and if she'll survive. I should be thinking these things, but my mind is not able to work it out. Instead, I will think about fish. There are enough worms to catch a whole mess of them, but now they're burning in a heap that was once a home. A happy home.

The fish swim up to the night sky in swirls of orange-white smoke, and I wish I could climb the swirls like Jack up the beanstalk, up and away from here. I have never seen a fire this big. Fires should not get this big. Maybe it'll swallow Levy.

I wish I could go back to before. *Please, God, let me go back to before I ever met him. Before the train came to town. Let the fire burn up all the time and seconds and let's just go back to before I ever heard her cry. I pray it . . . I pray it . . . I pray it . . . Amen.*

I open my eyes but the fire rages. Will she forgive me? Will she ever forget?

Can I?

ONE

Annie

It started when Miss Magnolia got this great big package in the mail on the very same day Mister Joe moved in, just a few doors down from her. At the time, I didn't put two and two together, but I know better now. Something was different about that very morning—the air was cool and crisp on an August day, the birds were quiet, and the cat was prowling some other corner of the house, not the first floor like it usually did . . . waiting for some old folk to die.

Nobody died in Harmony House that day the man come hightailing in the front door, carrying that package all in a hurry. None of us aides had ever seen anything that big, so we was all eyes, you know, wondering who it could be for. I seen it said *Mrs. Magnolia Black Jacobs*, and I remember feeling pride 'cause she was one of my own and being so surprised 'cause I never known she was a Black. In the two years I'd known her, she'd just been Mrs. Jacobs, Miss Magnolia, George's wife, to me. That package hinted she had a life before—before Harmony House, before age came and stole her away, before she ever married George Jacobs and had a family with him.

I walked with the package man back to room 101 and asked what was in it. "Don't know," he said. "Maybe some kind of painting?" It was a large, rectangular thing. The address was from New York City, but there weren't a sender's name.

I opened the door and found Mister George and Miss Magnolia still sleeping sound in their bed. It had been a rough go for them, 'specially the last six months, for Miss Magnolia losing her mind with each pin stroke, losing her independence, her ability to communicate. But for Mister George, I declare, it was even worse. For a while, his wife seemed to be forgetting everything and everybody. Even him, her husband of seventy-some years.

After the man helped me heft that package into the room, I leaned it up against the wall. I tiptoed on over to the bed, and Mister George stirred. "Goo-ood mornin', Mister George," I sang in my brightest, happiest voice, wanting to wake him with a Southern smile. He deserved some sweetness.

George

I open my eyes and see Miss Annie hovering over Maggie, her large frame blocking the sunlight, her face hard to wake up to. I've been spoiled by my lovely wife. "Good mornin'?

Sheesh, maybe for you—you got all your teeth." I reach over and fumble, trying to find my glass.

"Over to the right a little," says Annie. As I reach into the water, I realize what a stupid thing I just said. Miss Annie, the colored woman who takes care of my wife, has terrible teeth, all crooked and small and yellow, like little bits of corn left out in the field too long. And a face like a beat-up frying pan, but sweet like an angel. *Think, George, before you speak.* That part's never come easy for me, thinking. I pop my teeth in.

"Ah gee, I didn't mean . . . I'm sorry, Annie."

"For what? I ain't understood a thin' you said, what with your no-tooth self." She winks at me. "You sleep good?"

"Yeah, reckon. Fair to middlin'."

"Mornin', Miss Magnolia," Annie sings. "How we doin' today? Rise and shine. The Lawd done give us a new day together."

I turn over because I don't really know how my wife is going to react to being woken up. She doesn't know me anymore, and I'm pretty sure she doesn't know Annie either, and I just don't want to see a whole production right now. It's something that's hard to prepare for, and you never know when it might happen. Not too long ago when Maggie could still speak, Miss Annie was putting her to bed one night, and she turned and looked at me and said, "Where's he sleeping?"

"Right here, in the bed."

"With me?" said Maggie.

"Of course," said Annie.

"The hell he is."

My wife had never used a profane word in all her years,

but it's not what bothered me. I was a stranger now, just like everybody else.

Miss Annie knows enough to leave me alone every now and again. Occasionally she finds me lying on a bed of white towels in the bathtub, crusty tracks on my face from crying half the night. It's been hard. I won't lie.

I sit up slow and hang my legs off the bed, struggle to find my slippers. I rub the back of my head and my whiskers, my unshaven face. And I tell her about my dream, hoping to smooth over any unpleasantness on the other side of the bed.

"Miss Annie, last night I was young again. How 'bout that."

"That right?"

"Yes, ma'am. Old George. Dreamt I was sitting at this watering hole we used to have near the farm. I'd sit there as a boy, eight, nine, ten . . . with crickets or worms on my hook. I'd get bream on a good day, catfish any other. Sometimes we'd sell 'em at the store, Jacobs Mercantile. In this dream I had, there was somethin' on the line. It was a big somethin'. I was pullin', haulin' it in. The water was dark and I couldn't see, but I was pullin' and pullin' and pullin' and—"

"Well, what it was?"

I realize my hands are stretched out like I'm fishing, so I stop. I turn and watch Annie helping my wife sit up, the powder white of her hair like snow on her sweet little head. I miss touching that softness. I miss those shoulders, that body. I miss the woman who knew me. I miss my wife. But I'm not complaining. She's still here, see. That's more than some people can say.

"No, Annie, I never did see what it was. I woke up before I could reel it in. I tell you this though, it was somethin' mighty big. And in that dream I felt like if I could just pull that thing up from out of the water, it'd be like winnin' the lottery, like finding a pot of gold, you know?"

"Magic fishes, imagine. You find one, bring it to me, hear? Miss Annie gonna fry it up and get rich. There you go, Miss Magnolia. Give me this leg. All right. Careful now."

I could help Annie get my wife into her wheelchair. She's thirty-something years old and strong as an ox, but still, I could help her. I might be in my nineties, but I'm not useless. This morning I just don't feel like it. I can't get my mind off of that dream. I can't stop thinking what could have been under that water. Maybe tonight I can go back to sleep and figure it out, what I was supposed to pull up. Maybe there's treasure waiting for this old man, after all . . . though at this age, what in the world would I do with it?

"I brung you somethin', Miss Magnolia," says Annie as she goes to the windows and throws open the blue curtains. Yellow morning spills over everything, and I rub my eyes. I slide my feet into my slippers and hold myself propped on the edge of the bed.

"Good-looking white man drivin' a FedEx truck brung you this great big package here. All the way from New York City."

New York? I pick up my glasses and stick them on my nose. Hey diddle, she's right. The biggest box I've ever seen, long and skinny, is leaning up against the wall behind the card table. It's almost too big for our little room.

"What is it?"

"Don't know. You want me to open it?"

I tell her yes and look over at Maggie who's studying the big brown box as if Miss Annie's let a perfect stranger into the room. "There's a letter opener in that drawer there."

Annie grabs the box and attacks the edges, sliding down one seam, across another, and my heart stirs. What in the world has come for my wife? Who does she know who would ever send her anything, except for Alex or Gracie, and they could deliver it themselves if they needed to.

"Alrighty then," she says, pulling the side open and reaching in. "Wrapped it good." She pulls it out, huffing. Finally she cuts the Bubble Wrap off and there we are, Annie standing back, and me on the bed, Maggie in her wheelchair, staring at the biggest, most beautiful portrait of a young girl I've ever seen. She's lying on her stomach at a swimming pool, pushed up on her elbows, with wavy hair and full bosoms and all sorts of curves.

"You okay?" Annie asks, as I must have gasped out loud.

"I don't believe it. It . . . it's Maggie."

"Naw. Wait. Lawd have mercy, sure 'nough! I never seen a body so lovely . . . Miss Magnolia?" She crosses over to her and pushes her wheelchair to within two feet of the photograph. "You see this? This is you, ain't it? Weren't you were the prettiest thang? I swanny. Look at you!"

I watch Maggie, sitting there with her hair still uncombed and white and pink pajamas on. She studies the life-sized portrait of herself in a bathing suit. It must have been taken around the time we were married—she's only, what, seventeen or eighteen? Maggie lifts a trembling hand and puts it in her mouth. "Annie, grab her a washcloth."

She does so, and Maggie chomps down on it instead of her raw knuckles.

"How come you never told me she was such a beauty? Where's this picture from? Some magazine?"

"This is new to me . . . unless I've forgotten," I say now, low and inadequate. "Which is entirely possible. I—my goodness. No. I've never seen this photo in my life."

It dawns on me then: *There are things I still don't know about my wife.* After all these years, how can it be? But then again, there are things she still doesn't know about me either.

The thought of it all makes me want to tell Miss Annie to leave us alone awhile. I've got to study the young face of my wife. It's the pretty face that used to smile only for me. Apparently she smiled for some other creep too, somebody living in New York City now.

TWO

George

Maggie and I are walking down the hall toward the dining room. Well, I'm walking, anyway, and she's riding quietly in her wheelchair. From here, all I can see is the white-soft top of her head. I lean down and kiss it.

We tried to prepare as best we could, Maggie and I, for getting older. We talked about what would happen if one of us should go first, about how we would get along, would we remarry, that sort of thing. Of course, I said *no way in the world*, but she teased that she might—and she might have, but we'll never know now. She's stuck with me for the duration.

What we didn't prepare for was just how long we might live. You read about some Chinaman who drinks green tea and lives to be 114, or one of those Joes in the Bible who lived to be a hundred, maybe seven hundred years old, but you know that's not going to happen to you. Well, now, look, it's nearly happened to me. To us. We're antiques.

Now that Maggie's quiet, it's lonely at times. I live off my sense of humor, my good looks, my friendships. We have friends who still come to see us every morning for breakfast, Emmet and Jessica—they live upstairs. Emmet and me, we're rare in this home. I'd say, oh, eight out of ten here are women, widows. For married men like Emmet and me, don't mean a thing, it just means sometimes we got to change a lightbulb or fix a television set, or fight off the affections of a lonely old lady with wandering hands.

Emmet volunteers to cheer up the single ladies on our Alzheimer's ward. All it takes is a smile and a caring look, really. He walks them, one by one, to the dining room, mixing them up, the talkers with the nontalkers. Here he comes now with Smiling Betty on his arm. She's a looker still, but she doesn't talk much. Just smiles. Not a bad date. He could do worse.

"George," he says.

"Miss Betty, how you doin' today?" I say, charming her. She just smiles. "Well, that's nice. Emmet, you lookin' sharp today. Mighty sharp."

"Why, thank you, George. Say, you heard the one about the three old sisters in their nineties?"

"Can't say as I have, sir."

"The oldest was upstairs," says Emmet, rubbing his lanky Irish hands together to warm up his jokester. "She was putting her foot in the water when she called out, 'Hey! Can anybody remember if I was getting in or out of the bathtub?'

The middle sister put her foot on the stairs to come and help, but stopped. 'Can anyone tell me if I was going up or down the stairs?' she said. The youngest sister was on the couch, petting her little dog, rolling her eyes, listening to the whole thing. She thought to herself, *Sheesh, I hope I never get that senile,* and she knocked on wood for good measure. Then the dog started barking, and she said, 'Hold on, I'll come up there and help you two just as soon as I see who's at the door.'"

I laugh and Emmet looks over at Miss Betty. "Get it? The dog was barking? She was senile? Oh, never mind. Maybe it'll hit you later. I'll see you at breakfast, George? Let me just go walk Miss Betty to her chair."

"See you then, good man. See you then."

I watch as they shuffle by. I may be old as the hills, but it doesn't mean I feel like I belong here. Look at all these old folks. Dang, if they aren't cute. I wonder if anyone thinks I'm cute. I wish my wife still did.

Betty's so cute because she smiles all the time. What's not to like there? Maggie used to smile. At me, and apparently other folks too. I'm reminded of it in life-sized fashion these days. We put that Bathing Beauty picture of Maggie up against the wall. Not sure what to do with something that big or that beautiful. It hurts me to look at it. I remember feelings I had down deep inside from so long ago. Feelings of being a man. Things I've shoved aside for so many years. My wife. My wife, Magnolia, was the prettiest gal I'd ever seen. Still is. For the life of me, I cannot figure out who would send her such a large photograph of herself. Some old flame? Some secret admirer? It's driving me crazy. I know of no man.

I'd love to see Maggie smile again like that. At me. For real. But she doesn't think I'm funny anymore. Maybe that's it.

I push Maggie's chair to the table and scoot her up nice and close. I take a napkin and drape it across her lap. "Here you go, dear." Then I put my fingers to my ears and wiggle them as I'm sticking my tongue out and bugging my eyes at her. Nothing. No smile at all. She looks at me with those faded blue eyes as if they've been washed a few too many times. She blinks. I'll take that as, *Thank you, George. I love you. And you're still funnier than a one-winged chicken.*

Emmet comes back to the table, leans in, and kisses Maggie on her cheek. She startles and I study her face to see if there's any recognition there. Is it the same way she looks at me? Like I'm crazy? Some old coot? She's always been fond of Emmet. I think I detect a smile, some curling of the lips. Yes.

"Good morning, Maggie," Emmet says, loudly in case she can't hear him. "Do you know who I am?"

"Sure she does. You're the one who used to eat us out of house and home when you'd come over to supper. Come with a bottle of wine, leave with all the corn bread. You remember that, Maggie? You remember Emmet, Jessica's husband?"

Maggie looks at neither one of us, but at a little square saltshaker on the table. She picks it up with slow hands and turns it over, watching the grains of salt roll onto her empty plate like seconds.

"There now. We'll get you some breakfast in just a minute," I say. "You want grits this mornin'? Oatmeal?" I look at the salt in the plate. "Grits it is."

Emmet is staring at something behind me. He stands up slowly and pulls a chair out beside him for his wife.

"Good morning, Jessica," I say. "How are you?"

"I am here for another day. *C'est la vie*," she says.

"Beats the alternative."

Jessica is wearing her nicest housecoat. Looks like an oriental thing with red and gold dragons on it. Black wig. She's French. Always dressed to the hilt. Was an opera singer once, and well, once an opera singer, always an opera singer I guess. Just like I'll always be a corn farmer, though I've got no corn anymore. And Emmet will always be a taxi driver, even though he can't see to drive. And Maggie, well, she'll always be the prettiest girl in the world . . . and my bride.

We all sit down in our respective seats just as we do every morning for the past, I don't know how many years. Fantasia, our waitress, sweet colored girl, comes over like she does every day. "Mornin', what can I get you? The regular?" She sets a big pot of coffee in the middle of the table with cream and sugar packets and spoons for stirring.

"Miss Maggie will be havin' grits, and I'm mixin' it up today. I've got my good teeth in." I smile to show her. "I'm goin' with the bacon, extra crispy."

Emmet says, "Fantasia, you heard the one about the old man who ate too much bacon?"

"No, what happened?"

"He died," I say, flashing my pearly whites again. "Happily, I might add. Worse things could happen."

"Worse things indeed. That case, bacon for me too," says Emmet.

"You're not serious," says Jessica. Emmet sizes her up.

"Apparently that was not a serious order, Fantasia. You see, my wife would kill me before I could die happy if I ordered pork fat."

"Oh, Emmet." Jessica pops him on the arm. "I'll have the usual. Emmet will too."

Emmet reaches for the pot of coffee, but then stops. He's watching the door behind my back again. "Don't look now—Father Time's coming for you," he says. "I'd say you got at least an hour."

I turn around and see Miss Annie coming toward us with a strange old man on her arm. He's older than sin, and they're moving like molasses. Not so unusual in this place except they seem to be heading straight for us.

I grab onto my armrests to brace myself. I have this thing, see, about strangers. I just don't like them, never have. Nothing good has ever come from a stranger, even if he does happen to look like the kindest, saddest man you've ever seen. Looks can be deceiving—I am old enough to know that.

THREE

George

"Yoo-hoo. Mister George, Miss Magnolia, Mister Emmet, Miss Jessica?" Miss Annie calls over to us. "I'd like you to meet Mister Joe. Mister Joe, these are some real nice folks here—him even." Annie winks at me. "These the folks you gonna be livin' with now. I'll see to it you got everythin' you need. Now, I thought on your first day here, you wouldn't mind breakin' bread with some of Harmony House's finest. How 'bout scoot on over and make room for Mister Joe?"

"Sure, sure. Make room for Joe. Make room for Joe." Emmet stands up as do I, and we shuffle our chairs around. Emmet borrows one from another table and makes a place for the old man between himself and Maggie.

"Which floor does he live on?" I ask. It's a loaded question, but I need to know who I'm dealing with here. If it's the first, like we're on because of Maggie, it means he has dementia or a stroke or Alzheimer's, that sort of thing.

"The same one you do," Annie says, looking me in the eye, daring me to complain. She can be tough like that, it's part of why I love her. Great. So Joe's not all there. His eyes are moist. He looks like a good man. Only lost. Wonder what happened to him. Stroke? Dementia? Alzheimer's? I resist the urge to say, *What you in here for?* Like a prison. Like a joke, see. I doubt he'll get it.

"I know you're gonna be great friends," says Annie. "I understand he's real smart, like a genius."

"Genius, huh? Which kind?" I say. "Beethoven or the Rain Man variety?"

"Be nice," says Annie, popping me on the back. Then turning to Joe she says, "I'll be back after breakfast and take you to your room or show you 'round some, okay?"

Joe nods at Miss Annie and then she's on her way.

"Here, here, good fella. Welcome to our senior sanctuary." I tip my imaginary hat. "Genius, huh? Glad to have you. Listen, can you recite any part of the Gettysburg Address?" I ask him, folding my arms. "Four score and seven years ago . . ." Joe just looks at me. "Shoot, in this place, Joe, you're a genius if you can remember what you had for breakfast, so pay close attention. We'll be havin' a test later."

"George, you're going to scare him off," says Jessica. She turns to the new guy. "He's harmless, Joe, really. He just likes to hear himself talk sometimes." Jessica extends her hand over the table. "*Bonjour.* I'm Jessica. Pleased to meet you." Joe looks at her and nods, but keeps his hands on his lap. "And this is my husband, Emmet Conlan. He's Irish, so get used to the driving hat. Honey, take off your hat, you're at the table."

"The hat stays, woman."

"Oh, Emmet."

"And I'm George." I reach over and touch him kindly on the shoulder. "And this here is my wife, Maggie. Don't mind her if she doesn't say hello. She's a mite quiet these days." I see Maggie fiddling with her hands again, thinking about biting her fingers. They're already raw to the bone as it is. Her hands have become so nervous in this last year, when she started leaving me for good and forever. "Fantasia, can we get some tinfoil over here? The missus would certainly appreciate that."

After Fantasia comes back, I sit and watch my wife perform the most amazing ritual. Some may think it strange, but I think it's beautiful, hopeful. I see my wife in every shiny facet.

◦◦◦

Magnolia

I am making a wand. I marvel as my knobbed knuckles move and pulse with skill. I feel no arthritic pain when I have the silver in my hand. I'd like to make a circle, maybe. A ring would be nice, or a crown. But no. Once again, I have produced a long, thin wisp of a wand, another useless instrument to add to my pile.

There is nothing pretty about getting old. It's a travesty, really. Some crime against nature. My beauty has long since left me, though my husband says he still sees it. Dear man.

Now that my looks have faded and my years have grown long, I sit in this wheelchair, unable to do for myself. Somehow the Good Lord saw fit to take away my voice too. But my mischievous hands have a life of their own. I used to guide them. Scallywag that I am, I used to tell them what to pick up off the dinner table or out of the colored girls' aprons, but now they do as they like with no instruction from me at all.

The first wand I ever made was shortly after I went mute. It was a strange episode, mostly involuntary. My hands grabbed some aluminum foil from leftovers one evening in the dining room, and they just got to pressing and squeezing, and next thing I knew, I had a long, skinny silver wand. I like the looks of them. I like the feel of them in my hand. Occasionally, I like to bop George on the head with one, as if trying to turn him into a frog or back into the prince I once knew.

I do not know why I do it. I can feel my hands making it, see the wand in front of me, but I cannot control the movement of my fingers nor the making of wands. Yet each one is more perfect than the last. It's as if some bad-acting, childish, and magical creature has taken up house in my ancient body.

I have quite a collection now, long ones, thin ones, short ones, ones with little pieces of food stuck in them, mummified forever. I do not know why George doesn't throw the whole lot of them away, but he doesn't. He keeps my collection of wands right next to a shoe box full of stolen sugar packets on a little bookshelf. He thinks of these things as my art form. As if they are my communication to him, some kindling of magic between us.

I wish they worked. How I wish I could wave one of my

tinfoil wands and open my mouth again to say something intelligible. But it's no use wishing for things that cannot come true.

Look at George. Each year I've loved him more. He is ninety-one or ninety-two now. His ears have grown so, and those eyebrows! They're like two fluffy white mice nesting on his forehead. I'd laugh and tell him how handsome he is, if only I could. I'd tell him I love him too. He needs that, you know. To be told. But I'm trapped somewhere deep behind my eyes, waving . . . calling . . . but no one can hear me.

They think I don't know anything, but I do. They think I don't recognize anyone, fear anything, think intelligent thoughts, but they're wrong. I am every bit as with it as the next guy in this place. How many years have I been here, anyway? Glory be, who am I to grumble? There are blessings, I suppose, and I count them. I do.

Much to my delight, I have a memory of things I haven't thought of in years—my daughter when she was adorable in pigtails, my husband when we would giggle and swim and make love underneath the moon. But I also remember my childhood, my mother, my brother. Where were these things locked away? Some vault? Some time capsule? They ebb and flow in my mind like the Lowcountry tides, except with less warning.

Oh goodness, here I go again.

We are newlyweds, George and me, standing arm in arm in front of our very own cornfield. It's the corn that keeps us alive these days. George tends the farm and I take the corn into the market and sell it along with anything else growing—string beans, squash. People buy corn from us for feed and food. They make cornmeal of it, and I bake corn bread almost daily. It keeps meat on our bones. We may not be rich, but we have it all, here, in this field.

Look at George. How I love him. His lips are full, his jaw firm. His hands. I love his strong, capable hands.

George's pant legs are rolled up to his knees. We've been wading in a nearby creek in bare feet, and we're still giggling from it all. A lock of his hair blows across his forehead, making his receding hairline more apparent. But it matters none to me. It only means he's maturing, and there's nothing better than a mature man.

"Here, grab this," I say. I pull out a blanket from my picnic basket and George holds the two other corners. We straighten it out in a nice patch of grass in front of the cornstalks. "There. Isn't this nice?" I sit with my legs out in front of me, crossed at the ankles, for George. He loves my legs. I put my head back and bask in the sunshine, hoping George will kiss my neck and finally, he does.

"Why, Mr. Jacobs, are you trying to take advantage of a young girl in your cornfield?"

"Young? Why, you're twenty-two already."

"Oh, stop it." I pop him on the shoulder and reach over for the picnic basket. "I made your favorite."

"Rhubarb pie?"

"No, your other favorite."

"Um, pumpkin?"

"No, George, peach pie!"

"Oh, right, right. Peach is my favorite." He grins and I

see those dimples, that manly cleft in his chiseled chin. The curls at his temples.

"That's what I thought." I bring out two plates and two forks, and strain for the pie, but George puts his hand on the basket and pushes it away.

"Let's save this for later," he says.

"Later? Why? The ants are going to come."

"I'll take my chances." George leans in to kiss my cheek, but I turn to him, full on.

"Oh goodness, well, I suppose a few little ants won't be too much trouble."

We make love right there in our very own cornfield and time stands still. *I love you, George Jacobs, I love you. I love you . . .*

George? Oh drat. I am bound to this chair. *Speak to him.* I try to move my ancient mouth, but it won't work properly. I look at my husband, George, now, sitting at the breakfast table, a crumb stuck on his chin. I'd like to remove it for him or at least tell him about it. But I'm afraid that's impossible.

When I was a child, I didn't speak for a full two years. For survival, I suppose. And I used to not speak to George for days on end when we were younger and just married and I needed to prove a point. But now, now I wish I could speak to him. With all my heart.

There is a woman here who takes good care of me. Miss Annie doesn't mind my silence. She knows I can't help it. She talks enough for the both of us. But it hurts George. I know it does. George shouldn't be punished. Oh, he's been difficult from time to time as husbands can be, but a sentence of long life is hard enough. Silence—I wouldn't wish this on anybody. Something about my last stroke must have disconnected the wires from me to the rest of the world. I don't know what my face is doing half the time. I can't make my hands work the way I want them to. And every now and again, yes, it's true. I forget. I forget where I am, who I am, who everyone is. If I'm being punished, I'd like to make up for it now. *Please, God, if you're listening, let me say my piece.*

George looks at me sweetly. *Reach out and touch him, you old fool. Let him know you care.* But my hands have a mind of their own, now don't they? They press and cajole this tinfoil like life itself depends on it. My husband and I, married for seventy-some years, sit here at the Harmony House breakfast table in our golden days as perfect strangers with oceans between us. Oceans, not magic. If I had a real wand I'd wave it and make myself new again. For him.

Look at this. My hands are pushing the silver wand toward a gentleman, a stranger, sitting next to me. Who is this? I don't think I've ever seen him before, but I declare, he seems to know me. Part of me thinks he's my husband and I've forgotten him. But no, George is right there. This is just a strange old man.

Now he's a strange old man with a wand in his hand.

FOUR

Magnolia

I saw magic once, real magic, and there's something I've come to understand after all these years: magic can either come from one of two places, up above or down below. It's sometimes hard to tell the difference, but I can. It's all in the eyes. The magic of heaven comes through as miracles, Divine Providence, and there's a light in the eyes that tells you there's something beautiful inside a person. But for those who are filled with darkness, the darkness itself seeps out of the pupils and tries to pull you in. I have seen this kind of magic. I have seen this kind of darkness. It came to our little town of Levy, South Carolina, in 1929.

There was nothing much to Levy, just two roads that came together in a T where a big sign stood that read FRESH CORN, or sometimes FRESH WATERMELON or FRESH TOMATOES.

The store behind that sign was owned by the Jacobs family, Jacobs Mercantile, and it was something to marvel at.

My brother Ash and I used to walk barefoot down to the Jacobs Mercantile to see what-all had been dug up out in their ten-acre field. On homemade dusty shelves sat Civil War bullets, arrowheads, bottles. Up in the rafters, you might find a waffle iron from the late 1800s or a pair of rusty hinges from the one-room schoolhouse for coloreds. That school had closed down some time ago. Most of them had left and gone up north to New York or Chicago to find work.

Levy was somewhere between Savannah, Georgia, and Charleston, South Carolina, so it was a hot spot for traveling folk. Miss Tillie Jacobs had a room in back of Jacobs Mercantile where she let boarders stay for a night or more. Occasionally she even let a Negro stay there. She didn't mind, saying, "The color of a dollar don't change with the color of the hand."

Miss Tillie would always give Ash and me fresh apples for coming and visiting with her. I always thought she was a kindly woman, but looking back, I can see she was doing it out of charity. We were from the poor side of the tracks, if there was such a thing, in Levy. It was my brother and me and Mama and Daddy—Daniel and Juanita Black. We lived in a little house on Togoodoo Road, named after the Indians that once roamed those parts.

My father was the local postman and he carried the mail by mule and cart three times a week. We had twenty-three mailboxes in a little room in the front of our simple clapboard house. I knew all of them by name and used to help Daddy sort the mail into the boxes when he would let me. Mrs. Kline and

Mrs. Abrams always got the Sears Roebuck catalogs, and I liked to look through those before depositing them in their rightful places. Mrs. Benchley was a dressmaker like my mother, though not so stylish, and Mama looked over her *Vogue* magazine before passing it on, getting ideas for new fashions.

Living near the railroad tracks, we would hear the Boll Weevil pass through at nine fifteen in the morning and five thirty in the evening every day. Ash and I would go to the train depot and watch the passengers get on or off. If you wanted to get on, you had to wave a white handkerchief and hope the train conductor could see you, else he'd pass you by.

The Boll Weevil was part of the Seaboard Air Rail Line that ran from Richmond, Virginia, down to Tampa, Florida. The train itself wasn't part of that route, but on a little branch that ran from Hamlet, North Carolina, to Charleston and on to Savannah. It was a gas-electric train and nicknamed the "Boll Weevil" by the Negroes after the beetles that had come up from Mexico and eaten all the bolls on the cotton crops. Eaten their jobs, too, and the cotton farmers' livelihoods. I wondered about that, why they would name a train—a beautiful train that meant to me that life existed outside our tiny Levy—after some destructive pest. Later I'd come to understand how appropriate that name was. The Negroes saw it and knew it was danger, chanting,

> *Death's black train is comin'.*
> *Same train. Same train.*
> *Same train took my mama.*
> *Same train. Same train.*

Set yore house in order.
Same train. Same train.

The Boll Weevil meant cruel change. Eventually it destroyed everything I held most dear.

It's a hot summer morning in 1929, and the Boll Weevil has slowed down without anybody flagging it. Ash and I sit there on a bench, with our dirty feet kicking up dust.

"Reckon somebody's gettin' off," he says.

"Mmm-hmm." We watch intently. It's the most excitement we have in Levy, when a stranger comes to town.

The screech of the wheels of the Boll Weevil crawls up our bones and settles into a big grin on our faces. I watch Ash to see how he'll react and then follow suit. Four years older than me, he's my compass. He's my everything.

"Somebody's a-comin'!" he says, standing up all tall and dignified, so I do too, straightening the pinafore my mother made for me. It's smeared with dirt from wiping my hands.

Next thing you know, a big man gets off the train, wearing a nice black hat and a black suit. He has a handlebar mustache waxed into two points. He turns around and lifts the end of a trunk, and the trunk begins to move on out of the train. On the other side is a boy, a real, live, honest-to-goodness boy who's not from Levy. He has shoes on that are shined and matched and pants with suspenders, not rope around the waist like Ash wears.

I wave my hand a little, and the boy looks at me and smiles.

I'll never forget that look because before we can say "Howdy do" or anything, Ash grabs my hand and jerks me. "Come on; let's go tell Miss Tillie there's boarders comin' in!"

"Boarders a-comin'!" yells Ash as we hightail onto the porch of Jacobs Mercantile. "Miss Tillie!" We know to look in the store behind the register, but when she isn't there, we head out back to the fields. Miss Tillie always says the closest place to heaven is being in that field where she can see God's handiwork. We find her, leaning over a watermelon and aiming to pick it up and place it on a wooden cart on the back of her mule. Ash and I bend down and help her with it and tell her all about the mustached man and his boy, headed for town.

"You reckon you got room for the two of 'em?" Ash asks, knowing full well there's only one bed in the spare room.

"Well, how big is the boy?" asks Miss Tillie.

"He's about Ash's age," I spout out, blushing, remembering his dimples.

"Well then, maybe he can bunk with George," says Miss Tillie. "I'm sure he won't mind."

Boarders mean money for the Jacobs family. They make a nice living off their produce, for sure, but the boarding is where the real money is. A watermelon can fetch two cents, but Miss Tillie can get a full two dollars from letting out her room for a week. She wants to make this work for the gentleman and his son, one way or the other.

"How-do, I'm Tillie Jacobs, and this here's my son, George. His daddy, Mr. Bruce Jacobs, is out yonder plantin' some seed."

"We're looking for a room," says the stranger.

"This your boy?" asks Miss Tillie.

"It is. He's a good boy, smart. No trouble a'tall."

"Good, well, I got me the one room out back, but with a boy this big, he might feel like bunkin' with my son, George. George! Come on in here, quick. Got somebody I want you to meet!" Miss Tillie calls outside, turning back around and smiling. "How long you be stayin' in Levy?"

"Oh, a good long while, I reckon, unless I can get my writing done sooner than that."

"A writer? You don't say. What do you write?"

"Oh, my manners." He takes his hat off and swoops it down before him, bending at the waist. "I'm Charles Stackhouse, author of *Modern-Day Spells for Whatever Ails You* and *Pulling the Rabbit from the Hat*. You may have heard of that one. It won an award." Seeing it rings no bell with Miss Tillie, the man says, "They're novels, not true life. I have a bit of imagination, you see."

I watch Miss Tillie's face. Her eyebrows rise to her hairline and she turns to me. "We don't do much readin' in these parts, well, 'cept for *Farmers' Almanac*—"

"Sears Roebuck catalog," I say.

"Yes'm, that too."

Just then George comes in with his ears and feet all dirty. He's always the last one in school and the first one in line for seconds at the Christmas supper every year at Levy First Baptist Church. Not sure why they called it that since there's only but the one, no second churches around, except for the Negroes'. George likes to elbow me in the ribs sometimes, trying to tease me or pull my hair. Boys that age don't know what to do when they like a girl. I think George is scrawny compared to my brother. They have a healthy rivalry, those two. George's hair is wet from the heat when he comes in, and he looks at the man and his son as if they've come straight down from the moon.

"George, meet your new bedmate, uh—"

"Joe," says the boy in suspenders, speaking for himself all of a sudden. He holds out his hand and waits for George to shake it, which he does finally after wiping a hand off on his pants.

"George has a nice big bed, don't you, son? Won't be no trouble a'tall." The boy reaches out for Ash's hand next and nods at me. "Good then, well, let's get your trunk put up and then you can rest a bit from your trip. Where is it you say you comin' from?"

"New Orleans," the man says, and for a second I see a flash of something in that boy Joe's eyes, something that reminds me of a hooked fish, like he's in pain but with no where to swim to.

FIVE

George

I look at the new old guy. Poor sap. Thinks they dropped him off for summer camp. Has no idea this is *it*. The last homestead.

"Where you from originally?" Emmet asks him, eager to tell his New York stories to fresh ears and how many times he's been to Ireland—seventeen. He doesn't get the chance though. This new fella, Joe, don't say a word. I watch him as he studies my wife's wheelchair. He looks down at the wheels, then up the arms, at the wand she shoved in his hands, and then over to her face. He lingers there, and I almost see a spark of something between the two—maybe they recognize a kinship in state of mind.

I am uncomfortable with this change of events. If there's one thing that happens as you get older, it's that you get used to things. You like things to be the way they are. Maggie and

I knew each other as children, and Emmet and Jessica—we've been friends with them for the last thirty years or so. We're all set in our ways a bit. We are a foursome. Period. I don't know how I feel about having a fifth wheel. Yes, I do. I don't like it a bit. Our conversation will be awkward. We won't be able to joke like we always do. Feels like we'll have to babysit Old Joe, here.

"Quick, Joe, what's three thousand divided by twelve?" I say, teasing really. I don't feel like making nice.

To my astonishment, he says, "Two fifty." His eyes are dim but honest.

"Oh, I . . ." I'm trying to count on my fingers under the table. "Is that right? Anybody know?" After a while, we're all quiet, struggling. I should do more crossword puzzles. Try that Sudoku or something in the newspaper. Brain's getting rusty.

"Gee, I think that is right," says Jessica.

Good gracious, he is a genius. I look at Joe again, impressed. "Numbers guy, huh? Not bad."

"I, well, I b-better be going," says Joe. "My friend is pro-pro-probably waiting for me."

I'm shocked that he speaks in full sentences, and I feel like a heel. Jessica looks at him and says, "Oh, Joe, I don't think your family is here anymore."

"No. 'Course not. No family. I—" Joe looks over at the door to see if someone's over there, waiting.

"You'll get used to this place," says Jessica. "You'll see. The people are very nice. Miss Annie is just wonderful; you're going to love her." Jessica smiles sadly at him. I really can't imagine what it would be like to be here in Harmony House without friends, with no family, not knowing a soul.

"Joe," I say. "Listen. Whatever you do, stay away from the house cat. If it comes near you, run like you-know-what."

"Oh, George," says Jessica.

"Seriously, we'll talk about that later. It's one of Death's henchmen. Listen, Joe. How 'bout after breakfast, I show you where the action is? You seen the courtyard yet? They got horseshoes, croquet even. What's your pleasure? You like shuffleboard? I'm the reigning king."

"We'll see about that," says Emmet.

"Care to make a friendly wager? By the way, I don't think I caught your full name, Joe."

"Stackhouse," says the man. "Joseph P. S-S-Stackhouse." And he holds out his trembling hand for me to shake.

I look at him, hard now, because something about that name rings a bell, a very distant bell. Dang memory, it's not what it used to be. I feel a chill as I shake his hand and look at the wand in his other. I picture myself holding that old fishing rod again, desperate to pull some memory back up.

But . . . I got nothing. I lean over and feed my wife, always amazed she'll open her mouth for me still.

SIX

Magnolia

George puts a spoonful of grits in my mouth. Grits always take me back to Mama's kitchen. Oh gracious, I close my eyes and I am seven years old in Levy. There are no grits because the kitchen's gone. Everything's gone.

Everything is black where our house used to stand on Togoodoo Road. I am walking through the soggy remains of our home with Mama's hand in mine. We step gingerly over what used to be her dressmaker's dummy, now just a twisted metal frame. I get shivers down my spine. I was in that dummy. I could have been charred and mangled like my doll. She has no arms left. She looks up at me from the wet ground, wet from buckets of water being poured on her, wet from the rain. She is dark and sooty, and I love her still. Maybe even more.

I look at Mama. She has a faraway stare as she passes slowly over the kitchen where she used to cook us meals in happier times. We stop in the sewing room where the fire started, where she once mended our clothes and made bed linens out of cloth she bought from money saved under the mattress, money from making dresses.

She squeezes my hand when she sees the doll, squeezes because she doesn't want me to pick it up. I do anyway.

"Mama, her arms. Can you sew her back together?"

Mama says nothing but shakes her head. The Singer sewing machine is melted on one side. She saved up for two whole years to buy it. She pulls me away from the wreckage and leads me over to where my brother is sawing scraps of wood. He's almost eleven, a big kid. I've always looked up to him. Always played with him. Always run to his arms when Mama and Daddy were having words. It's always Ash I run to, and I am only seven, but I think Mama doesn't like the fact that I run to him and not to her. I think that must be why she looks at him and whispers, "Go on, wash up. Train's comin'."

"But, Mama!" I say. I look at her. It's her face, but somehow it doesn't seem alive anymore. Like darkness has sucked the life from her eyes.

Daddy's standing off a ways, and I see him nod at Mama. Her arms are limp. Ash is holding a saw, blood trickling down his shins. His blond curly hair is damp from perspiration. His face is smeared gray around glistening blue eyes. He's been out here, sawing and sweating ever since the rain stopped. There's a desperation I've never seen in his eyes before, and it scares me. Then he nods.

"Somebody could have been killed," Mama says, mostly

to herself, her voice a fallen anvil. She turns and walks back into the wreckage.

I want to stop her; I want to say he didn't do it, that my brother was the one who saved my life. But I can't get the words out, only cries.

The next thing I know, he's boarding the train. It's the nine thirty Boll Weevil, taking him away, destroying our crops, our lives. My life. Just like the Negroes said it would.

I see it now, a brightly colored train, the one Ash and I used to dream of flagging down and hopping aboard together, seeing the country. It doesn't look as glamorous or adventurous as I always thought. We've grown up on these tracks. Ash and I go swimming down in the crick and then walk along the railroad tracks in the hot sunshine to dry off. Our hair sticks funny, slap-up against our heads, but the smell of the water drying on our skin is the best thing in the whole world. I can smell it now, the water on Ash, the smoke, the canvas of the dress form, smothering me.

I am on those tracks again, crunching over gravel. I am running after a train that has my brother on it, my everything on it. I am crying. I am wailing and hope the earth might open up and take me into it mercifully. Because I cannot stay here without Ash. He is my Arms to run into, my Joy in the summertime, my hot Sun on wet skin. He is my brother. And now he's gone.

The days come and the days go in this place. Decades have passed, and I must remember these things, like it or not. Some things are good to remember and go on about, but this—this is like I'm dying. Again and again. I'm dying, arms stretched out on these railroad tracks, and Ash's being taken off.

Far away from me . . .

Yet, look. I'm still here. I am still. Here.

SEVEN

Magnolia

LEVY, 1929

The new boarders for Jacobs Mercantile arrive in Levy on a
hot day in July when thunderstorms threaten to roll up out
of nowhere and pop and crackle above our heads.

There we are, my brother Ash and me, standing in the
store with George, Miss Tillie's son, just fuming he's got to let
Joe, the new boy, stay in his room. I can see the fire burning
behind his ten-year-old eyes. He usually gives me goo-goo-
eyed looks and twists the thin skin on the back of my arm to
make me squeal, but right now he's in a different place altogether. I can tell he's not giving me a thought.

"Good then," says Miss Tillie. "George, Ash, help Mr.
Stackhouse here put his trunk in his room. Joe, you like
sugarcane?"

What child doesn't like sugarcane? I hold my hand out,

too, and get a nice three-inch piece. I love the sweet water that fills my mouth with each chew. The man in the mustache looks square at Ash and says, "You're a nice-sized boy, almost Joe's age. What's that, ten? Eleven?"

Ash looks down at his feet and says, "Be 'leven next month, sir."

"That right?" He keeps a-staring. "Come then, show me how strong you are." I watch as the man hefts his trunk up with Joe and George and Ash on the other end, and then they disappear into the back room.

I've been in there before, though I don't follow now. It wouldn't be right. It's a small room with wood paneled walls that sometimes lets the sunshine through, sometimes the cold wind. On a hot day like today I'm thinking Mr. Stackhouse will be mighty pleased to have a little airflow. There's a single bed up against one wall with a little table and oil lamp beside it for reading and whatnot. Across the room there's a small wash bin and an outhouse out back for the Jacobses and their boarders.

When Ash comes back out, I hand him his sugarcane and, mouths full and nothing left to do, we turn and leave, headed for home.

"You reckon he'll be comin' to school with us?" I ask, scratching a stick in the dirt as I go.

"Don't know. Might not stay that long," says Ash.

"Yeah, but he might even." Secretly, I'm hoping it. I may be young, but I know good-looking when I see it, and Joe is one good-looking boy. I could never say that to Ash though. "Reckon they'll come to church on Sunday?"

"Could be. We'll see."

I look over at Ash and see his mind working. I've always been able to tell when my brother's got something going on in his head. He might not have gotten Mama's looks, but he sure did get a double heaping of brains from her.

"George didn't look too happy about it all," I say, snickering.

"Don't laugh," Ash scolds me. "What if you had to share your bed with some stranger? How would you like it?"

Here I am, thinking he'd for sure get a kick out of it, but no. I am wounded. I toughen up and walk two steps ahead of him. "Race you home," I say, then set off fast as my bare feet can take me. The sky bursts with thunder and we light off for home, laughing in the rain.

We're soaking wet by the time we reach Togoodoo Road. We find Mama in the sewing room, wrapping red flowered fabric across her body and noticing herself in the mirror.

"Dry your feet off 'fore you come in here!" she squeals.

"You won't believe it, Mama! Miss Tillie's got boarders and one of 'em's a boy!"

"A boy? How old?"

"Ash's age, I reckon."

"I see. Well, good. Maybe he can help Miss Tillie in the fields. Who'd he come with?"

"A man," I say. "He's a magician."

"A magician?"

"Naw, he's not that, he's a writer. Writes books," says Ash. "Something about a rabbit in a hat."

"Well," I say, "he looks like one, anyway, with a handlebar mustache and black shiny shoes."

"I don't like him," says Ash.

"Ash, what a thing to say. You don't even know him." I watch Mama's eyes flutter as she pins the fabric up on her dressmaker's dummy. "Run on now and get cleaned up. Supper will be ready soon."

I walk out of the room, suddenly wishing Mr. Stackhouse had brought a wife with him, or maybe even a daughter, somebody Mama could sell a dress to. Then I think about Joe.

"Mama?"

"What is it, baby?" Her lips are curled tight around pins and her blond hair falls light on her shoulders.

"Maybe sometime we could have Mr. Stackhouse and his son over for supper. You think so?"

"Ouch!" She pokes herself and takes the rest of the pins out, sticking them in a red sewing cushion that looks like a tomato. "We'll see, honey." I stand there, pouting a little, and she turns and looks at me. She smiles then. "Must be some boy. You can talk to your daddy about it over corn bread, okay? Maybe butter him up on a nice, full stomach. That always works."

EIGHT

Magnolia

HARMONY HOUSE

I'm starving. I hope somebody takes me to supper soon. I
hope they have corn bread sopping in butter. Macaroni and
cheese. Fried chicken, maybe, though they'll cut it up into tiny
unchokable pieces. I don't want that, I want flavor. And lots of
salt. Something chocolate and bad for dessert. Bad, bad food.

"Are you ready for bingo, dear?" Our friend Jessica knocks
and comes into our room dressed in her finest. Gold lamé
fluff everywhere. I forgot about bingo. *It's just bingo*, I want to
tell her, but I can't. Not that she'd listen anyway. She once
wore a mink stole to our granddaughter Gracie's Christmas
play, and several of the children cried when they found out it
was a dead animal on her shoulders.

Oh, maybe I already had supper. What was it . . . lima
beans? No . . .

"Good heavens, what is this?"

"It's Maggie when she was younger," says George.

"Oh my word, I have never! You were . . . you were in Hollywood, dear? What have you been holding out on me? George?"

"I wish I knew," he says. "It just came in the mail this morning. Somewhere in New York City. We don't know who sent it."

"New York? Well, that's where I'm from, I . . . you know, there's something about this photo. Almost like I've seen it before . . ."

"Really? What, in a store? A billboard?"

"I don't know. You don't think . . ."

"What?"

"Nothing, I—you don't think Maggie has a secret admirer."

"Jess, this is not helping."

"I'm sorry, I—" Jessica has a hard time breaking her eyes away from my photograph. I sit here, watching, helpless to say a word. I've wondered where this thing was for years. I wrote many letters trying to find it. And now here it is. But why? Why now?

"What a mystery. You are quite a beautiful girl, Magnolia. If I only had an ounce of your looks. George, could we put some color on her lips?"

"I don't do color, Jess. Can you do it for me? Annie's not here."

"Come here, sweetheart, *ma chérie*." Jessica wheels me in front of a little round mirror on the writing bureau. It's just small enough for me to see my face in and no wheelchair. I can hear her breathing to push me. She's as skinny as a twig, but with all that gold fluff, she looks a good ten pounds heavier. "Here we are." She leaves for a moment and comes back to me, holding my lipstick. "It's such a nice color on you, Mauve Magic. Yes, this is you." I would like to pucker my lips for her or at least be still, but I'm not sure if I'm doing either. I am watching in the mirror. I am seeing the face of an old woman, my grandmother perhaps. But no, I never met my grandmother. I am at my mother's dresser and sneaking into her makeup drawer. I am wearing a face full of cosmetics. I can taste the plastic-metallic stuff on my lips. I am too young to be wearing this. Mama will be angry, but there's nowhere to wipe it off, nowhere to rub it—

"No, no, leave it alone," says Jessica. "It looks very nice. You're just as beautiful as that young girl in the photograph. My goodness. Shall we go? George, I'll go ahead and take Maggie to bingo if you need a few more minutes."

"Thank you, kindly," says George. "Be right along."

George

Friday nights are bingo nights; that's one thing I never forget. Don't knock it until you try it—beats knitting night or hip-hop dance. Sheesh. Trust me, those are for the birds. I love the thrill of thinking I might actually win at bingo. Because I could. I do sometimes. I put a card in front of Maggie too, but she can't really play, so I get two—*double*—chances at winning. Yes, I know, it's ingenious.

Speaking of in-geniuses, Joe will be joining us tonight. It's only fair we initiate him properly. Shuffleboard was a bust. Joe just sat there alone on a bench, staring at the big oak tree. And as soon as that cat came around, he pet the thing.

"Joe, not the cat," I told him. "Please. Whenever somebody dies here, that cat has been stalking them for days, sitting in the dying person's room, soaking up their very life! It's true!"

It is true, but Joe didn't listen to me at all. I can see we're going to have a hard time getting through to him.

He's all the way down the hall and to the right, room 123. I knock on his door. "Joe? You decent? It's George Jacobs. I'm your ride to bingo. I would have brought my Rolls but the drive is just too short." The door swings open on its own.

"I'm Joe. Joe Stackhouse. Hello." He smiles a yellow smile.

"I know it. We met at breakfast, remember?"

Joe is sitting in a wood chair with no shoes on and black socks. He's looking around at a room he doesn't recognize. And I can see why. He's got a queen-size bed with a brown and blue striped cover on it, looks new, like from that Target store, maybe. Young stuff. Looks like somebody sent him off to college instead of an old-folks home.

"You, uh, you ready to go play some bingo? It's sort of what we do here on Friday nights. Not much else to do. 'Course, if you want to be alone, I can respect that, being new and all. Ahem."

I walk toward him and can smell a distinct sweet-sourness. "Ah, Joe. Where's your phone?" Joe points toward the wall. I go and pick it up. "Hello? Hello, this is George Jacobs." I

lower my voice. "I'm in the new guy, Joe Stackhouse's, room.
Yes. Listen, we gotta problem. Is Annie here? No? Well,
somebody needs to get down here pronto and help him . . .
get cleaned up. Yes. Well, thank you. You too."

Makes me so mad. How could Annie leave him sitting
like this? If there's one thing that makes me mad it's people
not feeling dignified in this place. I look at Joe and he seems
not to care. "Right, then." He puts his hand out to me. "I'm
ready." I look at this man in no shoes and stinking up the
place to high heaven, and I have to stall him. "Wait just a
minute, there's somebody coming for something and . . .
well, I'll come back for you in just a few minutes, hear?" And
then I am bolting out the door as fast as I can make it. I wait
in the hallway, catching my breath, till Miss Candy comes by.
She knocks on his door. "Mr. Stackhouse?"

"Get him cleaned up real nice and then bring him on
down to the bingo room," I whisper. "He needs to make a
good impression. It's his first night here."

I walk away, muttering to myself. I don't know what
I've gotten into. I don't know why I've taken it upon myself
to look after this wayward new fellow, but it's just human
decency. When you're the only sober one in the room, you
can see how helpless the drunks are, I suppose. And somebody's got to help him.

I'd want somebody to help my wife, for instance, if she were
all alone in this joint without me. Hypothetically speaking.

As I walk down the hall, holding on to the railing and
minding my own business, that Harmony House cat crosses my
path. Gray and white with bright green eyes, he's right there in

the middle of the hallway like a stoplight. "Shoo," I say. But he doesn't move. Instead, he looks me straight in the eye and lifts a paw, licking it, then rubbing his face. "You better not try to be all cute with me," I tell him. "I know all about you. Steer clear from the Jacobses, you got that? Now . . . outta my way, cat. I'll be late for the first round."

But the cat doesn't go anywhere.

"Go on, what are you waiting for?"

"Who are you talking to?" There's a voice behind me. A voice I know all too well. I stop and turn around slowly, hoping it's a mirage.

"Casey," I say. From the looks of his face, I know this isn't a pleasure visit. Casey Burnett has been my doctor since he was out of diapers. Or practically. He still looks too young to be a doctor, but Emmet and Jessica talked me into him. Nice enough fella, I guess. Makes house calls, which is great . . . except when you don't want them.

"George." Casey puts out his hand and I reach out, trembling to shake it.

"I imagine you didn't come down here just to join me in bingo."

He sorta smiles. "I wish I did, George. Listen, is there somewhere we can talk in private?"

"Sure, sure, uh . . ." I'm nervous and I search around, thinking of what place I'd most like to hear the bad news. Something like this sticks in your craw for a while, the memory of it, so I want to choose wisely. "How 'bout out there by the gazebo?" So I lead him. He's walking a step behind me, out the exit and across the courtyard, past the horseshoes and the oak tree and the benches and the chessboard table. I can hear my odd breathing as I walk. I am suddenly aware that maybe it doesn't sound so healthy. The trees, bright green, and the glowing blue sky of dusk seem to be mocking my eyes. I can see them so clearly—it's all so pretty now.

"So give it to me straight, doc," I say when we step up on the gazebo. Last year a couple seniors got married right here in this very place. It was touching. "It's not good, is it?"

"The tests . . ." he says. "Well, they came back and confirmed . . ."

"How long do I have?"

"Weeks. Couple of months, maybe. I'm sorry—"

"But I've been feelin' so good! Are you sure?" Then his sturdy young hands grab onto my arms and hold me up, because I don't think my feet can do it anymore.

NINE

George

They say bad things come in threes, and today, well, I've had
my fill. First, Maggie's life-sized photograph comes waltzing
in from some New York admirer. Then Annie forces Joe on
us, some old needy stranger—like we need one—and then Dr.
Casey makes a dad-blum house visit. It's the end of my ride.
Game over. Sayonara. I look to the ceiling and scowl at whoever might be orchestrating this crappy day. Then I walk into
the bingo hall.

The room is decorated with stars and stripes leftover from
Fourth of July. There's no other holiday until Labor Day
and no knickknacks you can put up for that. It's not really a
bingo hall, but a multipurpose room used for birthday par-
ties, karaoke, that sort of thing. Miss Arlene Simpson is the
caller tonight as she always is. She's bossy and just likes to be
in control.

I find my wife sitting at a long rectangular table next to

Jessica. Emmet is across the way and he's left me a place. I see cards lined up and colored daubers, but the room goes fuzzy a minute and I have to hold on to Jay Milton's seat. "'Scuse me, Jay."

"You feeling all right, George?"

"Sure, sure." I make my way to my seat.

"George, you're just in time—"

"B-eight," calls Miss Arlene.

"Got you a couple cards—"

"You okay? You look white."

"I am white," I say.

Miss Arlene glares at me over her bifocals.

"Sorry I'm late—"

"G-thirty-three."

I sit still, staring at my cards.

"Well, look, George, you got that on both of them." Emmet reaches over me and makes round blue marks on my G-thirty-threes. He looks at me in the eyes. "What's wrong with you? You seen a ghost or something?"

Just then I hear a commotion and turn to see what it is.

"Well, I can't really go on with all you comin' in late, now can I? Might I remind you bingo starts promptly at six thirty."

"Miss Arlene," says Candy, "everyone, this is Joe Stackhouse. He's a new resident here. I want you all to make him feel welcome."

Smiling Betty and a couple other ladies near the window start clapping and Joe looks toward them, eyes sparkling.

"Over here," says Jessica, and she points to an empty chair at the end of the table. Miss Candy walks Joe over slowly, and

I grab ahold of myself. Look at this old man, chugging along. So what, I'm sick? We're all one foot in the grave, like it or not. And who says Dr. Casey knows what the heck he's talking about? He's just a kid. A sixty-five-year-old kid.

"Joe, you clean up good," I say. "Prepare to put your game on. I'm in this for blood."

I smile at him and Emmet gets him a red dauber in his hand and shows him how to press it down on his card. Joe seems to like this game and wants to play along.

Maggie's sitting across from me, chewing gum. I can't stand when they give her gum, but it keeps her from chewing her fingers, I reckon. I'd much prefer the tinfoil, but I wasn't here to insist. She looks at me with watery eyes, chomping, chomping, and I wonder if she knows I'm sick. Can she tell? How I wish I could tell her. Or maybe it's better this way. Maybe it's better that she's oblivious to the world around her. She won't have to know the difference if I'm here or gone or whatnot.

Forty-five minutes later I haven't won a lick, but Jessica won one round and she's wearing the silly red ball cap that was her prize. It goes so well with her shiny goldness. I much prefer the money rounds. About the fourth set, I start hearing an echo of the calls, except the echoes are happening *before* Miss Arlene reads the number.

"O."

"O-forty-one," she calls.

"I."

"I-sixteen," calls Arlene.

I look up in wonder then. My ears aren't playing tricks on me. It's Joe. His lips are moving before each call. I can't believe it.

I nudge Emmet. "Watch Joe."

It happens again.

"B."

"B-two," calls Arlene.

Emmet's eyes go wide and he turns to me. "Genius?" he says.

"I guess so. Or a mind reader, one."

For a while, I just sit there dazed, watching Joe's tricks, and I hardly remember my visit with Dr. Casey. But I know it happened. It seems like a dream, but he was here, wasn't he? Yes. He did say I'm dying.

"G, no, N," says Joe.

"N-twenty-five."

"Bingo," I say. And Miss Arlene informs me that I've won free coupons for peanut butter from the Publix store. She's much too excited about it.

Emmet slaps me on the back and says, "Well done, George."

But Maggie is looking at me from across the table. She's studying me as if she knows something's wrong.

Magnolia

Something's wrong with George. He's not funny tonight. He's not happy he won bingo. He's much too quiet. I study the short white bristles of hair on his head, the length of his ears, his yellowed eyes, but then the blue-green light from the windows calls me. I like this time of day when light glows. When night's blowing in . . .

"Ash, you're awful quiet tonight," my father says. There is a candle in the window that blows and casts shadows across Ash's face. We are bellied up to the table, the rain pounding on our roof. There is a nice spread of biscuits and butter in a dish along with lima beans and a small pork roast, all cooked on the wood burning stove.

"He's thinkin' 'bout the strangers come to town," I say.

"Strangers?"

"The children met a man and his boy about Ash's age today. They're stayin' over at Jacobs Mercantile," says Mama, serving my plate with a spoonful of beans. "Get you a biscuit, Maggie."

"Well, where'd they come from? How long they stayin'? Ash?"

"You can ask him, I reckon."

My eyes pop open and we all turn to look at Ash and how disrespectful he is tonight. It's not like him. No one can utter a word. Finally, Daddy lets it slide.

"I'll go down and meet him tomorrow, this Mister . . ."

"Stackhouse," I volunteer. "His son's name is Joe. And I was thinkin' maybe you could ask them for supper sometime. To be friendly. You always tell us we ought to be friendly, right, Daddy?"

I feel sheepish and pull my ankles together. Daddy looks

at Mama who's smirking. "Runs in her blood, I'm afraid," she says. "How 'bout ask him if he wants to come over tomorrow night? We got a little chicken and some potatoes. A couple more mouths won't hurt."

My father is a good man. He's the kind of man that would stop to help a colored on the side of the road with a drink of water. Never ask for anything in return. Why, when the colored preacher lady, Miss Maple, broke her ankle, Daddy knew she didn't have children to care for her, so he insisted she stay on our sofa so Mama could tend to her. I remember being a tiny thing and sharing my cut-up watermelon with her because Daddy said she was our honored guest.

Mama likes to hold on to Daddy and smile like she's lucky to have him. She loves him. I do too. Ash has a harder time with him than I do for some reason. Must be he's a boy, and there's something between the male folk that scratches a little. Mama says Daddy just wants Ash to turn into a fine young man, and I think he is. 'Cept when he's ornery at me. My brother can go from being happy-go-lucky to mad-as-all-get-out in seconds flat. He's nursing this new boarders thing right well, going on 'most a day.

It's yellow and crisp this morning like all the moisture from the air got dumped on the ground last night. It's a relief not being so hot. I put on my nicer dress that Mama made me with little pink flowers and green leaves. It ties around my waist. I run Mama's comb through my hair, which is not an easy thing to do.

I even wear my Sunday school shoes. And it's only the middle of the week.

Ash is not impressed.

"He's just a boy, and he's older than you. You're seven and a girl, so don't be gettin' all caught up on him."

"I ain't!"

He looks at my shoes and shakes his head. "Just come on. You're gonna get that dress all dirty, you know."

"Ain't neither."

Ash grabs his fishing pole and I grab mine, and we walk over to the Jacobs Mercantile to see if we can borrow some worms.

George Jacobs is behind the cash register, taking money from Mrs. Benchley for some collard greens and ham hocks. I watch his eyebrows lift up at the sight of my dress. I feel pretty all of a sudden, in his eyes.

Miss Tillie sees me and goes on and on, "Look at you— my, my, my. You going fishin' in that dress, Magnolia?"

"Yes'm."

"Well, okay, then . . . here. Ash, some nice juicy worms for you. And some for you, Magnolia. Bring me back a big one, hear? And, Joe? You gonna go fishin' with 'em too? George, you run along now. You can do yer chores later."

Joe comes out from the boarding room, and Mr. Stackhouse comes to the door. "You be good, son, you hear? We're having supper over at the Black residence this evening, so no funny stuff." His eyes glow with warning and he touches his mustache, straightening his points. "Met your daddy today, little lady. He's a fine man. Postal worker."

Prickles go down my spine when he says *postal worker* like it's a dumb thing to be. Miss Tillie gives him a wary eye. "Don't stay too long now, George. Be sure and give Joe the best spot, all right? You children be careful and whatever you do, don't go swimmin'. There was a gator down to the waterin' hole just last week. Might still be there."

"Y'ever swum with a gator, Joe?" Ash says as we get near Togoodoo Creek. It's a long skinny creek a little ways back behind our house, jumpable in a few places, but it empties out into a large pond. Black water. Cattails. Crickets jumping on marsh grass.

"N-not that I know," says Joe. I look up at him as the sunshine hits his face, his brown hair, and swoon. It's a hot flushed feeling. I don't believe I've ever swooned before. There's no one but Ash and George and a handful of other kids younger than me here in Levy. Nobody like Joe.

"Ain't no gator here today, reckon. You think, Ash? Prob'ly gone."

Ash is quiet, unraveling his fishing line. He pulls out a handkerchief of worms from his overalls. I watch as he opens it, and George and Joe and I all circle round, hoping to get a good juicy one. They squirm the most and the fish like to eat them. I don't mind hooking them neither, but Ash has to take my fish off if I catch one. Once I cut my hand up pretty bad and Mama fussed and made him swear not to let me do it again.

We're sitting there, four poles over the water, and a quiet

breeze blowing ripples under my bobber. "What you look for is a black bumpy back or tail, Joe."

"What?"

"Gators," I say. "Or you might see a head and two eyes, real still-like, watchin' you. But I don't see none. If one does get after you, run zigzag 'cause they can only go straight. Or maybe climb a tree. They can't climb."

"We got gators in the bayou," Joe says. "Saw a m-man get his arm bit off."

"Naw. Really?" George scoots closer, his knees up by his ears, his pole out deep. I'm on the other end beside Ash who smacks the back of his thick neck.

"Dang skeeters." Then he says, "Well, what happened?"

"Yeah, to the man?" says George.

"Only had the one arm after that," says Joe. "Then he d-d-died. Went looking for his arm every night, saying, 'W-where's my g-golden arm?'"

"That ain't true," says Ash. "That's a ghost story. I heard it 'fore."

Joe gets real quiet then.

"You makin' up stories, Joe?" says George.

"N-n—"

Ash rolls his sleeves up. "I reckon yore daddy don't want you tellin' lies, now does he? 'Cause we ain't liars round these parts. Don't care what you done down in New Or-leans. Yore in Levy now. Don't forget it."

"He . . . h'ain't my daddy!"

Ash and me look at each other, eyes round as silver dollars. "What you mean he ain't yore daddy? You lyin' again, Joe?"

"I–I just meant—yeah, I'm lyin'."

Joe looks awful pained to be a liar. I know I never want to be one just by looking at him. I feel bad for him and want to tell him it's okay, but I can't. Not now. Not ever.

And the whole day is more of the same. Joe catches three bream and I catch one. George and Ash reel in four apiece, and then they argue over whose is the biggest. Joe stays quieter than the rest of us, I reckon not wanting to spout any more lies.

When the sun gets too hot, we pick up and take the fish back to Jacobs Mercantile. The boys clean them—blood, guts, scales, everything but the heads. Miss Tillie keeps two as payment for the worms and sends the rest home in brown paper for Mama to cook up. She knows we're entertaining strangers tonight, and we don't often have much to offer.

I turn around before we leave, and Joe gives me a last look that likes to pierce my soul. He almost looks scared. I wonder if he ain't a liar then.

TEN

George

"You're a liar," says old man Whalen from across the room.
He's always making trouble. Apparently a little white-haired
lady next to him called bingo when she didn't really have
it, and there's all sorts of commotion going on over there.
Nurses are being called. Putz. Just let her win the dang
socks.

This new guy Joe's making eyes at my wife, and she's
staring back at him, tiny blue marbles. Seems interested.
'Course, she probably can't see so well, what with her macu-
lars degenerating and all. Sort of like the Harmony House
cat when he stares at a curtain or some spot in the air, like
he's eyeing a ghost, something you can't see. Gives me the
gee-willies.

I don't care how old we are, I can take still take this guy.

I push up my sleeve. "Dear, you ready to go?" I put my arm on Maggie's chair. She's my wife. *Why don't you look at somebody else's wife?*

There's a vacancy sign cropping up out of Joe's head, out of his combed-over silver hair. Not much in there. He drums his hands on the table like he's waiting. There must be something going on in that mind. He did guess all those bingo letters right. Who is this guy? What's his problem? Where is Miss Candy when you need her? Oh, right, she's taking care of the kerfluffle across the way.

"Joe, we're headin' back to the room now," I say. "You, uh, you don't want to come with us, do you?"

Aw, gee. Babysitting. Here we go.

Joe smiles and his eyes crinkle up and I swear I've met this man before. Déjà vu or something like that, though I never much believed in it. Strangest thing. Then it passes.

Emmet stands and says, "George, you and Maggie go on. We're calling it a night too. Jessica and I'll take Joe back to his room. Which one?"

"123. You sure?" He nods and I'm glad. I want to be alone in my room with my wife all of a sudden. I'm a dying man, and I'm thinking I might be real tired now. Maybe more tired than usual. I want to hold my wife in my arms and let her love me while I cry myself to sleep. I want her to hold me and tell me that everything will be okay like she used to when we were young and in love and the crops weren't coming in as plentiful as they should or when Alex was sick with the whooping cough and we steamed the room with hot, healing fog. Maggie always knows how to make it better, and maybe tonight will be the night that she can speak to me again, love me again.

I wipe my wet face. It's scratchy from whiskers this time of night. I push Magnolia's wheelchair to our door, and even though it's on the first floor where dementia lives, even though we are older than dirt, she is lovely and sweet and she is my bride. We are crossing the threshold together. I shut the door and want to lock it but I can't. Miss Annie will be coming back soon to put my wife to bed. She will undress her and brush her teeth and hair. She will do all the things I used to do for my wife. She will do these things without breaking a sweat, and with a smile on her face, because she was made for a job like this.

I was not made to be alone at ninety-two with my wife, not knowing me.

I was not made to be dying alone with a stranger in my bed.

It pains me to say it but Maggie and I have become strangers to one another, and this, yes, this is worse than dying any day.

I leave her in her chair in front of the television. *Jeopardy!* is on. We used to like this show and try to outdo each other. Maggie is smarter and usually won. I take off my shoes and sit on the edge of the bed. I lie down on my feather pillow and look toward the large photograph of my younger wife. *I wish we could go back, dear. I wish you were that young girl again, and I was young enough to hold your attention.* A tear escapes my eye and falls wet to my pillowcase. I am glad for Alex Trebek tonight. He can keep my wife company while I feel sorry for myself. There are days when an old man simply has to.

"G'night, Maggie," I muster before the door slowly opens and Miss Annie comes swooping in like she always does, taking care of my wife like I can't anymore.

Taking my place.

ELEVEN

Magnolia

LEVY, 1929

"Here, take my place," Daddy says, standing up and grabbing a chair from the sewing room. The man with the handlebar mustache thanks him and removes his hat.

"I'll take that," says Mama, and I watch as they each hold a rim of it. Their eyes lock for just a second, and something like ripples roll up Mama's spine until she is firm and straight like a board. She leaves the room and heads for her sewing machine to set down Mr. Stackhouse's hat and coat. She stays there for a while. Maybe too long.

When Mama finally comes back in she looks like she might be sick. She is holding her stomach and I ask her, "Mama, you okay?" She just nods and heads to the stove for the pot of potatoes. She sets them on a trivet in the middle of the pine table, and we all sit and get ready to say grace.

"Lord, bless our conversation," says Daddy, "and this food that you have provided. Let it go to the nourishment of our bodies. Amen."

"And God bless the cook," says Mr. Stackhouse. His mustache twitches, and his eyes seem to be hungry, but not for food.

For Mama.

There is a large photograph of me in our little room here in Harmony House. I'm not sure where it came from, but I do remember it. I do remember being that young. I do remember the man who took it. I have not known where this life-sized portrait was, though I have asked for it many times. No matter how much you want your beauty to stay hidden, people will go to great lengths to reveal it to the masses. But it's dangerous, beauty is. I've always known it. And it doesn't last. Just look at what happened to my mother.

We are sitting there around the supper table in Levy. I am just a child. Ash is there to my right and Mama to my left. Daddy is across the table from her, and Mr. Stackhouse and his son, Joe, are across from Ash and me. Thunder rolls through the growing darkness outside. A lantern flickers beside us. "What brings you to Levy, Mr. Stackhouse?" asks Daddy, cutting a piece of chicken off the bone.

"I needed a little quiet place to do some writing. I'm an author, you see. I heard about Levy."

"We don't get too many writers this way. Uh, Joe, are you enjoyin' it? I heard you went fishin' with Ash and Magnolia today."

"Ye-yes, sir."

"Did you catch anythin'?"

"Sir. About th-th-three bream."

"He's a smart boy, just can't talk worth a cuss, can you, son?"

I look over at Joe, horrified for him, then at Mama. She seems to have a chicken bone stuck in her throat. She grabs her chest and says, "'Scuse me."

"I hear you're a magician," says Daddy. "That right?"

"An amateur, I suppose."

"It's a shame what happened to Houdini. I always hoped I'd get the chance to see him one day."

"You know, Mr. Black," says Mr. Stackhouse, "I had the good fortune of watching Houdini about five years ago. He was doing a show down in New Orleans. Was hanging by his feet on a long rope and wrapped up tight in a strait-jacket."

"That right?"

"Darndest thing, after a while, he broke free. Just like that. I guess it's always something that's fascinated me . . . people who can break out of captivity or whatever holds them bound." He looks over at Mama and says, "Must be what got me interested in magic."

"Mama, Mr. Stackhouse is gonna do a magic show after supper," I say. "He did one for George and Miss Tillie today. They said it was really good."

"Oh." Mama nods and grabs her glass of milk. She drinks some, holding it in both hands.

In the sitting room, which is our living room and Mama's sewing room put together, I am perched on the sofa. Candles are lit and the place glows with dancing light.

"Now, if you'll kindly put your attention here," says Mr. Stackhouse, "you'll see what I have is just an ordinary hat." He's wearing a black cape and shows us the inside and top side of a big black hat. It's empty. "With just a wave of my wand here . . ." He waves a long skinny silver wand over the hat in a circle and all of a sudden, flowers pop out.

"Oooh!" I squeal.

"For you," says Mr. Stackhouse, handing me a bouquet of fresh daisies and bowing down real low and dramatic. I hold them and breathe them in.

"And now . . . my faithful assistant, a budding magician in his own right, will read your very minds." Mr. Stackhouse pulls out a deck of cards from his pocket and holds them up for us to see. He fans them, then holds them flat in front of my mother.

"Madam, if you'll do the honors . . . pick a card, please, and hold it to your lovely bosom." Mama doesn't move, just stares at Mr. Stackhouse.

"Go on, honey," says Daddy, enjoying this. It's the most fun we've had as a family in a long time.

Mama reaches a slow finger toward the deck, and Mr. Stackhouse's mustache rises up as he smiles. "Good, good.

Now, don't let anyone see it." He hands the deck of cards to
Joe, who is standing directly in front of me in a clean brown
shirt and black suspenders. Joe seems uneasy. He looks to
Mr. Stackhouse to be sure he's doing it right. "Now, remember what I taught you, son? Put the deck up to your forehead
so you can think hard about them." Joe does. "Good. Now,
fast as you can, turn them over and fan them out for one
second, then back over."

Joe takes the cards down from his forehead and tries to
fan them out, but instead he fumbles, and the cards go flying
out all over the place. They're all over the floor, this way and
that, some up and some face down.

"Stupid boy!" Mr. Stackhouse growls.

Daddy stands up. "Now, here, sir. The boy did his best.
Let me help you."

I watch as my father is down on his knees with Joe, struggling to get all the cards back together. Mama's eyes are white,
glaring at Mr. Stackhouse, who is staring back at her. Joe is
sniffling. He stands back up.

"I don't think my wife is feelin' real well," says Daddy,
standing next to Joe and handing him the cards he picked
up. "You understand if we cut things short."

"Sure. Absolutely. Your wife, she's not feeling well. I do
understand."

Mama gets up and walks slow toward the bedroom, one
foot padding soft in front of the other. In a small voice, Joe
calls after her. "A-a-ace of spades?"

Mama stops and turns around. She almost says something but then doesn't. Instead, she drops the card from her

chest and lets it fall to the floor. I run and pick it up. It's a crumpled ace of spades.

"Maggie, go and grab Mr. Stackhouse's hat and coat for him." So I do, and I find Mama in the bedroom, white as a sheet, sitting in the corner on the hard floor, head down in her knees. "Mama? You sick?"

She shakes her head and manages to whisper, "Just tell me when they're gone."

Before they leave, I smile at Joe and hand him his card. "It was a good trick," I say. "Best one I ever seen."

The next day Mama's up before any of us, mending and sewing like a machine. She doesn't speak much to us, but Ash and I know something's wrong. We know our evening didn't go well.

"There's somethin' wrong with Mr. Stackhouse," says Ash, as we head out into the blue dawn. I'm still rubbing the sleep from my eyes, but he roused me and said we just had to go.

The sound of early birds chirping and an occasional bat is all we hear as we walk along the railroad tracks. Ash is thinking, and this is where he does it the best. We stop when we see a deer family, a mama and her two babies, run across the tracks, white tails flicking, as if they're scared. As if they're running from something.

"I'm gonna ask Joe straight out," says Ash, watching them disappear into the woods. "I'm gonna ask him why they came here. He's hidin' somethin', I know it."

I stay quiet on this. Ash's older than me, and something is wrong, this much I know—so I'm going to let him handle it. I don't mind the fact that I get to see Joe again. I wonder if we can go fishing. I wonder if I should put on my pretty dress, but I don't have time to turn back around. Ash grabs my hand and says, "Just do what I say, Maggie. Don't say nothin' to nobody. Come on. I got a bad feelin'." And we run back the way we came and then off toward Jacobs Mercantile.

TWELVE

Annie

I don't mind waking up early. Mama always told me, "The world don't wait for nobody, Annie. Either live it or don't, but don't show up late." It was the opposite way her family raised her. She told me so many times how much she hated waiting for her mama or daddy to pick her up from some place, sometimes leaving her in the dark and scary for hours on end, white folks eyeing her. My mother is never late for anything. She'll be early to her own funeral. Mark my words.

I'm here before the sun comes up most days. I don't like my residents to linger in bed, in what might be soiled sheets. I figure, they got numbered days; I certainly ain't gonna be the reason they wind up living them in bed. Some of those white folks who eyed Mama are probably in my care these days, but times were different then, I understand that. And age . . . well, age changes everything.

This morning there's a small box sitting in front of George and Magnolia's door. I pick it up and see it's addressed to *Mr. George Jacobs*, but the mailing address is the same one from yesterday, that one in New York City. I push the door in and find Mister George already awake, which is strange. He's sitting on a wooden straight-back chair by the window. The curtains are still closed, but there's blue light coming through them, falling on Mister George's face like sky, like his face is turning into the sky. I rub my eyes. "Hey there, Mister George. You all right?"

He nods and rubs the back of his neck, looking at me. "What'd you bring today? Another surprise?" He don't sound good.

"Found it sittin' out front the door. It's for you. You want me to open it? How long you been up?"

"For me? Who in the—no, no, just bring it here. Lord, what now?"

I set the box on Mister George's lap and notice how frail he seems through his pajama bottoms. He's wearing a white T-shirt and has white stubble down his neck. He looks at the box and holds it away from his eyes so he can see, squinting. "New York City? What the heck? I don't know anybody there. Is this the same guy who sent the picture of Maggie? Bring me that. Yeah, right there."

"Just don't cut yourself."

I move over to Miss Maggie who's got her eyes open now. She sure is a sweet little thing. When she's lying there so helpless, I can't help but think about a child. I can't help but think the Good Lord done give me all the children I need right here in Harmony House, even if I won't have none of my own. It hurts a second, the longing, then I say, "Good mornin', sweet Magnolia. How's my favorite girl today? You ready to wake up?"

I lean down and put my arms around her shoulders and gently hug her to me. She's a tiny little thing and don't weigh but a minute. "There we go, sit up now." I've maneuvered her in her wheelchair more times than I can count, and now I don't hardly have to think about it. I look over to Mister George who's sawing slow around the edges of that box, like he don't want to mess up whatever might be inside it. Far as I know he never gets packages in the mail.

I get Miss Magnolia brushed and cleaned and dressed for the day and set her in front of her big beautiful picture. "I sure do see that pretty young girl in you still," I tell her. And I really do—her delicate little nose, her strong cheekbones, her shoulders, even that wavy hair. My, my, my, a beautiful woman. When I go to leave, Mister George is still sitting right where I found him over by the window. He's holding a card in his hands or something.

"Who's it from?" I ask, knowing it ain't none of my business. I'll be okay if he don't want to tell me, but I got to ask.

"A stranger," says Mister George, with a far-off look in his eye. The blue sky is glowing behind him now that the curtains are opened up wide.

"Everything okay?"

"Yeah. I mean, yes. Thank you, Annie."

"My pleasure, Mister George. I'll be seein' you later now, hear?"

Then I head off to my next resident, Mister Joe Stackhouse. I'm praying my first morning with him goes well.

Mister Joe's room is down at the far end of the hall. There was this little old lady named Sallie who used to live there. She was from England and had this hard-to-understand accent. She was long and fragile and thought I was her old nanny. She went back to being a child, a little girl, there at the end. And she loved me, I mean, she loved her nanny. I tried to make her as comfortable as I could.

But now Mister Joe is in her room. I turn the knob, not really knowing what I'll find. I remember finding Miss Sallie on the floor and that just sent me crying through the halls. It was unbefitting, but what you gonna do? I'm human. So I turn Mister Joe's knob real slow. I walk in the darkness and turn on the bathroom light so I can see a little. "Mister Joe? It's Annie. You sleep good? I thought we could get you up and have you some breakfast."

I move over to the bed and see the coverlet ruffled a little. But other than that, no Mister Joe. "Yoo-hoo."

I find him over toward the windows sitting in a chair, long and crumpled. Looks like he been up all night. "I need to go home," he tells me, "but the d-door is locked."

"Oh, now, Mister Joe. You're gonna like it here. I promise you will. The people are real nice and the place is real pretty. Just wait till we get you some food. Everything'll look a whole lot better with a full stomach."

He sits there a-watching me.

"You been up all night, Mister Joe?" I take his hand and pull him up to standing real slow.

He doesn't answer but I 'spect he has. It always tears me up. Yes sir, it does. This first night always gets to me.

THIRTEEN

Joe

Joe Stackhouse was handsome once. He still is, bar for the yellow teeth and strings of combed-over hair. His eyes are damp. They always are now. His shoes are worn—tan leather wingtips from many years ago. They lean out to the sides. His shoulders struggle to hold up a brown bomber jacket he insists on wearing, and his pants droop long in the back, slightly soiled from the walk over. But he's here in the outdoors where he can be close to nature, listen to the birds, and that's all that matters to him. However he got here. Whoever brought him here.

Joe stands in a little gazebo in a courtyard. He's always liked outdoor structures, things that reminded him of tree houses and playthings for children. Joe always envied children who had tree houses and people who would build them tree houses. For Joe had no one. He catches his breath from the walk and the climb up the step into the gazebo. He looks at a plaque nailed to a bench, and his lips move as he reads it. ERECTED IN MEMORY OF AVERY BAUER. The lips moving—it's something he only started once his hearing and eyesight wore down. Like his shoes.

Joe is kind and possesses the valor of yesteryear. A young lady is walking with an elderly woman along the sidewalk. The girl is pretty. He smiles at the pretty girl and says, "Hello." She smiles back. A cardinal comes and sits on the ledge of the gazebo just a few feet from Joe. It's bright red and flicks its tail. Today is a very good day. Joe is alive.

A cat comes and sits on the floor next to Joe. Joe watches its ears twitch, sees its long striped tail dance while the rest of the body is so still. He likes the bird and he likes the cat. He wonders if the cat will get the bird. He hopes not. Then again, he hopes, for the cat's sake, that it gets the bird. The cat takes one slow, calculated step forward and the cardinal flies off, up to a tree.

"Too bad, old boy," says Joe. He finds his way to the bench and slowly sits. He pats the top of his legs and the cat watches him. It sits on its haunches, green eyes looking around for more birds, but seeing none, it comes and sits on the bench beside Joe.

He lifts a shaky hand and rubs the soft fur on its back. The cat arches with pleasure and Joe smiles. He hasn't a clue how he got here to this gazebo with the cat, but he is happy here. He's always been alone. Now he is alone with a cat. He sticks his hand out and lets the cat rub its jowls on his gnarled fingers. "What are you doing here, kitty cat? Did someone

send you? Hmmm? Did they send you to find me? Oh goodness. Is it time to go back to work?"

Joe stiffens for a moment and thinks about messages. He
once had a job in the war, decoding messages. *Is this cat a spy?*
he wonders. Then, no, that's silly. A cat cannot be a spy. Still,
Joe is nervous. About the war. About work that must be done.
He feels that there's somewhere he needs to be. There are
messages he should be reading, lives to save.

The cat stands and presses itself against Joe's arm, wanting to be closer. Scratching his chin, Joe lets the tiger-striped
cat jump up on his lap, and he smiles very contently. He
doesn't much want to get off this bench now. Perhaps he can
stay awhile. It's been so long since any creature at all has given
him love.

"Joe? Mister Joe?" A woman comes to him, arms out-
stretched. "You 'bout ready to go in for breakfast, honey? I
swanny, that cat. Shoo." She comes close and the cat runs off.
Joe is a little sad now. And a little alarmed. He does not know
who this woman is or why she knows his name. The closer
she gets, the more he can see the color of her skin. It's light
brown and golden, like maple syrup. Joe thinks he remembers
a woman this color once. Has she come to get him? His heart
jumps. Has she finally come to take him home?

FOURTEEN

Magnolia

LEVY, 1929

Ash and I left home early this morning, and we're sneaking up on Jacobs Mercantile while black crows dance on the ground, pecking at spilled seed. We peek in the window. George is in there, stocking cans of condensed milk up against the far wall. He's tiptoeing and aiming to be quiet about it since that wall backs up to the boarding room. The door is closed, so we knock real light on the window. George looks over his shoulder, stops what he's doing, and comes to us.

"What are you doin' here so early?" he says, unlatching the door.

"We got to talk," says Ash. "It's about—" and he motions his head toward the boarding room. "Is Joe up?"

"Yeah, he's out back helpin' Mama pull weeds."

"What about his daddy? He up?"

"No. I been tryin' to be quiet. He sleeps late. I can hear him snorin'."

"Good. Go get Joe and meet us at the church."

"Why?"

"Just do it."

So Ash and me hop across the street and go sit on a bench on the side of the Levy First Baptist Church. After a minute or two, we see George and Joe, walking along, quiet, peering back every now and again to see if anybody's looking.

"What's this all about?" asks George, popping sunflower seeds in his mouth and crunching. Ash sits up and says, "Joe, have a seat."

My face goes flush because he's sitting beside me now. His cheeks are ruddy. I can tell he's nervous, and I have to hold back the urge to reach over and touch his hand.

My brother starts pacing in front of him, seems to be struggling for what to say.

"Listen here, Joe. Last night was . . . well, what I aim to say is . . . look." He stops and faces him, hands on hips. "I think you're a nice enough fella, but I gotta ask you honest. What you hidin'?"

Joe's head starts shaking slightly and he keeps his gaze on Ash. He doesn't say anything, then slowly moves to standing. Ash and George come stand close in front of him to block.

"I don't want no trouble," says Ash, "but I know somethin's goin' on. Tell me. You scared o' yore pa? That what this is? That why you won't talk?"

Joe looks like he's thinking of running. He glances over

to the store, then creeps to the hidden side of the church. We all follow.

"I told you," says Joe, looking at the dirt.

"Told us what?"

"But if you say anything, he'll kill me. With his b-bare hands, he said."

And that's when Joe opens up and tears roll down his face. He leans back against the church and whispers, "I was w-w-walking along the tracks 'cause I left home. I didn't know where to g-go. Then I seen the train and I thought about getting on. He c-come to me then, off the train, and tells me he's a magician and he needs an a-a-apprentice, and I got nowhere to go and he says we'll have adventure, so I get on the train. After while, we stop in Georgia and he gets me some c-clothes, some food, gets me cleaned up. He says p-part of the show is I got to pretend he's my daddy, and if I do, everything's s-s-swell, and if I don't, well, he'll throw me in front of the tracks. I don't mean no harm, I just—"

"All creation." Ash puts his hand on Joe's shoulder, and Joe shakes and tries to cry as quiet as he can. "Listen, I knew somethin' was wrong. I knew it. Now, we're gonna help you, Joe. We are. But you got to help us too."

Joe looks at him and nods. He wipes his nose.

"Why'd you come to Levy?" says Ash.

"I don't know. Honest. But I think there's s-something here he wants."

"How long you stayin'?"

"Don't know."

George has been listening and his eyes are tearing up. I

see him in a different light now. There's a kindness I didn't know he had. "He's got that trunk," says George. "You looked in there?"

Joe shakes his head.

"I'm bettin' he's got secrets in there. I'm bettin' we look in that trunk, we're gonna find out who Mr. Stackhouse really is."

"His name ain't S-Stackhouse," says Joe, looking up at Ash in the eyes like he's getting some nerve. "It's my name. He took it."

"Well, what's his name?"

"Don't know. I don't know."

George wraps his arm around Joe—just two days ago a perfect stranger—and says, "It'll be all right. We just got to figure out how to keep him busy while we look in that trunk." So we sit in silence for several minutes, all of us trying to figure what to do. Finally, I have a thought. "Sometimes I sneak cookies while Mama's sleepin' real hard. Maybe we could go in when he's sleepin'."

Ash thinks about that and says, "Maggie, Mama only sleeps that hard after she's been to see Miss Maple."

"Uh-huh. She gives her sleepin' medicine."

"It's not medicine, Maggie. It's moonshine."

And I've never felt so embarrassed and affronted in all my life. I have no idea what moonshine is, but these boys all seem to know. Sometimes I hate being younger. I wish I could go and hide.

"That's what we need . . . some of that moonshine," says George. He rubs his hands together and looks over toward the colored side of town. "And I think I know just how to get it."

FIFTEEN

George

I've never been one for drinking, but I sure could use a good scotch and soda right now, even if it is eight o'clock in the morning. I can't believe it. I just can't believe what I am seeing.

Maggie is over near the card table. She's sitting in her wheelchair where Annie left her, looking down at her hands. She's got washcloths in them so they'll be still. She seems to be studying the cloths. I wonder if she's thinking anything. I wish I could get in her head. The life-sized portrait is behind her, a long, lean, voluptuous account of my younger wife. She lies there, smiling behind Maggie, like the stranger she's become.

I know who sent that portrait now, and it's more than I can handle. For a split second, it makes sense I'm dying, because I don't know how I can live through all this. I never thought I'd see the day.

I lean the card toward the light from the window and read it again with a shaky hand. Slower this time.

July 28, 2010

Dear Mr. Jacobs,

You don't know me, but I am your nephew, or rather, your wife Magnolia's nephew, James Black. You may remember your wife had an older brother named Ash. I am Ash's son.

I know this must be strange to receive a note from me, but my father was ill for a very long time, and before he died, he wanted me to send you the letters he'd written to you over the years. He never felt able to send them himself. My father spoke occasionally about you and Magnolia, always fondly, but when I asked why we never visited, he told me it was a long story and that it was impossible. As a child, this made no sense to me. I hope you don't mind, but I took the liberty of reading these letters before sending them on to you. I understand now that it is a difficult story. I just wish there had been some other way. I wish there had been some way to keep the family together.

It is my hope that I can meet you and Magnolia soon. I will be traveling down to South Carolina in a week's time to put my father to rest. He wants me to scatter his ashes over a little pond in Levy, where he—and you and Magnolia—grew up. I don't even know if Togoodoo Creek is still there, let alone Levy, but I will find out soon enough.

I am sorry that we have not had the chance to meet before this, but as you'll read, time and circumstance have kept us apart.

I understand that Magnolia has suffered some strokes as
of late. I am very sorry to hear that. My father always kept up
with her . . . and you . . . but from afar. He loved her very
much. Please give her my best.

Sincerely yours,

James T. Black

P.S. I have sent by post a portrait of your wife when she
was younger. I hope you'll have some place to put her as she's
very beautiful, but large. My father kept her in his study for
most of my life, and I had a hard time parting with her, but
I know the portrait truly belongs to you and Magnolia. Dad's
letters will explain how she came to be in his possession. I
hope to be able to meet you both soon.

I set the card down on my legs and feel dizzy. Good thing
I'm sitting. I close my eyes and try to remember. Honestly, I
haven't thought about Levy in years. There are some things
you work hard to forget, and there are others that do the honors and erase themselves from your memory all on their own.
Levy was one of them.

It's been gone for nearly eighty years. Why must I bring it
back? Why? I look out the window at buzzards in a far-off tree.
You're waiting for me, aren't you? Well, I won't let you have
me without a fight. I won't remember Levy. I won't remember
Ash. I won't.

I look over at Maggie. "Honey, you ready for breakfast?
You hungry? Just give me a minute to wash up." She watches
me with anticipation. I'd like to think it's because she knows

who I am, but who am I kidding? She's hungry. That's the only reason she's looking at me with any interest at all.

I stand up and take the card and box of letters and shove it all on the shelf next to Magnolia's stolen sugar packets. Occasionally, over the years, she's had spells of pilfering little things, knickknacks. One time I caught her taking a piece of chicken off an old woman's plate. Another time she had so many packets of saccharin in her purse, she couldn't carry it because of the weight. My eye catches the glint of her aluminum wands and for a second, just a flash, a memory hits me square between the eyes. Dag-nabbit. I shake my head to clear myself of it. There's no way I'm going back to Levy. It's too bad Ash's gone, but he might as well have held his peace and taken those letters to his grave.

SIXTEEN

Magnolia

I'd like to ask George who sent him that package. I'd like
for him to tell me what's going on. He's not himself. He's
up early, he's staring out the window, he's quiet. *George? Are
you all right?* I wish the words would come, but they don't,
dad-blum. He's dressed now and pushing me down a long,
narrow hall. I can hear his breathing. There's a rattle, a
stress there. More breathing, more sneaking . . . and then
we're gone.

We are running through the woods on the colored side of town
where only five houses have people anymore. Most everybody
left awhile back, and the empty places have paint peeling,
boards sagging. The full houses aren't much better.

There's a blue house at the end of a dirt road. This is

where Miss Maple lives. Her daughter died when she was just a baby. Her sons took off on the Boll Weevil and headed north for better lives. Miss Maple's all alone now. She sits on her porch sometimes rocking, waving to neighbors, sometimes coming into Jacobs Mercantile and is always real sweet to me. She preaches at the colored church. Imagine that. A woman preacher. I've never seen her do it, but I picture her, ears close to God, him sitting next to her, whispering secrets of creation and salvation. Every now and again when Mama's ill she has Miss Maple come make our supper. My favorite are her corn muffins with little bits of corn inside. She says she makes them just for me.

Miss Maple's got a shed out back behind her house. Ash and George seem to know it.

"In there," says George. "It's where she keeps her still."

The sun is rising up over the pine trees. We heard roosters calling on the way through the woods, and I imagine most everybody's up by now.

"How we gonna get in there?"

"Shh," says Ash. "Stay quiet, Maggie."

"How come I always got to be quiet?"

"Shhh!" George looks at me, finger to his mouth, and I hate him right now. Square, up and down. Don't tell me to be quiet. You be quiet.

"Maggie," whispers Ash. "Go on up front and listen out for us. If you hear her stirrin' around, knock on her door real loud so she'll come up to you and not round back to us. Keep her talkin'. Okay?"

"What do I say?"

"I don't know, anythin', just get goin'. We only got a minute."

Not sure about this, I walk around the edge of the house, past dark windows, a square vegetable garden, and an old, rusty crab trap. I get to the front and wait, trying to listen for my brother and Joe and George out back. I hear a bump, some footsteps, and my heart races till it might burst. I put my hands to my mouth and hold my breath. Then a light comes on in the front of Miss Maple's house, and I set on fire. I move up those steps quiet and quick and stand there at her front door, hand raised to knock. *Knock, Maggie. Knock!* So I do.

A dog barks off in the distance and makes me jump.

I knock again, louder. Finally, the doorknob turns, and Miss Maple's blue-handkerchiefed head peeks out. Her skin is light and her eyes are dark and puffy. They're looking straight at me.

"Chile, what you need? Everythin' all right?" She wipes her mouth.

"Yes'm, Miss Maple, I just . . ." I turn to look behind me. I'm searching for the words. I lick my lips. "I was . . . just wonderin' . . ."

"Spit it out, now." She's covered with concern.

"I was wonderin' . . . could you do me some lady preachin'? I ain't never heard none before." It sounds even worse out loud than it did in my head.

"What in tarnation?" Miss Maple looks behind me, clutching her housecoat at the neck. "Somebody send you over here? Your mama all right?"

"She's fine, I just—"

"Why you out so early, Miss Magnolia? I ain't never seen you this time o' day. Yo' daddy need me to watch over you?"

I bite my lip. Please have something to say. *Please, God, whisper in my ear like you do Miss Maple.* She watches me with suspicion.

"No, it's just I . . . I'm thinkin' 'bout being a preacher lady myself someday. I don't want nobody to know, I reckon."

Her eyes lift and soften, and she looks around and smiles. The door opens a little more, and I can see some wood chairs and a round colored rug. "Come on in, chile, Lawd have mercy. He musta woked you up early this mornin' and touched yore heart. Imagine that . . . feelin' the call at . . . how old you is now?"

"Seven," I say.

"Well then, come on in. Praise Jesus. I declare. Seven year old. All dat prayin' I done, done you some good!"

The door shuts behind me, and my knees shake as I imagine Ash and George and Joe stealing moonshine out of Miss Maple's shed this very minute. A flash of guilty runs over me, hot and rampant and vicious, and I get to thinkin' the Lord won't look too kindly on me for lying—about wanting to be a preacher on top of it all. I reckon he'll have to deal with me later over that. Miss Maple offers me a cold corn muffin and I take it greedily and sit, wondering how I'll ever get out of here.

She comes and plops down next to me and all of a sudden starts boo-hooing. "Oh, Lawd, thank you, thank you for this chile!"

"Miss Maple? Why you cryin'?" She looks at me and

reaches for my face, then pulls me close into her bosom and rocks me like she always has.

"De Lawd done took away my only gal, Miss Maggie, and I never done understood why. Not never . . . till this very second." She sniffles and makes me look her in the eyes. She smiles real sweet and says, "I know now, he done give me you."

SEVENTEEN

George

Emmet, Jessica, and Joe are already at the breakfast table, waiting for us. Joe is shaven and cleaned up, wearing suspenders over a small potbelly. Emmet, as usual, has on his gray cardigan and driver's cap, souvenirs from his days in Ireland. Jessica is bright in a yellow blouse with ruffles at the wrists. Almost hurts the eyes. "Mornin', folks."

"Good mornin', George. Hey there, Maggie. Here, put her next to me," says Jessica. She takes Maggie's napkin and lays it across her lap. Maggie reaches up, slow and shaky, for the middle of the table. "You want a muffin?" Jessica moves the sweetgrass basket closer to her and lets Maggie grab one for herself. Then she holds it out over her plate and crumbles the edges. "Here, let me help you." Jessica pulls off a small piece and holds it to her lips. My wife takes it like a pretty little bird. Every time she eats it makes me happy. Nourishment to live. Appetite is a good thing, except I'm not sure I have one today.

God, I'm going to miss my wife. The feeling is too intense for an old man, yet there it is, hot, wet metal under my skin. My eyes well up. She has always been by my side through thick and thin. How shallow life would have been without her. How empty. *Can you miss somebody, you know, when you're in heaven? Up there?* I wonder. *Or does the missing part end?* I reach over and touch Maggie's arm.

"Fantasia, honey, bring us some coffee."

"Comin' right up."

My wife nibbles, and I smell her powder. I inhale deeply, but my lungs hurt. I cough and I can't stop coughing.

"George?"

Fantasia comes over and pats my back. "You all right, Mister George?" I nod with tears in my eyes. I wipe my mouth with my napkin and set it in my lap. I hold up a shaky finger to let everybody know I need a minute. Ah, dang, I don't want attention. If I'm gonna die, just let me do it in peace.

Finally, I muster a smile and push back a cough. "I'm fine," I say, my voice scratchy.

"Here's some water," says Fantasia. "Drink it. Let me know if you need anythin' else. You ready for some food? You havin' bacon again this mornin'?"

"No, I don't think so. I'm not sure I'm man enough for that today. Couple of scrambled eggs, please. Oh, uh, and one piece of wheat toast."

Fantasia takes all the rest of the orders and I look over at Joe. He's been watching me this whole time. I nod at him and say, "Mornin', Joe. Sorry for all the excitement." And he looks at me and holds his old hand up in greeting.

"Hello. I'm Joe."

Heaven help me. Here we go again.

"George, I was telling Emmet about that portrait of Magnolia you got in the mail. You think we could come by and see it after breakfast?"

"I—sure."

"Do you know who sent it to you?" asks Emmet.

"I think I might." I watch the cars in the parking lot through the window. I'd give anything to be out there.

"Well?"

"You know, I'm really not that hungry after all. I think I'll just take a muffin to the room and lie down."

Jessica's painted left eyebrow rises to her wig. "George?"

I push to standing and say my good-byes. I'm not ready for this. I'm not ready to be interrogated. I've been comfortably fussing over my wife and bellyaching over all that's gone on with her over the past however-many years, exactly because I don't like this.

I don't want anyone's questions, or pity, or anything.

I am trembling as I grab two muffins from the basket and lean down to kiss my wife's head. "Why don't you all enjoy breakfast? Bring Maggie on back after a while. Take your time. Do you mind?"

"No, not at all. You sure you're all right? Should we get a nurse? A doctor?"

"No doctors, I'm fine. Y'all excuse me."

And I walk with my back to my best friends in the world.

I simply cannot believe at my age I'm being forced to rehash all this childhood nonsense. But I can't stop thinking about Levy. I've got nothing to do now but think. Nothing to do but read those dang letters and suffer over lost time. Waiting for it all to end.

EIGHTEEN

Magnolia

LEVY, 1929

"Now some folk think nothin' happen when you dead and gone," Miss Maple says, "think you go to sleep forever, nothin' but black all roun'. Can you 'magine? Them folks is wrong, I'm here to tell you." Miss Maple looks at me and hands me another corn muffin. I wipe the crumbs off my chin and stick the new one up to my mouth. In the corner of the room a cat lies in a ball, curled up and uninterested in what she's saying. Miss Maple doesn't sit, she just holds her hands behind her back and paces slowly in brown slippers, sliding over the floor, back and forth in front of me. Her head goes down when she's thinking, then up to the ceiling, then she speaks again, long and blustery.

"Now what you's feelin' is prob'ly confusin' on you. Young gal like yo'self. I'm just a-thinkin' . . . thinkin' maybe your mama past done caught up with her . . . see, now, Gawd works in mighty mysterious ways, and yore mama been makin' good on her life. Yessir. Good with Ash, Mister Black, and you, baby gal." She smiles real sweet and pets me on the head. "Yessir, I'm thinking this is an answer to prayer and good livin' . . ."

All the while I keep looking out the window, wondering what the boys are doing. Did they escape? I want so bad to join them. Miss Maple tells me all about how the Lord calls a body, how his spirit crawls up in your soul, how you can't help but shout out his name and the holy truth of Jesus. I sit there and nod, scared half to death. We're going to be caught. I wonder if she can see the guilt all over my face.

I eat a whole 'nother three muffins till there aren't any more for her to offer. After a while of me not talking and such, Miss Maple sends me on home to give my best to Mama. Tells me if I get the itching to preach again, to head on back and she'll teach me some more. She'll keep my secret, just between us. She kisses me hard on my forehead as I walk out the door, and I can feel her love and my betrayal still sitting there, smack dab between my eyes.

My feet barely hit the ground as I run back over to Jacobs Mercantile, and there they are—Ash, George, and Joe. I try to calm down my breathing. I've been locked up in Miss Maple's house for what seems like forever, and you'd think somebody could welcome me back. You'd think somebody could say *sorry you had to lie* and *thank you for saving us*, but no. "I'm here. I'm back. Had to sit there forever and eat muffins and listen to preachin' . . ."

"Hey, Maggie." George smiles at me. His right front tooth is coming in all big and crooked. It's a smile hard to resist, seeing as I'm missing a tooth of my own, so I smile back. At least somebody's glad I made it out all right. "I never thought he'd drink the whole thing, Ash. You reckon he'll be all right?" George peeks through a long gap in the clapboard wall of the boarding room behind Jacobs Mercantile. I watch his ears rise. "Think he might die?"

"You cain't die from moonshine," says Ash. "Can you?"

"Sure you can. You 'member Anson Swaggs? Member how he fell in front of that train?"

"Yeah, but that was an accident. That was just a side offerin' from the moonshine. Weren't the moonshine itself, what did it."

"Well, if he does die, I don't want it on my head."

"He ain't gonna die," says Ash. "Hush up, now."

I look at Joe, trembling in his shoes. "How'd you get him to drink it?" I ask.

"Just set it on his night table whilst he was in the out-house," says George. "Then we sat here and watched. He eyed it, held it in his hands, wondering where it come from, maybe thinking it'd been there the whole time. Then he stuck it in a drawer for a while like he didn't want it. Later he come back and threw it down. I ain't never seen nobody drink that fast."

I peek in and see Mr. Stackhouse lying there, still, like a dead man, arms and legs sprawled all over the bed. I listen. "He ain't snorin'. You sure he ain't dead?"

"Yep, he snorts every now and again. He's all right." Ash

turns to Joe and says, "You ready to go in? We got to get in that trunk."

"There's a-a key," says Joe. "In his pants pocket."

"Maggie, you stay here and keep watch. You're real good at it. If anybody comes, you keep 'em busy."

This time I don't argue with my brother at all. There is no way I want in that room when the man could wake up any minute now. No sir. I nod and watch as Ash and George and Joe tiptoe past the creaky door. I hold my breath for them and look around, trying to keep watch. I don't want to see the boys as they enter the lion's den. Don't want to see them rifling through that strange man's pockets. Don't want to see it when he wakes up and kills them all dead.

NINETEEN

George

I sit here, an old man in our tiny room and think, *How could it come to this? How could a whole lifetime together come to this? To this little room? To this letter I hold in my hands? How could all the years just strip away like this and rub me raw?*

I can hear Ash's voice in his letter. It's him, all right. No matter how many years pile up, some things, some bonds made as children—well, I guess there's nothing stronger.

Ash's letter is dated April 12, 1997, twelve, thirteen years ago.

George,

As I'm getting older, as my body slows, I'm finding it hard to stay busy enough to fight back the memories, but they're there, pushing up like weeds. I imagine the same must be happening for you, old friend. I hope you've come to terms with the past. At least as much as I have.

I can't go into everything that happened in Levy just yet.
Can't force myself to write about it, but I will tell you about
the years after. They weren't so bad. I got used to it. I rode the
trains till I couldn't ride anymore, stowing away in cattle cars
or anywhere I could find. I lived for a while at an orphanage
in Portland after a nun found me sleeping in the train depot.
It was good to have a bed again. There was a girls' home on
the same grounds, and I didn't make many friends, but there
was a little girl there who looked a lot like our Magnolia. She
had strawberry blond hair and big blue eyes. I couldn't imagine a parent giving her up, but her parents had died. I almost
thought she was lucky. It would've been easier to have your
parents die than what I went through, I thought.

Miriam was her name. She was a sweet, pretty child. We
became friends and would look at bugs and worms and frogs in
the yard when we could get together. I wanted badly to go back
to the good times in Levy, for there were so many, but then . . .
well, then somebody thought it was strange for a boy my age—I
was about thirteen by this time—to be friends with a girl of six
or seven. They put an end to that real quick, and I didn't fight
it. She tried to play with me, but I told her to scram. I was hor-
rible to her. Made her cry and everything, but my life would've
gotten much harder than it already was. I was just biding time,
anyway. Another two years and I'd be gone. No big deal. I'm
not complaining, just explaining things as I saw them.

I ran away from St. Mary's Home for Boys after midnight
in the summertime when I was fifteen. I caught a train, fell in
with some hobos, and found myself working for a carnival in
California. Nobody cared where I was from or how old I was.

Everyone there was a misfit of some sort, so they didn't mind me. I was young and strong and a good worker. I liked the work. I liked pounding in tent poles and feeding horses and seeing the pretty ladies.

We'd make a town happy for a while and then move on to the next. Some towns were better than others. Some had boys who wanted to fight, in others it rained all the while. But every time we set down in a new town and stepped foot on the empty fairgrounds, I would look out and see nothing but a blank slate. A world of possibility, of starting over. A world that could be anything we wanted it to be. We had no idea whether it would be a good time or not. That was part of the fun, the not knowing. I sometimes dreamed that I would be working a fair and all of a sudden, Maggie would come over and tug on my shirt. I would know her face the second I saw it because I'd memorized it and studied it every night with my eyes closed in bed. Some people counted sheep. I would study the gentle features of her face, the freckles that dotted her nose. The way her tiny hand felt in mine. I would see her face and know it was her and pick her up and swing her around. And then I'd talk her into running away with me. I'd take care of her until her dying day.

But it never happened like that. Every town, every new fairground brought the possibility of Maggie, but it never actually brought her.

And then, well, then there was the New York World's Fair. And that's when everything changed. Everything.

You're a lucky man, George Jacobs. I hope you know that. I hope it's settled down into your bones so there's no doubt in your mind: *you have led a blessed life.* Mine has been filled with its share of blessings too, but it's always been void of her. I still love and miss my baby sister. Please tell me you've treated her right.

Your old friend,

Ash

There is a knock at the door and I have no time to hide.

"George?" It's Jessica. She is pushing my wife in the door. *Maggie. Oh, Maggie.* I don't want her to see me like this.

"Emmet, come here, take care of Maggie." Jessica hurries over to me and kneels down. I am a wreck, wet stuff all over my face, my body shaking. There's no controlling it. "George?" Jessica holds my shoulders and her eyes begin to tear up. "Honey, are you all right? What's wrong? Emmet, go get a nurse!"

I shake my head no, *no,* but I can't get the words to come out. Through a haze, I see my wife in her wheelchair, watching me. She is old and fading. Behind her, a large portrait of a seventeen-year-old beauty smiles as if nothing could ever go wrong with the world. And in my mind's eye, I see the young Maggie standing there, the seven-year-old girl with freckles and a missing tooth, whose world changed when her brother went away. She is lifting something now and pointing it at me. It's a wand, a hand-pressed silver wand.

I fall to pieces then. *I love you, Maggie. Please tell me I've treated you right.*

TWENTY

Magnolia

My husband is blubbering by the window. The last time I saw him like this was . . . well, when we were expecting our little boy and lost him. I've always been so sad that George didn't have a son, but it wasn't meant to be, I reckon. I do hate seeing him cry.

I wish I could comfort my George. I push myself up and find that I am standing on two legs. I want to move. I want to take a step . . .

"Goodness, it's all right, Maggie."

Don't make me sit! I want to see what's wrong with my George! Diddly, Emmet. I am sitting again. I am clutching the arms of my wheelchair. Miss Annie is coming in now, concern all over her face. *Annie, tell me what's wrong with him.*

"Mister George, you okay? Let me look at you." She takes a cloth and wipes his face. He's sitting by the sunlight, clutching a piece of paper. "What you got there? A letter? This what has you so upset, or you sick? Which one? You sick, Mister George? Here, let me get you over to the bed."

"I don't want to go to bed!" says George, finally catching his breath and finding his voice. We're all around him, me, Emmet, Jessica, Annie, gaping at him. *I'd be mad, too, if I were you, sweetie. Let 'em have it.*

"Take a deep breath for me, all right? There. Miss Jessica, would you be a dear and grab me a glass of water? There's a cup in the bathroom." Miss Annie kneels in front of George and takes his hands in hers. They're always big and warm like bread dough. She takes the letter and folds it, not looking at what it says. She sets it down on the ground and says, "Look at me." And my husband obeys. "What you want me to do? You want to be alone? You want company?"

George sits there a minute, then he shrugs. His ears stick out, and it reminds me so much of when he was a boy. He still is that boy, stuck in an old man's body.

"Thank you, Miss Jessica." Annie takes the water and puts the glass up to George's lips. "Drink this now." He does and takes the glass from her. "How 'bout you and Mister Emmet go on out for a little while. I'm gonna let Miss Magnolia and Mister George here rest a bit."

"Oh, okay," says Jessica. *Thank you for understanding, Jess.* "We'll be . . . well, you let us know if you need anything at all." She takes Emmet's arm and they walk out quietly. I am glad when they're gone and the door is shut.

Miss Annie breathes in deep and lets it out slow. "The letter, Mister George. It's got you all torn up."

He nods and takes another sip of water.

"Somebody die? That it?"

He scrunches his face.

"Is it from the same person what sent that picture of Miss Magnolia there?"

I wait to see and after a second, he mumbles mmm-hmm.

"Oh, Lawd have mercy, I see. You think you wanna tell me about it now? Wanna get this off your chest?"

"No, Annie. I can't."

"Alrighty then, I won't press you. But I will say this: Ain't nothin' I won't help you get through. You know that? You know I'd do anythin' for you and Miss Magnolia?"

He nods. "I do know that. Thank you, Miss Annie. You're a true friend."

Miss Annie hands him a tissue and leans up and kisses George on the cheek. Then she comes over to me and whispers in my ear, "Miss Magnolia, you take good care of your sweet husband now, hear? He's a good man, that one. A real keeper." I close my eyes and listen to her mumbling as she heads out the door. "Somebody died and he cain't even talk about it. Somebody *died* . . . sweet Jesus, have mercy . . ."

I hope he's not dead, but part of me hopes he is so he won't wake up. I've decided to watch. I've decided that if the magician wakes up and grabs my brother, I can at least haul off and run go get Mr. Jacobs out in the field. But he's not waking up. He's still lying there on that bed, not moving. Ash and Joe and George are on the other side of the wall, just feet from me, kneeling down at the big black trunk. They've opened it up. I watch their eyes to see what might be in it. The breeze blows and I catch a whiff of manure mixed with something musty from inside the boarding room.

"Wow," says George.

"What? What is it?"

"Turn around, Maggie! Keep a lookout!"

I obey and listen to Ash, dying to hear.

"Whoa, look at this. He really is a magician."

"Look, a hat. Can you pull a rabbit out?"

"Abracadabraaaa."

I turn back around and peek through the hole. Ash is wearing a top hat, George is wrapping a long black cape around his shoulders, and Joe is holding something in his hand.

"Is that a wand?" I ask. "Give it to me! Please!" Joe pushes the wand through the little slot between the boards and I hold it in my hands. It is long and skinny, silver and shiny, and I run it through my fingers, almost feeling powerful. I point it at a big black ant and close my eyes, trying to turn it into a frog. It doesn't, but I pretend it does anyway. I point it to my dress, pink gingham, dirty around the hem, and I close my eyes, pretending it's a white ball gown with glass slippers. I open my eyes and really believe it for a second. Then I hear, "What's it say?"

"Hold on."

I look back into the room. The magician isn't moving and neither are the boys. My brother Ash is holding a newspaper out in front of him and looking at the front page. His brow is furrowed and his eyes are racing back and forth. He licks his lips.

"What?" asks George. Reading isn't his strong point. He doesn't like to study much.

"It says . . ." Ash breathes out heavy. "I cain't believe it."

"What? What's it say?"

"It's about . . . Mama."

"Who? Your mama?" says George.

Ash nods, and my stomach fills up with bile and sap. I don't like the look on his face, but it makes sense now. After dinner last night, I reckoned the magician knew my mother somehow. I just didn't want him to.

"Ash?" My voice wavers.

"Maggie, turn back around." So I do.

"Here, put these things back." I hear shuffling and crinkling, and I blink and think of Miss Maple's face. I almost wish I was back in the safety of her room, nothing better to do than eat corn muffins and get an earful.

"George, your daddy's comin'!" I watch as he moves through the rows of corn, straight at me. He's a tall thin man, wears a black faded hat and overalls. He's carrying a bushel at his side. I hear the *swish, swish* of cornstalks as he pushes them aside.

"Mornin' Maggie," he hollers. "You seen George?"

"M-me? No, sir. I ain't a-seen him." I lie so easy, it nearly scares me. After he walks around front, I say, "Hurry, hurry up!"

Next thing I know, all four of us are running through the woods toward the creek like a gator's after us, 'cept we ain't zigzagging, we're straight like bullets. Ash's in the lead with folded newspapers under his arm. He's hightailing it, running like there's no tomorrow, and for a scary second I half-believe it's true—maybe there isn't. Something's real wrong. Maybe tomorrow won't ever come.

TWENTY-ONE

Magnolia

LEVY, 1929

The newspapers from the magician's trunk talk about Mama with pictures and everything. Ash reads them to me and I listen, eyes closed.

November 2, 1917—SCANDAL BREAKS OUT AT STATE FARM WHEN GUARD "ELOPES" WITH PRISONER. Man Deserts His Family; Woman Leaves Her Mother Behind Bars.

November 8, 1917—GUARD COMPELLED HER TO ELOPE, GIRL SAYS. Beautiful Girl and Guard from State Farm Are Captured in Tampa When Their Funds Gave Out.

November 9, 1917—ELOPING COUPLE FROM PENITENTIARY WILL BE BROUGHT HOME TUESDAY. Juanita Dyes Her Hair Red for Disguise; Dans Seems a Little Chilly. Ex-Convict Points Out Prison Guard to Tampa Police.

November 10, 1917–CHAMPION PRISON ELOPERS ARE NOW RETURNING FROM HONEYMOON. Juanita Will Resume Her Task as Water Carrier; Dans Will Have a Cell in Jail on Felony Charge.

November 11, 1917–CLAIMING THAT HER LIFE WAS THREATENED BY DANS, JUANITA WELCOMES ARREST. Dyed Her Hair from Blond to Bright Red to Throw Pursuers Off Track. Says Capture Came as Relief, as Husband Kept Close Watch of Her.

November 11, 1917—DANS THE LOSER EVEN IF JUANITA PAID THE BILLS. Eloping Prison Guard Denies He Married Fair Prisoner, but Charges Her with "Vamping" Him away from His Job.

December 21, 1917—JUANITA AGAIN ESCAPES FROM PRISON; RETURNS.

January 18, 1918—DANS RECEIVES TWO YEARS. Prison Guard Who "Eloped" with Fair Juanita Pleads Guilty.

August 15, 1918—GOVERNOR FREES BLOND BEAUTY OF THE PRISON FARM.

Ash is on his knees in the dirt. He's got dust on his forehead from wiping the sweat away with the back of his hand. The papers are sprawled out in front of us—me, George, and Joe. Joe looks as if his eyes might pop. George is clutching the chest of his overalls, and I am too stunned to cry.

"Is Mr. Stackhouse's real name J. W. Dans?" asks Ash, sounding afraid of the answer.

"I don't know," says Joe. "That could be him, but he's got a m-mustache now. You sure that's your mama?"

"I'm sure."

"And you never knew?" asks George.

"What kinda question is that?" says Ash. "'Course I never knew. Did you know?"

George shakes his head pitiful-like. He didn't mean any harm. Ash looks over at me and sighs. "Maggie, it's time you grew up quick. We got to get to the bottom of this, and it ain't gonna be easy. You in or you out?"

"I'm in," I muster, not missing a beat. The look in Ash's eyes is different than I've ever seen. He looks hard, older than ten.

"Okay then. George, you go on back and help your pa with the farmin'. Joe, you go act like nothin' at all is wrong. Keep a lookout for Mr. Stackhouse, er, whoever he is. You think he's startin' to wake up, run on over and let me know." Ash takes my hand. "Come on, Maggie. We gotta go home and talk to Mama now."

My mother is standing out in the side yard at the clothes-line. There are dresses of hers and some of mine hanging, some socks, some of Daddy's underwear. The breeze blows them around her as we walk up, and her hair pulls back. When she looks at us, she's as pretty as I've ever seen, wearing a green dress with tiny orange flowers. She smiles, and I feel like running into her arms. I don't care what-all she did before. She's my mother. I love her no matter what. In fact, I was just over at a lady preacher's house lying about the call of the Lord. Who am I to judge? I know without a doubt, I am fiercely forgiving of anything Mama ever thought about doing.

Even if it was going to jail.

Jail, to a child, is the worst thing that can happen to you. You hear about chain gangs, you hear about stripes and bars and, oh my goodness. I'm amazed that a body can live to see the outside of jail. I'm amazed, if it's true, that Mama made it out. I fill up with warm love and think of it as a miracle.

"Mama, we got to talk," says Ash. He doesn't sound as in love right this minute. I'm wishing he would change his tone.

"Just a minute, let me finish up."

"We got to talk now," says Ash. Mama lowers her arms from the clothesline and slowly lays a wet shirt across a laundry basket.

"What's wrong?"

Suddenly Ash can't speak.

"Ash? Is somebody hurt? What happened?"

Ash shakes his head, fighting for the words. "The stranger, Mama. That stranger who come to town, come to dinner last night . . ."

She hesitates. "What about him?"

Two black crows come cawing over our heads and they sound so close, I duck.

"You know him, don't you? I mean . . . he knows you . . . who you are."

"Why, Ash Black, what's gotten into you?"

"Mama, is this you, or ain't it?" Ash pulls his arms out from behind his back and holds the folded newspapers in his hands like an offering. Mama steps forward real slow and takes them, her eyes growing big as a jack-o'-lantern's.

"Where did you get these?" Mama falters and seems she might lose her feet.

"Come sit down." And Ash leads us both inside the house, a silent procession, much like the time we buried the pieces of Anson Swaggs after he fell in front of the Boll Weevil.

"He had these in a trunk?" Mama's eyes run over the head-lines. "Oh heavens, I never wanted you to know about this." Mama sits on the sofa, ankles crossed. She sets the newspapers aside and picks up a handkerchief, fiddling with it in her hands, staring at it. "I never thought there'd come a day . . ."

"So it's true? You went to jail? You married some prison guard before Daddy?"

Hearing it coming from Ash's mouth makes my stomach queasy, and I get off the couch and walk to the doorway. I think about leaving, but I want to hear. I need to hear. I sit down against the wall and hug my knees. I feel the cool hard wand in my fingers.

"It's a long story, Ash." She looks at him and her eyes fill up. "But I guess it's time I told you the truth." She takes a deep breath and dabs at her eyes.

"It all started with a pair of stockings," she says, "that, and being at the wrong place at the wrong time. Bad luck, really.

"Before you two, before your daddy and Levy, I lived in Hebron, Georgia. I grew up there. I was a seamstress and made dresses, always up on the new styles. I was hoping for a proper man to marry, so I always looked my best. I had no family around . . . see, my mother and brother were both in jail, serving time. Shelby was in Kansas for doping . . . that's—"

"I know what it is," says Ash.

"Well, and my mother, your Gran, she was at Milledgeville State Farm for highway robbery." Ash looks out the window and rubs his face. I feel as if I've entered some strange new world on the other side of the looking glass. "I know this is hard to hear," says Mama. "Levy is such a small town and nothing like this happens around here, and I know it's hard to imagine me having a life before—"

"Just go on," says Ash.

"All right, son. I'll tell you. It wasn't easy having everyone you love in jail. The only thing I had going for me was my looks. They were a blessing and a curse at the very same time." Mama stares off at the wall and seems in a daze. When she comes to, she shifts in her seat, real animated all of a sudden, like she's just telling us a fairy tale. "So the stockings, see . . . I was always partial to real silk. They'd started making these artificial ones that were cheaper but shiny, and I didn't like having to powder my legs, didn't like how baggy they got around the ankles by the end of the day. Well, I had a very nice pair of silk stockings that I would wash by hand and set out to dry in the cool evening breezes . . . I took good care of them.

"Well, one day I was walking along Gleeson Street, minding my own business, when a man, this drunken sailor . . . he grabbed me. I struggled free and ran off, but I was humiliated, angry. I looked down and saw my stockings were ripped, and honey, I shouldn't have, but I knew I didn't have enough money on me. I marched right down to Beazlebanks Five and Dime . . . I was just so angry."

"And you stole somethin'," says Ash.

"I stole something, yes. I don't ever want to catch you doin' something like that, young man, hear? I got no right tryin' to explain myself, but it's just how it was. The Beazlebanks' son, a fat little thing with a lollipop in his mouth, hollered for his daddy when I tried to walk out the door."

I look down at my hands and realize I stole the wand from Mr. Stackhouse's trunk. I don't want to give it back. I don't want to go to jail either. I slip it in between my knees and hunker down so nobody can see it.

"It was the first and only time I'd ever shoplifted, I promise," says Mama. "And everythin' might have been fine for me, maybe, if I hadn't been caught. I might have married a lawyer or doctor or had a nice life entertaining politicians or maybe just making dresses and an honest livin' till my final days. But my fate weren't so kind. It was in my blood, I reckon. Our family brewed trouble like some folks make black tea."

"If it's in your blood, it's in mine," says Ash.

"Ash Black, I don't ever want to hear you say that again. Honey, look at me." Mama reaches over and touches Ash's chin. "You want me to stop? Maybe this is all too much."

Ash stands up and puts his hands in his pockets. "You ain't told me about Mr. Stackhouse, Mama. Is he that Mr. Dans in the newspaper? Did he come here to get after you?"

"Oh, Ash." Mama puts her head in her hands and her shoulders start bouncing. Her blond hair springs up and down. "He didn't come back for me, honey. I 'spect he come here . . . for somethin' I got."

TWENTY-TWO

George

That old photograph of Magnolia at the swimming pool is a dead ringer for her mother. It's hard for me to look at it and not think of Mrs. Black. I turn away. I close my eyes. *Why, God, why? Why are you doing this to me now? I'm dying soon enough. Can't you just have at me when I get to the other side? Can't you just let me enjoy what time I have left here with my wife? With my friends? Why are you tormenting me now? I'm an old man. A harmless old man.*

"Maggie? What's wrong? Are you crying?" I go over to my wheelchaired wife. She is holding a tinfoil wand and seems to have tears in her eyes. I try to take the wand, but she looks hard at me and holds on to it. Won't let it go.

"It's okay. I'm here." I take her and pull her over to the window to get her some light. "Oh, Maggie. Are you in there? Talk to me."

She doesn't answer me, just sits there, staring with wet

eyes. Must be someone in there. "I don't know who else to talk to. I miss you."

I bend down on the ground, which takes some doing, a full five minutes, it seems—bones creaking, popping—and put my head in her lap. For a long time she doesn't touch me, but she doesn't scream and doesn't clock me on the head either. It's been so long since I've felt her body next to mine. I breathe in the clean fabric of her pants. I feel the warmth of her legs and it takes me back to when I was safe as a child on my mother's lap. And it takes me back to when we'd lie naked for hours, Maggie and me, laughing and loving and . . . a tear rolls sideways across my cheek.

"Oh, Maggie, Maggie, I don't know what to do. I'm scared, honey." Something hard and sharp pokes me. I sit up and realize my wife just stuck a tinfoil wand directly in my ear, nearly impaled me, and I laugh, and laugh, and smile again. It feels good.

"Thank you," I say. "Hoo, Maggie, I needed that." I wipe my eyes, then sit back in my comfy chair and pull out the letters from Ash. Maybe her wands *are* magic. I feel like my old self again. The humor. The humor seems to be back, and I thank God for it. Without humor, getting old is a much worse sentence.

"Maggie, I got a surprise for you. Not sure what you understand from me these days, but . . . Do you know how much I love you? More than you can imagine. I don't want to hide anything from you, so I'm going to tell you all that I know. You know that big portrait of you, honey? You know who sent that to you? It's your nephew, a nephew you never even knew you had. That's right. He's Ash's son. You remember Ash? Yeah, Ash. Maggie, I'm sorry to tell you, but . . . your brother has passed away." I study her face to see if any of this is registering. She is pressing the wand, pressing, pressing, and seems to be just fine. She must be sheltered from all of this. Good heavens, maybe it's a blessing, this losing her mind. I just told her that her only brother is dead, and . . . nothing. It almost makes me feel better. Maybe Maggie won't even know it when I pass away. She won't suffer at all. It'll be like switching out pillows.

A weight seems to be lifting off my shoulders.

"I think I'll read to you. Would you like that? Would you like me to read some letters from your brother, Ash? That way I won't have to do this alone and you can just sit back and relax and not give two hoots. Okay? Here we go then."

"It starts out *Dear George*, and it's dated April 15, 1992. Maybe he got done with his taxes and had nothing better to do than write an old phantom from his past. What do you think?"

Dear George,

In May of 1939, I was working the World's Fair in Queens, New York. I could feel the buzz and bustle of it in my blood. I'd seen parades and presidents, celebrities, sports figures . . . people hadn't been this excited since the Yankees beat the Cubs in their third consecutive World Series. Do you remember that year? I was at the heart of it all.

I got to watch people's faces, ones that had been cleaned up from the lean years of the Depression, ones that were hopeful for the first time in years, eager to see what the future

119

held. I was happy for America. I loved my country, still do. Love the optimism it musters when it needs to. I loved working at the fair and seeing that the world is small. You could walk from Poland where "Polonaise" blared at all hours, to the Vatican to see Michelangelo's *Pieta* on loan from Rome, in minutes. The lines never stopped. We kept them all moving.

For a while, I was assigned to Billy Rose's Aquacade, and I liked the water shows well enough, but after seeing folks in their skivvies diving and swimming in formation a couple dozen times, it sort of loses its appeal. The fairgoers were more interesting than the acts to me.

I watched the families. It was hard not to watch them laughing, smiling, experiencing the fair together, and not wax nostalgic. I didn't feel sorry for myself, no, but I was only twenty—my childhood wasn't so far off and it still stung. Sometimes I imagined you were working your daddy's field in Levy. I imagined Magnolia living in a city, Charleston or Savannah, maybe, going to school to be a teacher. I imagined Mama missing me, the way I missed her.

I worked for three hours at a time at the Aquacade and then had twenty minutes for break. One day I headed out past the LifeSavers Parachute jump and listened to the screamers as they floated back to earth. I left the Amusement area and grabbed some nuts at the Mister Peanut exhibit. I passed a throng of people headed to General Motor's Futurama. I'd seen it before, and every now and again, I did like to sneak back in. It's not as if I believed that a future city of 1960 would actually look that way, it's more that I liked the sensation of sitting in chairs in a circle and looking down on the model. I liked the feeling of being high up, like God almost, as if in an airplane and looking down on all the little people, cars, and buildings. Everything looked so insignificant reduced to miniature.

But this day wasn't for the Futurama. I was headed to the Court of States. I'd already been through Pennsylvania, Louisiana, Texas, and was learning a lot about my country—this day I was headed to North Carolina.

Words can't describe what I felt when I walked into the exhibit room and saw her, hanging there. She was the most beautiful woman I'd ever seen. She was airbrushed in color, her hair strawberry blond, hanging full around her face, draped over her shoulders. Her arms were slender, and I could see the small round scar from her smallpox vaccination. I touched my own arm in the same place and put my hands over my face. It was just too much. I never expected . . .

I stumbled back to a bench. It was Mama's face. My own mother. I wanted to cry, but grown men didn't do that. I pulled my eyes away from hers just long enough to read the placard down below:

Swimming is a favorite pastime in North Carolina. This bathing beauty is eighteen-year-old Magnolia Jacobs of Charlotte. She is but one North Carolinian who enjoys the good health provided by the Piedmont's warm climate.

It was Maggie! I couldn't believe how she'd grown. She was the spitting image of our mother, but there was sweetness, an innocence Maggie had that Mama lost along the way. She was life-sized and full of light. This pretty girl was the one person I loved most in the world—I'd recognize her anywhere—and I sat there day after day, dreaming of going down to North

Carolina to find her. I knew I would someday. I didn't know how or when. I just knew I would.

That was the first time I knew Maggie was still alive, George, the day I walked into that North Carolina exhibit, and I can't tell you what it meant to me. The relief, the longing, the emotions stirred up. Finding her after all those years, and learning she'd moved to Charlotte, and by her last name, that she'd married you—

I wasn't sure what shocked me the most.

Ash

TWENTY-THREE

Magnolia

"Don't look so shocked, Ash. Mothers are just people. I never pretended to be an angel, did I?" There's gravel forming in Mama's genteel voice. She's not crying anymore; it's almost as if we aren't here, as if she's someone else—the other Mama we read about in the newspapers. I set my legs out soft in front of me on the floor and gape at her from across the room.

"Heavens, I was goin' off to jail to visit my own mother. What kind of child's mother is behind bars? Well, other than yours." Mama leans forward and puts her finger up to my brother's face. "Look, I am not one to be held down. I had spirit and then some, wild and free. Always did. A bit like you, Ash. I wasn't always the woman you see today, all working hard, poor as dirt, meek and humbled. My spirit once surpassed my beauty. Every baby is given a dose of life, but me? I'd been born with two helpin's—my body could barely contain me, and certainly no penitentiary.

"I would have been just like any other inmate there at Milledgeville except for . . . well, ever since I was a little girl, I'd known about my beauty. Look at your sister there. You see that? That was me, Ash. She's every bit as pretty as I was and will probably be prettier some day. No wonder poor little George is all smitten."

It's the first time anyone has ever said something like that about George to me, and for a second, I forget to listen to Mama. I'm thinking about my being pretty. I'm thinking that George is smitten with me. I guess I've always known it deep down, but now, now it's real, in the air. Solid-like.

"Maggie, are you listenin' to me? Come here, sweetie." She beckons for me and I rise up slow and slink over to her. She pulls me up on her lap like a rag doll, and I smell her soap. "As long as we're talkin' honest, there's somethin' I got to tell you. Your face is your most valuable asset, and don't ever forget it. Trust me on this. You can get any man to do your biddin', just never let him see your brains, you hear? Keep him hoodwinked into thinkin' pretty is all you got. It's safer, easier that way."

"Mama," Ash growls. "You still ain't said about the stranger."

"Oh, right. I was gettin' to that. Well now, what with my spirit and my beauty and my brains, I had to find a way to break out of the Milledgeville State Farm Penitentiary. And I did. Not once, but twice. See, I've never been one to learn from my mistakes. It seems I like to make them over and over again."

I am staring at a bug on the wall. It's a palmetto bug as big as my fist, crawling up the wallpaper. "The Milledgeville State Farm Penitentiary is an actual working farm," Mama goes on. "Sixteen acres on Highway 22. When I was there, there was a three-story brick men's buildin' across the highway and a ladies' buildin' with private rooms. The men tended the farm every day, hard labor, but us ladies had it a little easier. Some chose to farm, but others learned house-makin' duties . . . cleanin', sewin', that sort of thing."

I wish I could squash that bug, but I'm here on the sofa next to Mama, sitting still.

"There were male guards at our prison, and there was some fraternizin' that went on between the prison guards and the female inmates. This means they were . . . friendly, Maggie." She turns to Ash. "This, of course, is where I found my foothold. Dear God, help me for havin' to tell me own children these things. I met a day guard by the name of J. W. Dans, who had a wife, a son, and who had his eye on me."

The palmetto bug flies suddenly in a dizzying blur over to the window behind Ash's head, and he smacks it with his bare hand. It drops behind the sofa.

"Now, I'm not proud of any of this. I would never behave this way anymore, but I was young and desperate. Time moved slow at the farm, too slow. Few months in, they made me a 'trusty' for good behavior, and made me water carrier for the other inmates and prison guards. I only had one year to serve, but you think I could wait it out? Well, do you?"

"I know you didn't, Mama," says Ash, arms crossed tight, staring at the rug now.

"Well, I couldn't stand being held under lock and key. It was against my nature. I had to do *somethin'*. Mother was already at the same prison. Our crimes were alike—both steal-ing—but Mother had somethin' waitin' for her on the outside that I didn't have. She had money, and lots of it, put away for if and when she ever got out. I needed that money."

Mama gets up and walks to the wall. She touches a small framed picture of her mother and her when she was a little girl, the only one we have, hanging crooked on the wall. Neither one of them are smiling. She straightens it. "I couldn't use my looks on her, so I had to sweet-talk, cry a little. Every day I told her I was dyin' in that prison. And I lied. I told her I was fallin' in love with J. W. Dans."

Ash looks at Mama.

"But she knew better," she goes on. "She knew he was old, a good twenty years older than me. And she knew there was no chance I was in love with that man. But she also knew she'd raised a desperate child, and that she was partly to blame for it, and that I was gonna break out no matter what."

Mama stops talking. She looks at Ash and then me. She's thinking about crying. She walks to the kitchen real slow, and Ash and I stare at each other, confirming we've both been hearing the same thing. Mama's a jailbird. It doesn't seem real. What does that make us? She comes back slow and sits on the sofa. She straightens out her pretty dress. She has a mason jar in her hand with some amber liquid in it. I've seen it before. I know enough now that it came from Miss Maple. It's the same color as her, maybe a little more golden. Mama takes a sip, closes her eyes, and waits a second.

"On November second, 1920, my mother wired some money to a hotel in Tampa, Florida, and I convinced the guard it was now or never. I changed clothes, put on my nicest suit, and walked right out in broad daylight on the arm of J. W. Dans, who had a car hidden and waiting a little ways off.

"It was almost too easy. I should have known. I would soon find out J. W. was a hard man. We eloped and had a civil ceremony, Lord knows why. It was phony—we even used different names. Then we headed for Cuba by way of Tampa and stopped about halfway, J. W. eager to be a proper husband to me. He spent his last dime on a ritzy motel in Jacksonville, thinkin' there'd be more money waitin' for us. I dyed my hair red so nobody'd know who I was, but the next day when we got to Tampa and tried to get that money, there was none. We'd been duped by my mother, still behind bars at the Milledgeville State Farm."

"So you got caught," says Ash.

"We got caught. I was back behind prison walls, and J. W. was hauled off to another jail. I told everybody I'd feared for my life, which I had, soon as we got out on the road. He was a dangerous man. What kind of person would up and leave his family? I got off with just a slap on the wrist because the warden, the courts, even the newspapers were smitten. It was my looks, see. My beauty, like I was tellin' you, honey . . ." She stares at me.

Mama looks anything but pretty right now. Her skin is the same and her hair is the same, her curvy figure and all the same, but there's something coming from her eyes—it's so sad and dreary, I have to look away.

"A month later, four days 'fore Christmas, I broke out again. I was really gonna do it too, but the clay hills and ravines of Baldwin County were too much. Few hours later I turned around and begged 'em to take me back, lest I freeze to death."

"And they did?"

"'Course they did."

"So how'd you ever get out again?"

"I used my brain. I started writin' letters to the new governor of Georgia, Governor Hardwick. Month after he was sworn in, he pardoned me, and I walked right out of Milledgeville State Farm scot-free. That's the honest truth. I should have done that to begin with."

Ash gets up and walks over to the window. He presses his hands up to the glass as if he's trapped inside. He's quiet for a while, and Mama's sipping her drink. Finally he says, "Okay, Mama. Now we know. But you still ain't said about the stranger. I know he's here for you. He wouldn't have all those papers 'bout you if he weren't. And I know you ain't happy to see him 'cause I seen it in your face last night. Tell me the truth, Mama. Is it him? Is the stranger the same man in those papers? Is he that J. W. Dans you run off with?"

Mama stares into her glass. She rolls the liquid around and then puts it up to her lips. When the jar comes back down, it's empty, and she sets it real careful on the little table beside the sofa. She looks at me, or at least she seems to be looking at me. Her eyes are more far off.

"I had no money," she says, slow and slurring a little, "and my family was still doin' time, but I heard of a woman down in Levy who took in boarders and didn't ask questions. I crossed the state line and wound up in the back boardin' room of Jacobs Mercantile." Mama turns to look at Ash. She reaches a hand up for him, then lets it drop. "Three months later, Ash, you were born, right there in that very room."

TWENTY-FOUR

Magnolia

Ash? Ash, is that—Oh, it's you, George. Why won't you read to me anymore? Why won't you share with me Ash's letters? It's been so long. So long. Tell me, is Ash well? Is he coming to visit?

George has not slept from what I can tell. Miss Annie is not here yet to get me from bed, the windows are still drawn, and green dawn hangs over our room. George is sitting at the window in his chair beneath a lit reading lamp. He holds letters out over his pajama bottoms. He is unshaven from what I can see from here. His whiskers, through my hazy eyes, look like a dark shadow, as if someone's standing beside him, blocking the sun.

I turn and look the other way. Sometimes I am disoriented in this new life, this new body. Sometimes I think I will look over and see my daughter, my little girl again, waking me up early, ready to go play, or begging for breakfast. Most days it was a couple hard-boiled eggs mashed with a little salt and butter, but on Sundays, I would do it up right. Pancakes, sausage, scrambled eggs, and cheese. We were so happy, the three of us. A family. Now she has her own life to tend to. I rarely see her.

I open my eyes and see only a vague image of a young woman, lying on her front, smiling in my direction. She is quite beautiful, and I wonder who she is. Something about her is familiar, but from here, I cannot tell what. If only George would read to me. If only he would speak to me and tell me what he has learned about Ash. If only he would understand that I am not dead yet. That I am still here. I am alive.

After Miss Annie comes and does her business with me, I am exhausted. *Put your foot here, lift this arm, open your mouth.* So many instructions, sometimes I feel like a dull rag doll. But I know she means well. She almost reminds me of Mama. No, more like Miss Maple.

Oh, Miss Maple.

George is fit to be tied this morning. He looks like you-know-what, his hair all this way and that, his clothes not quite matching. There's a look in his eyes, a faraway but determined look. A scared look, like the one he wore when he was headed to Pearl Harbor. He pushes me to breakfast and I can't see him anymore; I can only smell the aftershave he pressed on his cheeks so no one would know he's been up all night.

This can't be good for you, dear, I wish I could say. But I can't.

We pass gaggles of old women, some flocked together, some lingering, lost on their own. A woman in the middle of the hall tells no one in particular she wants to take a nap. George doesn't stop to make small talk today. He almost seems in a hurry, as if we're in a hurry, but that's impossible. There's absolutely nowhere we have to go or have to be . . . in a hurry. We are in this home where time moves slowly.

I smell bacon. I would love some bacon this morning, not grits, not bland scrambled eggs with no salt. Give me salt. Give me meat. Give me flavor!

"Hello, dears." Jessica rises from her chair. She is wearing a more subdued ensemble today, no garish colors, just a simple blue silk top and pants outfit. There are hints of some other color swirled in there, but I can't see what it is, green maybe. Something oriental? Indian? I could sit here in my wheelchair and visit the whole world through Jessica's closet of clothes. I look down at my white bobby socks with the balls on the backs. George forgot to put on my shoes.

We find our places around the table and belly up. My hands instinctively grab for my fork, my spoon. They move them over an inch, then back. They touch the edge of the paper placemat, fold the edge, then straighten it. I get tired of watching my hands. I turn to look at George. He is watching Miss Annie walk a strange old man to our table. Something about him is familiar. They come closer and George sits the man between himself and Jessica. I can see his face from here. The old man is smiling in a sad sort of way.

"You all remember Mister Joe, here."

"Morning, Joe," says Emmet.

"How was your second night? Did you sleep well?" asks Jessica, beginning to fuss over him.

The man says nothing, but smiles. He grabs his napkin and holds it in his hands as if he doesn't know what to do with it. Maybe his hands have a mind of their own, too, like mine.

"Joe, I, uh, you know you never did say where you're from yesterday," says George, holding his fork and stabbing the vinyl tablecloth with it.

"His people say he's from here, 'round these parts," says Miss Annie. "Now you enjoy a good breakfast, Mister Joe. I got to go run on and do some other things, but George and Emmet and all, they'll take good care of you. Right, folks?"

"He'll be fine," says Jessica. "Run along, do your stuff."

"Joe, you ever been to a place called Levy, South Carolina?" says George. I watch the stranger's eyes. They graze over the table. He moves his lips as if he's repeating the name of the place. He shakes his head a little.

"George, isn't that where you're from?" asks Jessica.

"Joe, were you born in *New Orleans*?" says George, more forceful now.

The man is mumbling to himself.

"Listen to me closely, Joe. Have you ever been on a train called the Boll Weevil? Have you ever pretended to be somebody you weren't?!"

"What has gotten into you, George? You're upsetting him!"

"I got to know! I just—"

"George?" says Emmet. "Listen, let's go out and get some fresh air. Right now. Come on."

"I don't want air. I want the truth! Have you come back? Is it true? Can it be after all these years?"

TWENTY-FIVE

Magnolia

LEVY, 1929

We are in our little house on Togoodoo Road. Newspapers are strewn out all over the floor. "Is it true?" says Ash. "Is it him? Has he come back?"

"Oh no," I whine. "Is she alive? Is Mama okay?"

"She will be."

I sit, sullen and angry, watching her. She's left me. She's left us hanging midstory. She is lying back on the sofa, taking a nap while the blue light of dusk wraps around her. I always want Mama to finish her stories, whether it's Little Black Sambo or Peter Cottontail. What happens to the little boy? Is he stuck up in that tree forever? When will the tigers chase their tails and turn to butter? When will Peter escape from the farmer? You can't just leave a body hanging like that.

Ash holds a newspaper close to his eyes and studies the

picture of the prison guard. "It's him, Maggie. Look at the nose." Ash rubs his own nose, then his chin. He pushes the paper to me.

"What do you mean? Who is he?"

Ash stays quiet, head down. Finally, he says, "You're too young to understand."

"Am not." I look at the paper. I see that man's face. I see Mama's face. I wish I could read.

Maybe I am too young. Ash looks even older than ten right now. His eyes are moist. I want to go hug him. I want him to pull me to him and rub the back of my hair like he always does when I'm scared, but he doesn't. He is sturdy and breakable at the same time. His sandy blond hair is thick and curling at the temples. The look on his face, his hazel eyes now bright green . . . it all makes me afraid, like the ground is shifting.

"When's Daddy comin' home?"

"Not till tomorrow. Went to Savannah for a new wagon wheel."

"Ash, my stomach hurts. Let's go outside. Mama looks like she'll sleep for a while."

"No, Maggie."

"Why not? There's nothin' we can do here. Let's catch fireflies."

"Didn't you hear me? I don't wanna!"

My bottom lip quivers, and I think about crying. Ash never yells at me, but lately it seems it's all he's doing. I wish Daddy would come home. I wish today was mail day and he was just down at the train depot, unloading the post. He'd be back by now and sorting it all out. Maybe he'd let me help him. Maybe he'd hold me on his knee and I could nuzzle my head down in his shirt collar and everything would be okay.

"I don't wanna play with you anyway," I say, *humph*ing and turning around.

"Don't you see, Maggie? Don't you see what's goin' on?" I look at him. I truly don't.

"Mama's right, you might be pretty, but you got no brains."

"You're a liar!" I stomp out and he hollers after me.

"Don't you get it, Maggie? It's him! Mr. Stackhouse. Mr. Dans. He's my—"

"Ash! Aa-aaash!" We tear outside to see where the fire is, but it's only George and Joe. We hear them before we see them. They're heaving, trying to catch their breath. "Ran . . . all the way . . ."

"What is it? Did he wake up?"

George nods hard. His face is red, his body soaked like he's been swimming. "He . . . comin' . . . mad as all . . ."

I watch as Ash's eyes light up. His body tenses, fists form. I have the urge to run and hide from everybody, in the woods maybe. But there's no time.

"Go on, wake up Mama!"

I run inside and shake her as hard as I can. She comes to, and eyes wide sensing the darkness, jumps up and runs to the bureau. She grabs some matches and lights a lantern. It glows around her face and makes her look like a spook. I hold on to her dress, wishing I had my own light. We hurry to the porch in time to see a cloud of dust like smoke coming along the dirt road, and through the storm I can see that mean man a-coming. I do the only thing I can do then—I run back in and hide inside the dressmaker's dummy where we play sometimes. I stand there, quiet as I can. And wait.

TWENTY-SIX

Ash

April 16, 1992

Dear George,

The waiting was the hardest part. After seeing Maggie's face at the World's Fair, I went back every day and dreamed of finding her, but I knew I couldn't. Not yet. At the same time I felt hopeful for the first time since I'd left home. I had something to look forward to.

Maggie was okay. It meant more to me than all the riches in the world. I had suffered a decade over my leaving. I had abandoned her, and I wasn't sure I could ever forgive myself for it.

I'd been at the fairground in Flushing Meadows for a year, helping to set it up, doing whatever odd jobs were needed. Before that, I worked for the Ringling Brothers circus and lesser-known carnivals as they passed through the west coast. I heard about the World's Fair from a buddy of mine and we traveled by train for three whole days from California. The Big Apple was everything we dreamed it'd be—bright lights, skyscrapers, baseball. Life.

I made my usual visit to the North Carolina exhibit one day in 1939. I sat on the same bench in front of the life-sized photograph of Maggie. I cracked open a peanut and popped it in my mouth. A man came and sat down beside me. "She's a l-looker, isn't she?" he stuttered, and I kept my eyes straight ahead.

I looked down and saw his immaculate shoes. I saw the dust on my own. "She is."

"What I wouldn't do to marry a w-woman like that. You married?"

"Me? No, sir," I said.

"Well, you should get married. Everyone should."

I sneaked a glance at the man's hands and saw no ring. "And you?"

"Not in my cards, I'm a-afraid."

"You a priest or somethin'?"

The man laughed and slapped his knee. "No. I'm, well, I'm married to my w-work, you might say. My bride is the you-you-United States of America, and she keeps me busy."

I had to look at him then. The stutter, there was something familiar. His face was chiseled and good-looking. He was smooth with his fedora, his bow tie perfectly straight.

My heart nearly stopped beating. It couldn't be. "Joe?"

I waited for him to answer. He looked hard at me then and his eyes went moist.

"That you, Ash?"

And that's how we found each other after all those years, drawn there by the lure of sweet Magnolia.

We weren't children anymore, we were young men. Joe and I sat there on that bench that day, eating peanuts, oblivious to the people coming in and out of the North Carolina exhibit. I told him all about escaping from St. Mary's Home for Boys and running away with the carnival, and he told me about being the youngest recruit for the SIS program, some top-secret code-breaking operation for the navy. He was brilliant, you know. Remember how he always knew who was going to catch the next fish? Uncanny. He was almost a mind reader. It was unfortunate he'd had the upbringing he had, but to my relief, he'd turned out okay. He said he was in New York, meeting some English chaps about government issues. He seemed anxious about it. Nervous. He was that same way in Levy, remember?—when that man, I can't call him my father, tried to hoodwink us all. He'd used Joe, only a kid, just to get to me, and now, well, I prayed Joe was all right. I felt responsible.

George, I have to tell you, before I went off break that day at the fair, and Joe and I parted, he remarked about the photograph of Maggie. I confirmed it was her, and he was stunned silent. It was almost as if he was trying to reconcile the coincidence of it all.

"I'm writing a book on p-probability," he told me. "But the fact that you and I are meeting again, here in front of a picture of Maggie, is too much." He was trying to calculate things and mumbling under his breath. Just then Rose, this sweet girl who worked in the Palace of Knowledge, came in. Sometimes she would meet me there, although not on purpose, she claimed. I never minded her company. She was pretty and curvaceous and had a sweet laugh. A nice outlook on life. Anyway, Rose came in and saw me sitting there with Joe, and something came over her all of a sudden, something turned in her eyes. She looked at Joe and at me and at the photograph of Maggie and started shivering.

She went into a trance of some sort, and I was thinking this was part of her act. "It's too dark. Too cold!" she wailed.

"Rose? You okay, Rose?"

"Too dark. Too cold . . ."

I put my arms around her and held her close on the bench. Joe stood up, alarmed. "She's my friend, a fortune-teller." I shook my head. Something was wrong with her.

Rose seemed to be coming back around. She looked up at me and said, "I seen the past and the future. You all were there. You got to go back."

"What are you talking about?"

"I got to go," she said, still trembling. "I'm sorry. I don't know what come over me."

Rose left after that. I shook Joe's hand and wished him well. I tried to apologize on Rose's behalf. I assured him she wasn't crazy. She was a good gal. But he seemed a little shook up himself. Then he walked out of that room and out of my life. I never saw Joe Stackhouse again. Not in person, anyway.

George, I've often wondered about that encounter at

the fair. I've often wondered about Joe Stackhouse and even looked him up. I did see him on TV a couple times, and this is what my encyclopedia says about him, word for word:

Joseph P. Stackhouse (1918–)

Born in New Orleans, Stackhouse pursued mathematics at Cornell University, and eventually headed the US Army Signals Intelligence System (SIS), a group that decrypted secret messages intercepted by cable and radio. On September 20, 1940, SIS created MAGIC, an analog machine to decrypt Japanese diplomatic communications. Stackhouse and his team are credited with decoding the message that led to the shooting down of Japanese Admiral Yamamoto's airplane, the mastermind behind Pearl Harbor.

He's a national hero, George. Did you know that? He really made something of himself. Imagine, a kid stolen from the streets of New Orleans, overcoming and making good like that. His code breaking probably saved my rear in the war. And yours. And did you see the date he created MAGIC? It was barely a year after our encounter at the World's Fair.

I still wonder about him. I lost track. I don't know if he lives in Washington DC anymore. I don't even know if he's alive, but I still think about what Rose said that day. About all of us. Is there some way she sensed the terror we all felt back in Levy? Could she feel it there between Joe and me, a black residue that never washes away?

I asked Rose about her episode in the North Carolina exhibit later, and she said she didn't remember a thing. She looked at me as if I was the one crazy, and I started thinking, maybe I was. Maybe none of it had happened.

And then after the war, after I came back to New York from New Guinea, I found Rose working in a corner diner. The simplicity of it, of her, after what I'd seen in the war made me swoon. We courted and six months later she married me.

I opened a little antique shop and wound up poking around in an old warehouse on Fifth Street, looking for things to sell. What I found was treasure. Collecting dust and slightly worn around the edges was that very same portrait of Maggie, leaning against the back wall. I actually cried when I found her yet again. I framed her, put her in a prominent place in our home, and kept her in a prominent place in my heart.

My Rosie died last year from pneumonia after forty-seven happy years of marriage. We never once spoke of Joe Stackhouse again, and yet still, I'm an old man sitting here, thinking of him. Thinking of you and Maggie. Wonder what it all means.

Ash

TWENTY-SEVEN

George

Joe Stackhouse. Here at Harmony House of all places. After all these years, what, eighty? How is that possible? How can it be he's back?

"Mister George? What you doin' in there?" Annie knocks. "Been in there 'most an hour. You all right?"

I look at myself in the mirror. I lean down and turn on the faucet, get some cold water in my hand, and rinse my face. I need to shave. I look like crud. I'll probably scare Maggie if she sees me like this.

"Just . . . just a minute, Annie. I'll be out in a minute."

I reach for my razor. Dang hand won't be still. I hold it up to my face, but there's no shaving cream. I look into my own eyes, pools of faded blue, pools of water . . . *I see Maggie and Ash down by the water. I'm holding a fishing pole, wearing my overalls, my feet are bare, the sun is on my back.*

Good heavens. I've got to go back to Levy.

The weight of it. The pull of it—all that happened so long ago.

I put the razor down and open the door. Miss Annie is standing there, been listening to me the whole time, her head leaned in just so. She eyes me hard. "You feelin' okay today? Ain't had no more bacon, now?"

"No, no, I just . . . Miss Annie, some strange things are goin' on."

"Strange? What strange? Like, you woke up cravin' bananas and peanut butter strange, or ghosty strange? 'Cause I don't do ghosty strange." She moves over to Maggie and leans down, slipping a walking shoe on her right foot. She always starts on the right foot . . . superstitious maybe.

"I don't know," I say. "I shouldn't be telling you all this."

"Oh, okay. Yessir, you shouldn't be tellin' me all this . . . I ain't one to tell . . . I just take care of your wife here every day—*every day*—and you . . . but that's all right."

"Annie."

"No, no, I know my place."

"Miss Annie, hush up now. Come on, let me get dressed and we can take Maggie out in the sunshine. I'll tell you what I know."

A light comes into Miss Annie's eyes and she looks like a little girl for a second. She smiles and busies herself with Maggie's other shoe, and I wonder if I'm not making a mistake. Maybe I should tell Emmet instead. My hands grow sweaty and I sit down on the bed and pull on some pants. I look up at the picture of my wife when she was young and adoring of me and can't help but feel betrayed. I never knew about this photograph. Who took it? Who was she smiling for? And why didn't she tell me her photo went all the way up to the New York World's Fair?

Of course, I haven't told her I'm sick either. Haven't told her I'm dying and might only have weeks or days.

So many secrets. So many. It's hard for an old man to keep them straight anymore.

We're out here in the courtyard. Maggie is enjoying the fresh air and sunshine. I don't like her to stay indoors too much. She needs sunlight and vitamin D. She perks up a little with all the colors and sounds of the outdoors. Anybody can see how much it helps her.

Miss Annie arranges a light cloth over Maggie's lap, so she'll have something to busy her hands, then shows up at my side. She sits down across from me at the chess table.

"Don't mess up my game," I tell her. "I'm beatin' myself." I struggle to find a checkmate, then look up at her.

"Well?"

I look over at Maggie and lean in to Miss Annie. "All right. You know Joe? You know that new old guy?"

"Mister Joe? Joe Stackhouse? 'Course. What's wrong with him?"

"Nothin', nothin'. I just . . . well, I thought there was something familiar about him. From the first moment I saw him, there was something about him that made me feel like I'd seen him before."

"So? You know him?"

"I think I do." I look down at the chessboard and take down a white pawn. I set it to the side, taking my time.

"You know I do have things I need to do today," says Annie, folding her arms.

"I just . . . I didn't realize it was him, Annie . . . I mean, I didn't remember any of it, really, until I read the letter."

"What letter? Sorry. My bad. Go on . . ."

"Annie, if I tell you this stuff, I want you to promise me you'll keep it quiet. You can't tell another living soul. Got it?"

"Oh, now, Mister George, that don't sound like me. I don't know."

"Annie . . ."

"Oh, all right. But tell me quick 'fore I change my mind."

"The portrait of Maggie that came . . . and the package of letters I got? They're from Maggie's older brother, Ash."

"Brother? I ain't known she got a brother!"

"Shhh! Listen. He's dead."

"Oh, Lawd have mercy."

"But in his letter he said he saw Joe Stackhouse at the World's Fair, and that Rose the fortune-teller said we had to go back, and then Joe shows up here and—"

"Whoa, whoa, back up now! You got a letter from a dead man?"

I reach over and take Miss Annie's hand in mine, squeezing it. "Annie, focus now. When I was a little boy growing up in Levy with Maggie and her brother Ash, one day Joe Stackhouse showed up, just a boy, with this magician and . . . what happened next changed all of our lives forever, and now . . . now he's back." I can't help myself, but I'm tearing up. I'm just so tired. Let's get it over with.

"Mister George?" Miss Annie looks alarmed. Her voice is tender. She leans over the table and knocks the pieces onto the ground. "I'm here for you. You know that. But you ain't makin' a lick of sense."

"Annie, I'm dying." The words slice the air between us and sober me up. "I'm dying, and Joe shows up here, and I get these things from Ash, and his son's scattering his ashes on Saturday, and the timing, see?" I stare at her and my eyes screw up. She's foggy and her face is changing. I see a flash of . . . what? Dang it, there's something I can't remember!

"Mister George, honey, you all right?"

"Fine, fine, I just . . . Annie? I've got to go back to Levy. I'm not sure how or why, there's something I've forgotten, something escapes me. All I know is somehow, I've got to get there so I can make things right. I don't think I have much longer . . . on this earth."

"Oh no. Lawd Jesus, help me, the poor man—"

"Annie, pull yourself together."

Miss Annie's eyes flood, and a tear escapes and rolls onto her arm. She studies my pupils, one to the other. Then she looks over at my wife.

"Does she know?"

"About what?"

"About your dyin'? About anythin'?"

"No. I don't think so. You really think she would understand?"

"I wouldn't put it past her. She just can't say it no more,

but my bet is, she's still in there. Lawd have mercy, what I got myself into. Mama always told me not to work here. She always said it be trouble. Aw, Lawd have mercy—"

"So you'll help me?"

"Mister George, I got no idea what you're askin' of me!"

"Eighty years later, Annie, somehow, all of us—me, Maggie, Joe, Ash, well, his ashes anyway—are being brought back together again. And that's just impossible. There must be some reason for it. Don't you think? Aren't you religious or something? You know . . ."

"What? You mean 'cause I'm a black woman? Heavens, Mister George." She turns serious on me. "I got a close relationship with my Lawd and savior, Jesus, yes. But ain't nothin' to do with my color."

"I never said it did, Annie. So what do you make of it?"

"I don't know."

"Annie, I'm asking you to help me make right on something that happened a long time ago. I'm asking you to help a dying man make peace before he goes. There's still something I can't seem to remember. I think I might if I go back. I want you to take us down to Levy on Saturday." I look over at my sweet wife, who's sitting in her wheelchair, minding her business. She seems to be counting acorns on the ground, thinking of sleeping.

"But it's against the rules! How 'bout get your family to do it? Your daughter . . . granddaughter?"

"They have busy lives. They'd make excuses I don't want to hear. No, they wouldn't want to drive all that way, just wouldn't understand."

"Oh, they wouldn't? Shoot, you ain't know who you talkin' to, 'cause I ain't understandin' a bit of this." She looks at me, and I smile real sweet. "Why you gotta do this to me? Lawd almighty, Mister George. Great Gawd in heaven . . ." She's rocking and praying, eyes closed, hugging her chest. She sings a little and lifts her head to the sky, then she looks over at me and squeaks out, "Only got but one life to live. How long you got?"

"Till Saturday?"

"No, till . . ."

"Weeks. Maybe more. Maybe less."

"Oh no, Lawd."

Miss Annie searches my eyes and I jerk away, staring at my wife. "Don't tell the others," I say. "I don't want a big fuss."

"Not even Miss Magnolia?" she whispers. Maggie is biting her fingers.

"Especially not her. I'm not sure what it would do to her. Heck, it might not have any effect, and that—that, I just don't think I can bear."

"Mister George, I'm gonna live to regret this . . ."

Magnolia

LEVY, 1929

"You're gonna regret you ever messed with me!"

I am inside the dressmaker's dummy, hoping I'm invisible. I've never heard anybody so angry. Mama and Daddy don't yell like this. Nobody in Levy yells like this. I hear Ash's voice, "Leave him alone!"

There's a scuffle and wail. I don't know what's happening.

"I saw what you d-did!"

"Well, just wait till you see what I do to you! I shoulda left you where I found you, begging for food! I shoulda pushed you right off that train, you little ingrate!"

"Stop it!" Mama screams.

"Get outta my way!"

"Leave him alone!"

"Get off me, you—"

Then I hear a clunk, a loud thump. There's quiet and I can actually hear the blood pumping between my ears. Somebody's hurt! I want to peek, I want to run, but I can't move! It's dark. Too dark!

I hear a dragging sound. I hear breathing and grunts. A whisper, "Get out! Go on!"

Next thing I know it's hot. There is fire all around me. I try to run, but I fall, and my head hurts. This is all a bad dream. It'll be over soon. All be over soon . . .

"Now listen, this will all be over soon," says George. We are in the courtyard, and he's holding Miss Annie's arm over a game table. A red cardinal lands right in between them for a second, then flies off in a flash. "Like I said, all you got to do is get us there to Levy. The rest, leave it up to me."

We're going back to Levy?

"I'm gonna regret it, I know I will. Mark my word." Miss Annie bites her bottom lip. "But this is just crazy enough to be from the Lawd. And I ain't a-one to go question him."

Back to Levy? How can we go back? I grip the arms of my wheelchair and try to stand up, but when I do, my leg slips out from under me. I am on the ground, seeing sideways, a familiar pain in my head.

"Are you okay? Maggie, speak to me!"

"Maggie? Oh, thank God!"

I see Ash over me, holding my head in his hands. His face is all dirty and I smell smoke. Can't get it out of my lungs. Fire is all behind him, and people from Levy are throwing buckets of water on a burning house.

"Maaaaaggieeeee!" Mama screams a terrible sound I don't ever want to hear again. "Oh, my baby, my baby . . ." She is rocking me in her arms, pressing me into her. My head hurts. I open my eyes and through the light given off from the flames, I see Mr. Jacobs throw a bucket of water on the house. I am across the way, near the trees, feeling nothing but strange and heat. Things are not right. This isn't how it is. I see George and Mr. Jacobs helping with the fire and Joe, coming from the woods with two buckets of water. Ash is next to Mama and me, breathing heavy. He is crying, then not, then crying again.

"Oh, Ash, I'm sorry," Mama says in a pitiful cry.

Ash leans his head down and puts his hands on the dirt. He gets sick right there beside me, and Mama turns us away.

"I never wanted any of this," she says, rocking me, squeezing me tight. Then her voice changes. "Ash, where is he? Is he in there?"

I know she's talking about that awful man, and I want to see Ash's face, but I can't. Mama's blocking him. All I hear is Ash getting sick one more and Mama clutching me tighter and rocking me like I'm a baby again.

TWENTY-EIGHT

Annie

We're in Miss Magnolia's room, and I'm rocking her, rocking her on the bed, sweet thing. "There, there now." I look to Mister George. "Please don't ask me again. Ain't no way I can take you out of here, 'specially not now." *Trouble*, Mama told me. *Trouble. See?*

"But Maggie's all right. Aren't you, dear? The doctor said it wasn't a bad fall. She'll be as good as new."

"She's eighty-nine years old! I got to take better care. She could've broken a hip or worse. I was right there, Lawd have mercy."

"We were both right there," says Mister George, and he catches my eye. I turn away, lay her down, and pat Miss Magnolia's two purple stitches above her eye. Her hair is laid out, light snow on her pillowcase. I've had residents fall on me but never stitches on such a pretty little head. "There you go, Miss Magnolia. Pretty as a picture. You feelin' all right? You need anythin'?" I reach in my pocket and pull out something for a headache. I know she's got to have one but she never complains. Never a word. What a sweet one. I'd be fussin' up a storm by now.

"They're gonna be watchin' Miss Magnolia real close for the next couple of days. She cain't go on outin's . . . nothin' that could get her hurt again."

"But don't you see? You're hurting her worse if she doesn't get to go back to Levy. She'll get to meet her nephew. She'll get to pay her respects to her only brother."

"She don't know up from down," I say, and as soon as I say it, I regret every last word. "I didn't mean that! Oh, heaven above, Mister George, you know I don't mean that. She's in there, she is! I just . . ."

Mister George puts his hand on my shoulder. He leans over in the bed and kisses his wife real sweet near her ear and whispers something I can't hear. Then he says, "I know, Annie. I know. I'll talk to my daughter tomorrow." He rolls over and don't say a thing more. But I sit here and watch over them. I'll watch over them long as it takes.

When I'm sure Mister George and Miss Magnolia are sound asleep, I tiptoe over to the window and pick up that package marked *Mr. George Jacobs*. I nestle down in his comfy chair and flick on the reading light. Miss Candy's helping Mister Joe tonight, so I got some time. I start with the letter on the top.

August 3, 1996

Dear George,

It's been awhile. I've been busy, helping my son, James. He just got his divorce finalized, and I tell you, it breaks a father's heart. Makes me wonder if I didn't have something to do with it. Makes me think about the time my mother told me about trouble and how it was in her genes. I'm wondering if I haven't passed it on to my son. Will it keep going like tainted blood to his children and on to theirs for all of eternity? I don't know how much of a Bible man you are, but I've started reading it a little more over the years. It helps me make sense of some things, makes others more mysterious. I noticed that there are lineages in the Bible that are cursed by God. One king makes him angry and all his descendants pay. 'Course all it takes is one, right? All it takes is one fella to come along and do right in the eyes of the Lord for the curse to be broken. Likewise, you take a nice family and all it takes is one bad seed to get the curse started up.

I wonder if our lives aren't this way. I wonder if we're not bad seeds or good seeds, beginning or ending curses.

I've had all I can with sadness lately. My son, the grand-kids . . . if Rose were alive, it would kill her. So while I'm here, wallowing, I figure it's time I confronted Levy. Bear with me. I still haven't sent those other letters to you, and I may never send this one either. It's the only way I can open up, though, thinking you'll never read these things. It was Rose's idea. My sweet wife used to say I'd sleep better if I could get this stuff out. I'm hoping she was right.

So thank you, in advance, for being on the other end of this pen. It's time to get some things off my chest. Here goes.

Have I told you how angry I am you get to spend your days with Maggie? Have I told you how bad I miss that child, how I've never met her as a woman, how I wonder what she's like, if she has that same laugh that fills up from her toes, if she still knows how to hook a cricket, if she's as beautiful as ever, if she remembers all our wonderful days? Have I told you how angry I am at God that things had to end up this way? Why couldn't he have let me forget? So many friends died in the war, George. Sometimes I wonder if they weren't the lucky ones. Now that I'm old, my friends are losing their marbles. Maybe they're the lucky ones. They can forget.

I can never forget. I can never forget about the Boll Weevil pulling into Levy that day, about Maggie and me meeting that evil man and Joe Stackhouse when they got off the train. How we invited them into our town, their own little welcome committee. How we led the way to Jacobs Mercantile and watched as all our fates were being sealed. If only Mama had been there with us and recognized him right off. If only we hadn't stolen that moonshine from Miss Maple and used it against him. Maybe he wouldn't have been so angry. Maybe we could have talked it all out and I could have gone with him willingly. But no.

George, you got to believe me when I say I would do anything to undo that day. I'd do anything to just understand this was my father, come to take me away. How I wish I could've seen into the future. None of it would have happened. I could have gone with him and everyone would have been sad awhile, but the fire wouldn't have happened, the sheer terror that ripped through Levy, the family being ripped apart like that. Maggie, dear Maggie, crying after me as my train pulled away. I could have spared us all of that.

Some things haunt you in the middle of the night. I'm haunted by Maggie's face and the sound of her voice. I can still hear it over the train.

It was the end of our innocence. I never realized how good we had it: you, me, Maggie. We had some good times growing up, didn't we?

Remember that time in church I hooked a fiddler crab on Mrs. Benchley's hat and she screamed and hollered till we nearly wet ourselves from laughing? Remember all those times we walked the train tracks, imagining we could grow up and be engineers or aviators? And then there was Togoodoo Creek. The watering hole was ours alone. It was a special place, a sacred place. Until . . .

Well, I'm done. It's all I can do for now. I am old. I'm tired. My son's life is shattered, not to mention what my grandchildren are going through. I just keep thinking if there was some way to go back, if there was some way to undo all that happened in Levy, then his life would be better for it.

We would all be better for it.

Deep down, I know she's in good hands with you, George, but it doesn't erase this gnawing envy. It eats me alive. I miss my Maggie. I want things to be the way they were before, and sadly, the past can never be undone.

Ash

P.S. I will never send this letter because it's just an old man whining about the past, and I truly can't stand people like that. Can't stand the sound of my own voice. Time to stick my smile back on. Maybe I'll just burn this thing—but for some reason, I have an aversion to flames.

TWENTY-NINE

Ash

August 4, 1996

Dear George,

I didn't sleep a wink last night. I lay there wide-eyed, staring at the ceiling. Every now and again, I'd roll over and think that Rose might be there, but the mind, it was playing tricks on me. Rose has been gone for four years now, and I tell you, it doesn't get much easier. The smell of her can waft by at any moment and nearly knock me off my feet. I'll hear a song she used to love and think she's here again, but she's not. Cruel tricks, is what it is.

You know, it's the same way with Maggie. She's my little ghost. The sad part is, I'm not man enough to go find her and show my face. I'm not sure what would happen if I did. I just keep thinking about the last time I saw her and how it was so traumatic for her. I never want to do that to her again. I imagine she's happy now. With you, even. She's just that kind of girl. As a baby, she would wake up with a smile on, those chubby cheeks, that sweet curly hair. She would look at me with her pretty blue eyes, and I was in love. My mother would let me hold her on the sofa when she was tiny. It was Mama, me, and Maggie on my lap. Shoot, it's amazing how an old man can be so close to tears at times. I feel like I'm falling apart, friend. Do you ever feel this way? Do other old men feel this way?

My son, I saw him today, he's a mess. That's really what's bothering me. Says he didn't see it coming. Says he thought they were happy together. He feels like a fool. What do you tell your child when he's been hurt so bad? How do you tell him he should have seen the train coming? I tell you, if Rose were here, she'd be able to say the right things and make him feel better, but me? Sad excuse.

All right, here's the thing. I may never sleep again if I can't get all this mess out. I feel like I'm upchucking, some big sissy boy on the therapist's couch. If my friends from the war could see me now.

Here goes.

Levy. Who's stinking idea was it to go through the magician's trunk? Yours or mine? I can't remember. I do remember sneaking over to Miss Maple's house and into her shed. All those mason jars. Remember? All that moonshine. I tasted it, and so did you and Joe, and we all spit it up. It was like firewater. I remember wondering how a sweet lady like Miss Maple could make firewater and tolerate it. Did she drink it herself? I thought about grown-ups and what a strange lot they were. Ain't it true, now. Ain't it true.

We stole back over to Jacobs Mercantile and prayed the magician would drink the stuff. I doubted it. I doubted anybody in their right mind would ever put that in their mouth, but lo and behold, we watched through the slits in the wall. He drank it all down. Every last drop. I knew he was a devil then. In the pit of my stomach, I knew, only a devil could drink firewater like it was nothing at all.

Have you ever wondered what we could have done differently, George? Have you ever wondered if there was some other way to get in that room and go through that trunk without stealing Miss Maple's moonshine? Because I have. I've thought of a zillion ways. But as boys, we were too young, too stupid and excited to think anything through.

Why is it that one of the lovely side effects of living this long is you get plenty of time to think things through? Ain't it a laugh?

Sleep well, my friend. Sleep for the both of us if you can tonight.

Ash

⚜

Annie

Mister George is snoring loud. I don't see how Miss Magnolia can sleep through all that racket, but I reckon you been married that long, you get used to some things.

I want to just cry. I want to go crawl into that bed and lay right there in the middle of those two people and make all their cares go away. Lord have mercy, I think I might need a child. *Would you see fit to bring me a man first? It works better that way. See to it, Lord, that the man don't care what I look like. See to it that he love me all my days like Mister George and Miss Magnolia here. They got a love to envy. They got a love nothing can tear apart.*

"You still here?"

Scare me to death! My hand jerks and I crumple the letter. Mister George woke up. What time is it, anyway?

"Still here," I whisper, waiting for him to let me have it.

"Good," he says, and my heart calms.

"Just go back to sleep now, Mister George. Sleep tight. I'll watch over you."

I listen for him to see if he'll snore again, but he doesn't. He's still awake and he knows I'm over here, reading his letters. He knows it and he's glad. I'm a big believer in things happening for a reason, and I can't shake this feeling I was put here in these old people's lives for a reason. *It's right there in your hand*, the Lord says to me. *Keep reading, Annie.*

All right, Lord. You know I will.

THIRTY

Ash

December 24, 1996

Dear George,

Well, it's Christmas Eve here in New York. How many have we seen now? Seventy-seven? Seventy-eight? I can see outside my window, the cool moonlight glowing on the neighbor's snow-covered roof. I always loved this time, on the night before—James snuggled in his bed, Rose having put on all the finishing touches and filled his stocking, and me, wondering if a tricycle or other contraption I put together in secret out back would actually work. I loved the excitement of it all.

Sadly, James is here again this Christmas Eve. He's here because he has nowhere else to go. He and Cheryl won't be getting back together any time soon, if ever. I say it's sad that he's here, but I admit, it's nice having him safe in his bed again. Selfish of me. It's like time has rewound and I keep expecting Rose to come to bed soon and give me a kiss, tell me *Good night, Santa.*

Where's Maggie tonight, George? She must be seventy-four now. Hard to believe my baby sister is . . . dare I say, an old woman? I can't imagine it. I put her sweet creamy skin and strawberry blond hair on her still to this day. There can be no wrinkles. There can be no gray hair. Surely there's no stoop in her walk. I imagine she still skips everywhere and runs faster than any of us boys ever thought about.

I heard I have a niece out there, somewhere, and I'm glad. Glad that Maggie got to love somebody the way Mama must have loved us. She did love Maggie and me, you know. She did, and one of the things I regret the most is that I had to leave in order to give her peace. I wonder if I made it worse sometimes. I wonder if I shouldn't have stayed. I wonder, I wonder . . .

I think I hear sleigh bells and if I'm not asleep, the old fat man won't come. I know what I'm wishing for this year. I know what I want him to stuff in my stocking, but I'm afraid James is here, and that's the best I'll get. I'll take it, family in whatever form it comes in, broken, hurt, safe in his little bed again. He's fifty-one, you know. James. I wish you could meet him. He's got a little bit of Maggie in him . . . in the eyes. He inherited her beauty, but my stubbornness, and alas, all the trouble that trails along with it.

We do the best we can in this life, George, and that's all we can do. It's the only way for an old man to sleep at night.

Good night, George. Good night, Maggie. Good night, Rose. Merry Christmas Eve.

Ash

January 1, 1997

Dear George,

It's a new year today, 1997. Happy New Year. I have some resolutions, maybe you do too. I resolve to walk around the block once a day to keep my joints working. I resolve to stop flipping off bad drivers. I resolve to keep drinking my Manhattan no matter what James says. It has a longevity effect, I tell him. Pickles the liver so it'll keep longer. Here, I'll have another.

I resolve to let go of the past and get on with the future, but it's hard. I'm seventy-eight years old, no wife, no job, although I occasionally get a call for some of the antiques I keep in the basement. I used to have a shop, George. A real nice shop. Funny, you know what I had a lot of? World's Fair memorabilia—salt and pepper shakers shaped like the Trylon and Perisphere, Mr. Peanut dishes, postcards from the France and Egypt exhibits. You name it, I had it. Now I only have a few things, commemorative spoons, buttons and name badges from fair workers' uniforms, and of course, that large photograph of Maggie as a bathing beauty.

It's mine, you know. You might have the real thing, but I have this portrait to keep me company. I have her sweet smile always looking upon me from over the fireplace. I have her two-dimensional figure to remind me of what an old fart I am now. And you, you get to start the new year with the sweetest girl to ever live and breathe. Me? I got nothing. Rose is gone. And I'm here in this cold world alone.

I am here for another year, and I have to ask, why? Why am I still here? What use is there for an old man who can't comfort his son, can't contribute to society, can't climb the stairs well or get around much anymore? What use at all?

Happy New Year, George, old buddy. I resolve to stop writing these whiny letters to you. I resolve that you'll never get your grimy hands on this portrait of Maggie because she's mine. She's all I've got.

Signing off one last time. Happy New Year.

Ash

THIRTY-ONE

George

I'm lying still on the bed, on the peach-colored sheets my wife bought before we ever moved into this place. I've never thought about them much, except the color is her. It nearly matches our Cadillac out in the parking lot, which, sadly, neither of us can drive anymore. Miss Annie has my wife in the bathroom, getting her cleaned up and pretty for another day. But I am here, thinking about Levy. I am thinking about Ash Black and about Joe Stackhouse. I can't believe it's really him come back after all these years. Is it really him?

I sit up and, I swear, I can feel the hairs on my arms brush the sheets. I hear birds outside my window, a vacuum cleaner somewhere in this building. I can hear old people rocking in chairs on the front porch, the sunrisers who always watch the sun come up as if it might be their last. I can feel something in the air, murky and warm, like the steam of a summer shower. I can feel my blood pushing the cancer along in my veins. I stand up and walk to the window.

Miss Annie read some of the letters last night. Good. Maybe someone else knows what this is like. Maybe some other party understands what I've been forced to relive. Her keys must have fallen out of her pocket. They're there in my leather chair, the long loop of them, a dozen or so. One of them has to work. I scoop them up and stick them in the pocket of my old robe. Next I go to the game table.

I open the little drawer beneath the checkerboard and pull out my secret weapon, hidden in the back. I stick it in my other pocket and walk quietly out the door. I am aware of all my surroundings, the blood pounding in my head, the shuffle of my slippered feet as I move toward the old man's room.

He won't be expecting me. He'll probably be sleeping. I feel like I'm in Belgium again, 1945, except it's not cold. I remember the frigid chill that made me wonder what in the heck we were fighting for. I remember sneaking up to the camp. We didn't really believe the Nazis could be doing such a thing, but then when we saw—well, what we saw—

After all these years, I am still surprised at the atrocities of men, at the things we are capable of.

I am sneaking to the stranger's room, and I've never felt more awake. I watch as my arm covered in tan terrycloth reaches for his door. It's as if someone else is doing this. I look through the keys, slowly, methodically. There it is. I push it in the door and carefully open it without a sound. The room is dark and smells musty like age. Musty like memories.

There he is on the bed, asleep. For a second I picture

him young again, lying on my own bed in Levy. A few days of bunking and you get to know a fella. I got to know that he liked to sit up in the middle of the night and scream bloody murder, mumble to himself. I used to listen to him in the darkness. He never stammered when he was talking in his sleep, never when he was battling the demons of his dreams.

I walk to the edge of the bed and look down on him. His mouth is open wide as if he's gasping for air, but his breathing is barely there. I hold my hand in front of his mouth to be sure he's alive. Good.

I've got to hurry. Annie and Maggie will be finishing up soon and she'll know I'm gone. She'll know I've taken her keys.

"Joe?" I say, pushing on his shoulder. He doesn't move. "Joe. Wake up." I shake him harder. After a minute of pulling him from the depths, he stirs.

"Who . . . what?"

"It's me. It's me, Joe. George Jacobs. Remember me? You used to sleep in my bed. You were the magician's son come to Levy. Look, I've got something for you."

I click on the lamp on his night table and he squints.

"Hello? Do I know you?"

"Sure you do. I'm just old now. Like you. We're old. See? Still me, still George." I pull my ears out to show him what I looked like as a kid.

"Where am I?"

"You're in Harmony House, Joe. You're old as the dickens, you're stuck in here. You're in room 123 of Harmony House and there's nothing you can do about it." I throw his covers back. "Now get up. I got something I want you to do for me."

Joe does it, dutifully. He reaches for some glasses and I hand them to him. He shoves them on his nose crooked.

"Is this a drill?" he says.

"Drill? No. No, this is the real thing, Joe. Now look here, come sit down." I find a crutch leaning against the wall and hand it to him. I help him stand up and we dance slowly over to a table and two chairs. I turn on a floor lamp for more light and then pull out my secret weapon.

"You see this? You see what these are? I bet you're not any good at cards, are you, Joe? No, I bet you never touched them in your life. Here. Have a try." I push the stack of cards over to him and he looks at them, then at me. He smiles. *Yes, that's right. Take the cards. Take them in your old hands.* "Can you shuffle them?"

He picks them up and holds them in shaky fingers. He tries to cut the deck, but his hands won't cooperate. "No, never could shuffle worth a nickel, could you? Here." I shuffle the deck and pull out a card. I hold it to my chest and then spread the rest out in random fashion, face-side up, so he can see them. A second later I swipe them all to the floor. Joe looks at me surprised, alarmed. I smile this time.

"I'll pick those up later. Joe? You got any idea which card I'm holding? Any idea at all?"

Joe looks at my eye and then the other. He stares at the card hidden on my chest. He moves his mouth and seems to be counting. *Come on, come on . . .* Finally, he says, "F-four of hearts?"

My eyebrows lower and I turn the card around. I set it on

the table and push it toward him. When he reaches for the four of hearts, I grab his hand. It's him.

"Tell me what you're doing here, Joe! Who sent you? Was it Ash? Did he send you to torment me after all these years? He never could let it go. Tell me, Joe. Tell me!"

"Mister George! What are you doin'? Unhand him!"

It's Annie. Dangit, I've been caught. "I was just . . . we were playing cards."

"You were doin' no such thing! I declare, I don't know what to do with you!"

I look over at my wife who is dressed and fluffed in her baby blue outfit. She used to run circles around me in those sweat suits, but now she sits there in that chair, getting thinner, not much meat on those pretty bones anymore.

"Mister George?" Miss Annie bends down and gets right in my face. She doesn't quite look mad. "Go on now, get some clothes on," she says. "Miss Maggie's hungry, hear? You all go and have some breakfast, and I'll speak at you later. Mornin', Joe honey, how you doin'?"

She cuts her eyes at me, and there's nothing I can say. I was caught interrogating the new guy, but I have no regrets. I know now, without a doubt—it's really him. The implications are staggering. How could it happen? What are the odds? What cosmic justice is this? My heart pounds as I push Maggie down the hall. My head is a swarm of hornets. I see flashes of Joe's younger face. We're running through the woods, running out of time. We are all running out of time.

THIRTY-TWO

Annie

Never so upset in all my life! Never felt this much pressure on my shoulders. What a position to be in—two things so wrong both seem right at the same time. How can that be? Mister George only has so much time left on this earth. Wouldn't the right thing be to take him down to Levy like he asked me? I'm the only one who knows what-all he's been reading in those letters. I'm the one been watching him move to distraction . . . might even hurt somebody if he don't make peace before his time.

But then Harmony House would knock me right out on my ear if I broke the rules, and I love this job. People depend on me. I can't do that.

But the man's dying! *Lord, have mercy, what you doin' to me?*

I put my hand up to Mama's door and catch my breath. Thursdays are my day off in the afternoon, so I go and check on her. She don't like to think of it that way, but I tell her it's the only time I can visit. I ain't checking up on her. Just visiting. *Take a deep breath now, Annie. There.* Her house is brown and her door and window trims are painted blue to keep the haints out. It's old Gullah tradition—superstition, if you ask me. But Mama believes what Mama believes. No changing that woman's mind.

"Hey, Mama." She's sitting on a wood chair, pulled out way into the middle of the kitchen, eating a peach and squinting at the tiny television set in the other room. "What are you doin'? Gonna go blind tryin' to watch that from here."

"Don't like gettin' peach juice on my carpet. Don't fuss at me."

I walk into the kitchen, set my bag down, and look around. I see she left the bag of bread open and everything's probably stale already. I move over slow and fasten it tight. I open the fridge, acting like I'm gonna get me something to drink, but really I'm checking to see what she's eating, *if* she's eating. I see a quart of whole milk and open it up. I sniff it in secret. It's good. *Thank you, Lord.* I see Tupperware stacked up every-which-a-way and know this stuff's old. Somehow I got to get in there and clean it out, but she'll have my hide, thinking I'm here checking up on her. Thinking she's old and can't do for herself no more.

"Got some fried chicken in there if you're hungry," she says. She pulls her eyes away from the TV set and looks at me for the first time. "What's wrong with you, gal?"

"Nothin's wrong."

"Don't give me that. You think I don't know you? Carried

you for nine months, changed your diapers, sent you off to school, washed your clothes, picked up after your ever-livin' self—"

"Okay, Mama. That's enough. You don't want to hear it though."

"Why? Why I don't wanna hear about what's troublin' my little Annie? I'm your mama! I carried you for nine months—"

"It's work, Mama. Just work."

"Oh." Mama sits there and takes a slow bite of her peach. The juice dribbles down her chin, so she sops it up with her napkin. Her jaw moves once, twice. Then she says, "Them old people givin' you trouble? Told you that place was nothin' but trouble."

"I know it, I know you did." I take a paper towel and wet it at the sink. I clean off Mama's breakfast table in slow circles.

"What is it then?"

"It's just . . . Mister George. Miss Magnolia's husband."

"White folks?"

"Yes, Mama."

"I don't know why you let them old white folks get all up in your head and mess you up. Too much trouble. Mm, mm, mm. They think they got troubles? I got troubles. You wanna hear what Miss Essie Mae done on yesterday?" I wipe slower and move over to do the countertops. "Go on then. I'm listenin'," she says.

"Mister George is dyin', Mama."

"Oh. I see. Sorry, baby. But don't they all die? We all gonna die someday, you know."

"Mama. Please?"

"I said go on. What you waitin' for?"

"Other day, this package come for Miss Magnolia, great big pretty picture of her when she was young." I stretch out my arms to show her just how big. "My goodness, still is one pretty lady. Then Mister George be gettin' these letters from Magnolia's long lost brother. He the one had the portrait."

"Long lost? How long?"

"Real long. Ain't seen him since they was children."

"That so?"

"Mmm-hmm." I pull up a chair and sit down across from Mama. She forgets all about her TV show in the other room. She sets down her peach pit and wraps it up in her napkin.

"So, Mama, here's the thing. Strange things goin' on. Mister George let me read a couple letters from Miss Magnolia's brother. They mention a man by the name of Joe Stackhouse long ago. And guess who come and moved into Harmony House just this week?"

"Who?"

"Mister Joe Stackhouse."

"No, ma'am. Same one?"

"I ain't lyin'. So now all these folks what knew each other as children, done come back together at ninety years old. You believe that?"

"I cain't believe it."

"And Miss Magnolia's brother dead now. His nephew wrote to say he bringin' his ashes down here to scatter come Saturday."

"This Saturday?"

"This Saturday. Two day's time. So Mister George wants

me to take him and his wife down there. Says he wants to make peace after all these years 'fore he ups and dies himself."

"Lawd have mercy, chile, take the poor man. Take him!"

"I know, Mama. Ain't that easy."

"Why not? Dyin' man just wants some peace 'fore he go on to the Lawd. Ain't no problem with that I can see."

"It's against the rules, Mama. I can lose my job."

"Lose your job at the old folk home you been wantin' to stick me into? Cain't see a problem with that neither."

"You make me so tired, Mama. I don't want you in there. I said it a hundred million times."

"Not goin' neither."

"Good then."

"Good." Mama gets up slow and walks hunched over to the trash can. Her age is catching up with her. I got to get her involved in that new senior center. She's almost sixty-five. She needs to exercise. Take some walks. Make some friends. She's been alone too long since Daddy died, going on twenty years now. "How come his kinfolk cain't take him down there?" she says.

"He don't want 'em involved. It's personal, Mama. Some things you cain't share with family, you know that."

She comes back over and I can hear *The Price is Right* on in the other room. Somebody just won something good.

"Listen here," she says, licking her bottom lip. She *thwacks* the table right in front of me with the palm of her hand. "I'll take that old man where he need to go."

"What?"

"I said, I'll take him. I ain't mind drivin' some old white

fella off to do the Lawd's work. I ain't got no big job a-holdin' me back."

"But, Mama, I don't think that's a good idea."

"Why not? I'm able-bodied. I got my driver's license. They tried to tell me my eyes was bad, but you know what I telled that scrawny fella? I say, I can see *you* clear 'nough. Yes sir, I tell him, listen here, you gone give me that license if you know what's good for you. I been drivin' these roads since Daddy's tractor. Ain't no young punk gonna tell Miz Wright she ain't drivin' no more!"

"I know you can drive—"

"Well good, then. Saturday. It's settled. Where I'm drivin' him to anyway?"

"Levy, Mama."

"Levy? Like the Levy on down where Daddy come from? Oh, hail no. Uh-uh. Not in a million years. You ought to heard the stories 'bout what-all happened to his mama, your great grandmama in Levy. No sir, Annie. I ain't a-goin' back to that curs-ed place. Why you even gonna ask me a thing like that? Shoot. Sometimes, I declare, I ain't know what to do with you. Levy. Lawd have mercy, Annie, sometimes I ain't know."

"What happened, Mama? I didn't know we were from Levy. I thought you were both from James Island."

Mama looks at me cross-eyed, and I swear, she's the most infuriating woman I ever met. "What happened? I ain't a-gonna say! Lawd Jesus know and Daddy in heaven know, but that ain't somethin' for me to repeat. No sir. It be askin' for haints to come take up roost in here," she whispers now, "and I work hard as it is to keep that from happenin'. Hard as it is. My mouth stay shut."

Mama sits there, arms folded. She turns her attention to the TV set again, and I might as well be talking to the wall. My head's spinning faster than it was when I come in here today, and I'm halfway wishing I'd stayed home.

I have roots in Levy?

THIRTY-THREE

Magnolia

My hands are busy with a wand George gave me from my collection. He saw me eyeing them, and I do feel better with it in my fingers. My head hurts a little though, and my shoulder; not sure why. George pushes me to the breakfast table and I see an old man with a hat and an old woman in red. They're smiling at me, but I haven't any idea who they are. My hands aim at them and *poof*! The man and woman are gone now—Emmet and Jessica are there in their places. Thank goodness, I was hoping to see a friend. I want someone who knows George to watch him closely. He's acting strangely today.

"If I didn't know any better, I'd say you didn't sleep a wink last night, George," says Emmet. "Look like we used to when we'd have our all-night poker games."

"Those were lovely," says Jessica. "Emmet was always worthless the next day."

"I am guilty," says George. "Though not from playing poker." He looks at his fork, leans forward, and rubs his eyes.

"What is it, George? Something the matter?"

George looks at Jessica's eyelashes, we all know they're fake, and then at me. "I imagine I will regret this, but I got to tell somebody. You know Joe? That new guy?"

"Sure . . . where is he, anyway?"

"He'll be coming soon enough. Miss Annie's with him now."

"Something wrong with him?"

"I know him," says George. "I know him and Maggie does too. At least she would—"

Jessica leans forward on her elbows and whispers, looking around her to make sure the coast is clear. Her eyebrows are two painted upside down Us. "Well . . . who is he?"

"Knew him as a child. He was a boarder in the back of our store. Didn't stay long though. He came with a man, an awful man. Between the two of them, they destroyed the peace in Levy. Destroyed everything."

"Oh. Well now, it's been a long time, George."

"I know it has. But some things don't go away. Some things like wanting to protect the girl you love so much." He looks over at me and I want to smile at him. I want to tell him I love him. *I love you, George.*

LEVY, 1929

George is at my side. He hands me a flower he picked from the woods. It's yellow and white with bits of pink on it, but in the glow of dawn, it all seems blue. The stem is flimsy. I look at the petals, with the streaks in them. I look up at George. He is not smiling. He is covered in soot from head to toe. I've never seen him look so awful, so dirty. I've never seen such seriousness in his eyes. I've never wanted to hug him so badly.

"Sorry about your house," he says, looking at his feet. Behind him, my house is a flat black mess that still gives off heat and smoke, but the fire is out. It took all night. At least it's out. The men of Levy are walking around like the living dead back there, wiping their brows, leaning against trees, hands on hips, hanging their heads.

"The mail!" I say.

"Huh?"

"The mailboxes in there. Mrs. Kline won't get her catalog. Mrs. Benchley won't get her magazines!"

"That don't matter," says George, sitting down next to me in the grass.

"Yes, it does! Daddy's mailboxes, they're all gone! All gone, all gone . . ." And then for the first time since yesterday morning, since I woke up in the blue light, since I found out about Mama's being a jailbird, since I watched our house burn to the ground, I start crying a long, painful cry, and George puts his skinny arm around me and holds me close to him, rocking and rocking, until I can't feel the tears anymore, just George's warm body. I feel safe here.

"You're safe here, George. Nothing's going to happen in Harmony House. If you haven't noticed already, Joe's not quite all there."

"Oh, I know it, I'm not afraid of Joe," says George. "No, it's more than that."

Miss Annie comes up behind George and taps him on the shoulder. He turns and she whispers something in his ear. He nods and then Miss Annie leaves. When she comes back, she's got an old man with her. He's stooped over and leaning on her arm. He's got white combed-over hair and a white shirt on, slacks. He watches a few feet in front of him until he comes closer to us. There, he's clear now. I can see in his eyes. He looks at me and I know who it is; I see past all the years he carries on his shoulders and on his face. I see a boy I once knew. It can't be . . .

Joe comes to the tree where George is still holding me. He's been crying, and tear tracks run through the dirt on his face. He's still handsome, I think, though how I'm thinking this at a time like this, I don't know. Joe says to George, "I guess it's a-a-all over."

"They find him?"

Joe shakes his head. He turns and looks at the smoldering embers. "Nothin' left."

"Oh," says George. He loosens his grip on me and stands up quick. He runs down the dirt lane and then stops in the middle and falls to his knees. I can see he's getting sick over there and I should go to him, I should help him, but I don't.

I can't move. And anyway, Joe's here. He sits down beside me and I can feel him next to me. "Hey, Maggie."

"Hey."

"I'm sorry we come to your town," says Joe. "S-sorry for a-a-all of it."

"Shhh, don't be sorry. I'm glad you're here." I do it then. I put my hand on Joe's back and he heaves into his knees and cries real quiet. Mama and Ash walk over to us in a daze. He's holding her upright. "Doc Murphy's comin'," says Ash. "He's gonna fix us up."

The next thing I know we're all riding in the back of a wagon with hay at my feet. I am lying on Mama's lap, her eyes staring far off, and all I can see are flames—in her eyes, in her flowing hair, in the morning sun peeking through the trees. Then I look over at George and his blue eyes are watching mine like cool water, dousing the fire . . .

THIRTY-FOUR

George

It sure is hot in here. I can't eat a thing today. Fantasia brought
me scrambled eggs and buttered toast, just like I asked, but
there's a lump in my throat. Nothing will go down. I sit here
in my chair, pushing eggs from one place to another. There is
chatting going on around me, old people at the tables nearby,
Harmony House staffers clinking dishes and cups as they take
them away. All this noise, all this chatter. I look at my wife
who has a spoonful of coffee over her plate. Her lips pucker
as she leans in. The coffee is spilling, she'll never make it.
"Here, let me help." She looks at me cold. She knows, doesn't
she? She knows how worthless I am. It's why she doesn't love
me anymore.

I can't do this. I look at Jessica and Emmet, silently eating as they've done next to each other since the beginning of
time. They don't understand. Neither of them do. They say

they understand what it's like to have a wife who doesn't know you, but they don't. They can't possibly! I look over at Joe and watch as his head bobbles. He chews something slowly. He looks at his plate. He's absolutely gone, isn't he? He's lucky he's forgotten Levy. Maggie, Joe, they've forgotten Levy, but me? I'll never forget again. I used to be blissfully ignorant, but Ash's letters have broken through the fog, cursed me with a memory like an elephant. So I have to do this. For me. I am alone in this world now. I am leaving it alone. I understand that now.

"Excuse me," I say, folding my napkin and laying it on my plate. I scoot my chair back.

"But, George, you didn't eat anything."

"You don't look good, honey. I think you need to see Dr. Casey," says Jessica. "Let's make you an appointment today."

"No, I'm fine."

"You're not—"

"I'm fine, I said."

Miss Annie comes over and puts her hand on my shoulder. "You all go on, keep eatin', I'll take Mister George, here, on back to rest."

I don't argue with her. I've got to get out.

In the hallway, I let Miss Annie lead me back to the door of our room. Then I stop, look back down the hall, away from her face. "I'm leaving, Annie. I know you don't understand, but I got to go. If you can't help me, I'll find some other way, but—"

Miss Annie turns me toward her and puts both hands on my shoulders. Her grip is strong and I feel her strength rolling through me, fortifying me. "Look here," she says. She licks her lips. Her eyes are chocolate. "There are some things I don't know in this world. Lots I don't understand. But I know enough about the Lawd to know he's all up in this-here. He's a-callin' you on back to Levy. I don't doubt it. And he's callin' me to get you there. Now, Mister George, you like family to me." Miss Annie's eyes tear up. "I put in to Ms. Johnson today for a special outin'. It's the only way I can figure she'll let me take you outta this place. If she says yes, that's good news, but I still don't know what to do 'bout your wife. Miss Magnolia got them stitches—"

I lean in and kiss Miss Annie on the cheek. I have never kissed a colored woman in all my ninety-two years, but I have now, and I'd do it again in a heartbeat.

"Miss Annie, I'll admit I've never believed in much, but if I ever had doubts there are angels in this world, I don't doubt it now."

She smiles a corn-toothed smile that gives off heat, and she grabs my hand and squeezes it tight. "Oh, there's so much we don't understand, but God loves you, Mister George, 'specially you. Let's get you ready for your trip now, honey. Got lots to do. So much, so much."

THIRTY-FIVE

George

Miss Annie is packing a bag with changes of clothes for Maggie and me and all sorts of medications, hairbrushes, I don't know what-all. If we do go to Levy, it's not like we're staying overnight. We'll just go, pay our respects to Ash's son, and . . . and be done with it. I can hear her singing in the bathroom, some sort of spiritual, almost familiar:

> *Gospel train's a-comin'*
> *I hear it just at hand*
> *Hear the car wheels rumblin'*
> *And rolling through the land*
> *Get on board little children*
> *Get on board little children*
> *Get on board little children*
> *There's room for many more.*

Sitting here, I can hardly keep my eyes open. What time is it anyway? Still breakfast? Noon? There's a feeling in my stomach, something like hunger or nausea or both. It pricks at me long enough to keep my eyes open. I pick up one of Ash's letters and commence reading, painful as it might be. It's too late to hide my head in the sand. It's now or never. I know that. I'm ready for anything. Ready as I'll ever be.

February 8, 2000

Dear George,

Well, the world didn't end. I was kind of looking forward to what would happen if it did. I sat here on New Year's Eve, expecting that when the ball fell, all hell would break loose. Maybe a war, a bright flash of light, some gassy smell that would put us all in a deep forever sleep, but nothing of the sort happened. I sat here alone, no wife to kiss, not even a dog, just alone in this world that didn't end, wondering, why the heck not? Why the heck am I still here?

It's been a few years since I wrote you last, if you didn't notice. 'Course, how could you? I'm thinking of biting the bullet and coming down to visit my sister. I don't care what you do; you're an old man now. I figure, the two of us together are over 160 years old, and I'd pay to watch that fight, wouldn't you?

The only reason I can come up with for still being alive, for still taking up space and sucking up air, is because there's something I still need to do with Maggie. I can't get Rose back. I've tried every night in my dreams. She comes to me sometimes, she does, and when I wake up in the morning, I try to keep my eyes closed so she can stay in my head, but as the day wears on, I lose her all over again. It's excruciating. The house we lived in looks the same. The place where she used to sit. The stove where she used to cook. The bookshelf full of books she read over and over again—all evidence that she was here, but she's not. Never will be again. It's still hard to wrap my head around.

I imagine you don't have to suffer this way. You have your wife. You have my Maggie. You have her adoring eyes, while I have her—what? Scorn? Pity? Does she still blame me for all her childhood troubles? Does she even remember me after all these years?

Seeing her face-to-face, even if she hates me, is better than not seeing her at all. So I'm coming, George. I'm coming whether you like it or not. Have at this old man if you want to. You can't do any worse damage than has already been done.

Happy New Year.

Ash

February 9, 2000

Dear George,

Dangit all, I'm not coming. The gods must be against me. I tried to call and get a plane ticket to South Carolina, but I couldn't find my wallet to get the credit card number. Then I tried to call my son to drive me down, but he wouldn't answer the dang phone! I nearly pulled out what's left of my hair trying to remember where I keep my keys, and how exactly to back out of the driveway in snow, but for the life of me, all was kept hidden—the wallet, the keys, the plane ticket, the son to drive me. If that's not the universe keeping me in my place, I don't know what is. I lost my nerve now, anyway, so I'm staying here, George. I just thought you should know. Even though I'll never send you this letter, I thought I should tell you—you won. You won, George. I lost out. But apparently it's got to be this way.

You know, strangely, I'm relieved. No matter how I feel, I could never upset my Maggie again, and I realize—I do—how much my coming might upset the balance.

I'm looking at her big beautiful picture right now. She's smiling at me and gorgeous, and it calms me some. Just sit tight and take care of her, George. God trusted her to you, and not to me. For some reason I don't understand, it's the way it should be.

Hug her for me. Hug her for me and whisper how much she is loved by an old man living in New York.

Dangit.

Ash

THIRTY-SIX

Magnolia

LEVY, 1929

My brother Ash is hugging me tight in Doc Murphy's living room, and I'm trying hard to stop coughing. He's a head taller than me, but I'm catching up fast, he says. I wonder if one of these days I'll be as tall as Ash, if I'll be like him. I'd like to be like my big brother, brave, smart. I look up at him. He's the best brother there ever was. He saved me from that fire. I just know he was the one who came and got me. Mama's always telling Ash to watch over me when we go off in the woods, what to do if we see a snake, what to do if we get bit by one. Ash knows how to make a tourniquet and says he'll suck the venom right out of my leg if he has to, and I believe him. I always feel safe when Ash's around. But he's leaving now.

"You'll be all right," he says. "Doc Murphy's gonna watch

you and Mama tonight. Miss Tillie said I can stay at their house for a while."

"With George?"

"Mmm-hmm. And Joe."

"But the man with the mustache!"

"We don't have to worry 'bout him no more." I can see in Ash's eyes he's telling me the truth, so I relax my shoulders and let him walk me to the sofa, let the medicine take effect. I'm getting sleepy now.

Ash smiles at me, though how he can muster a smile after fighting a fire so brave, I'll never know.

"Ash?" Mama is on the sofa next to me, reaching for him, her hands shaking. She doesn't look so pretty now. She's worn, like her dirty green dress. Her hair is limp beside her flushed cheeks.

"What, Mama?"

"Can you send for Miss Maple? I . . . I need her here."

"I will, Mama."

"And, honey?" Ash turns back to her. "You're nothin' . . . you're nothin' like him . . . like he was. I want you to know that, son."

Ash nods and something passes between them, then he turns and walks away. When I'm sure he's gone, I close my eyes for sleep, and the longest day of my life so far is done.

The rain pours down outside the window, turning day into gray. I'm lying on Doc Murphy's sofa, feeling better, though my chest hurts. I rub my head and feel the goose egg on top.

It's tender. Mama is on some blankets on the floor and I study her. She's almost like an angel when she sleeps. Her face is clear, with so signs of trouble there, no worried look in her eyes, no lines in her forehead. She's peaceful. I almost want her to stay there, just like that, forever.

Daddy is here now, asleep, sitting up in an armchair. It looks mighty uncomfortable. I don't ever want to fall asleep in a chair.

It occurs to me we have no house anymore. Where are we going to live? We can't stay forever on sofas and floors and armchairs. Maybe we can move in with Miss Maple. I think of her corn muffins, of the round colored rug, of the cat that pays me no mind, sleeping in the corner. I think of the way Miss Maple looks at me with watery eyes, like she loves me. Like I'm somebody special. And Ash. Where is he now? Oh yes. I close my eyes and listen to the rain. I remember his face, his messed up matted hair as he hugged me last night. I wish he was here, but I imagine he's still sleeping sound at George's house.

The rain falls heavier and I pull a blanket around me tight. The sky lights up, a bright flash, and I know it's coming—One. Two. *Bang!* Thunder crashes outside our window and I pull the cover up over my head. There's a pounding, more banging, and I hope the storm passes. Then I hear voices. I pull the cover off my face and see Daddy and Doc Murphy standing at the door. There's a soaking wet boy there, hands waving, breathing heavy, and I rub my eyes to be sure of what I'm seeing.

It's George. He's screaming, "He's back, he's alive, he

come to take Ash! The man, that magician, you got to come fast!"

The rhyme of it dances in my head, dances, dances, and I play it over and over again while the men run outside into the rain and Mama holds me tight on the sofa. It's a rhyme, I like rhymes, so I rhyme it again and again in my head while she rocks me and carries on so. *Hey diddle diddle, the cat in the fiddle . . .*

Maybe I'm still in a dream. *Wake up, Maggie. Wake up . . . wake up . . . wake up . . .*

"Wake up, honey, it's time to go back to the room." I open my eyes and see blue fabric. I don't know where I am. I lift my head and see Jessica down in my face. When she's so close, I can see the wrinkles clearly. *Jess, you look better from back there.* I blink and see I'm still °in the dining room of Harmony House. Must have dozed off in my chair. I do that a lot these days. Sometimes there's no reason to stay awake.

"Here, George might like these." She places several skinny wands on my lap. My, the hands have been busy, haven't they? I didn't even notice. Imagine, even in my sleep.

"Joe, these are just as good as Maggie's. I declare, you two must be made from the same mold."

Joe? Joe made these wands for me? I look over and see an old man with sparkling eyes sitting behind a glass of juice. Behind him, the rain is coming down outside the windows and it makes me sleepy. I close my eyes. *Oh, Joe. I pray you're safe wherever you are. You can keep that wand, you know. Keep it and use it on that terrible man. Make a spell of protection so he'll leave you and Ash alone for good. Promise me. Promise me you will.*

God, please protect them wherever they are. They're just boys. Only, always boys . . .

THIRTY-SEVEN

George

"Come out, come out, wherever you are," says a blond perky lady with a tray in her hands. She smiles and cajoles the old people into the multipurpose room, like some pixie Pied Piper. The tables are covered in brown paper and there are plastic plates of paint every couple of seats.

I am shoving half of an apple into red paint and squishing it onto a piece of manila paper. This is for the birds. Whoever thought this was a worthwhile thing to do? The lady up front is awful excited to be sharing her fruit with this room full of old farts. I bet we're the highlight of her day. Delightful.

She comes by with her magic tray and hands my wife half of a green bell pepper. I watch as Maggie stares at the thing. Shaky hands, rolling it around in her fingers. She eyes the paint.

"Go on, stick it in the yellow," says the lady. "That will be lovely. You can make a sun. You want to make a yellow sun?"

I want to vomit.

Jessica is on the other side of Maggie. She takes her pear half and presses it in the brown. "I'm making a tree. See?"

Maggie looks at Jessica's brown pear and then at the yellow paint, then she takes the green bell pepper in her hands and shoves it up to her mouth. Attagirl.

"No, honey, that's not for eating," says Jessica. She takes Maggie's hand and pushes it down into the yellow paint. It gets all over Maggie's fingers and her eyes grow full as two moons. Jessica forces her hand down on the paper and when she pulls away, Jessica squeals, "See? What a beautiful sun."

Don't look like a sun to me.

How can time be passing so slowly? And why, *why* do we have to pass time doing this crappy craft? We only have an allotted amount left anyway. I keep looking over to the door to see if Miss Annie will come in and tell me she's got the go-ahead for the trip to Levy. And what if she does? What if she has to post that dad-blum thing out on the bulletin board for all these old folks to sign up? What if the whole place empties tomorrow morning and loads up on a bus to Levy? I look over at Miss Allison with that growth on her neck. Oh, heck no. She can't come. She'll talk the whole time about her grandchildren and then ask questions about Levy. *What is the population of Levy? What is the history of Levy? Blah blah blah.* I won't be able to handle it. I won't.

I feel itchy under my skin.

I look at Joe across the table from me. Wow, he's old. What is it about aging that melts the skin and years like tire tracks all over a man's face? I guess he's still not too bad look-ing, strange as that is. I watch his face. He's holding a star fruit in his hand and pressing green stars all over his paper, all in straight lines. *It's not how stars go at all,* I want to tell him. *You got to scatter stars, they're random, see?* But I don't say anything. His stars are all lined up just right.

But wait.

"You missed one there," I tell him. He looks up slow and catches my eyes. "Right there. You see? You got stars all in rows, but right there, you missed one." Joe goes back to press-ing, but he doesn't fill in that one spot. "Gee-manilly, Joe. Fill in that one place. Right there. You want me to do it?" He keeps going, green rows of stars with that dad-blum hole.

I think I might lose my mind! There's something miss-ing! Fill it in! "Fill it in, Joe!" He startles and the stupid lady comes over to me with her big tray of fruit and says, "We all express ourselves differently, don't we? I think it's lovely. You just work on your own paper. Press your apple down now." She presses my hand down, and when I lift it I have a big red splotch in the center of my paper with little spots where the seeds should be. It's ugly. *How dare you press my hand like I'm some old geezer!* I take that red apple and press it right on her rear end when she walks away. She squeals. "What'd you do that for?"

I fix my mouth and dip it in some more red paint and lean over the table and press it down on Joe's paper, right where that green star should have been. Good, no more holes. Everybody's staring at me. I hold my red apple up like a weapon. *Don't anybody mess with me. Don't anybody mess with George Jacobs today. I'm not in the mood.* Maggie is next to me in her wheelchair.

She's watching me. Almost seems amused. She's holding her stupid bell pepper in her hand, covered with yellow paint. Slowly she pushes it over to my mouth for me to eat, and I laugh and laugh and belly laugh until they ask me firmly to leave.

"Didn't want to be here, anyway," I say. "And I'm taking my wife too. This craft is for sissies and children. We are neither."

There is total silence, and then out of the back of the room, I hear a quiet clap. Then it spreads. By God, it spreads like wildfire, and I see my moment and take a bow. Jessica looks mortified and Emmet is pushing up to stand. "Enjoy the rest of your class, folks." As I take another bow, I lean down to Joe and whisper, "Come on, old man. You're coming with me. We got to talk."

THIRTY-EIGHT

George

"All right, troops, focus." My pretty wife is sitting in her wheelchair in our room, purposefully blocking the bosom on the large portrait of her former self. Joe Stackhouse is here too. I don't want him staring at her curves, so I placed her just so.

"Look right here, Joe. Right here in my eyes." I pace in front of him slowly, thinking. How should I put this?

"Now, I know we're all old. I know things that happened in the past could just stay in the past—" Joe wipes his nose and looks at the game table in front of him. He's behind the red checkers. He takes one and moves it forward on the diagonal. I'm losing him.

"Okay, scratch that. I can see there's no pussyfooting

around here. Here's the facts. Joe? Maggie and I used to live in a town called Levy. We grew up there. We were childhood sweethearts—at least, I was sweet on her. Anyway, you came to town with a man in a handlebar mustache in 1929. Remember that? You came on a train and you stayed with me in my very own bedroom. You were about ten, eleven. Is any of this ringing a bell?"

Joe takes a black checker and jumps himself backward. He puts the red checker off the board to the side. "I'm from N-New Orleans," he says.

"That's right. After you left New Orleans, where did you go, Joe?"

Joe holds his hand in midair, waiting to know what to do with it. Should he move the red or the black? He seems to be getting confused.

"Arlington," he says finally. He nods.

"Joe, I know you were in the secret service or whatever you did. I know you were a national hero, and I thank you for it, I really do. But do you remember coming to Levy? I swear it was you. You were in Levy with this magician fellow, and you did card tricks—"

"Three, one, fourteen, twenty," Joe mumbles.

"What's that?"

"Three, one, twenty, three, eight . . ." His eyes are far away swirls. He pushes the checkers and board onto the floor real slow and they *clinkety-clink* as they hit his leather shoe one at a time. His hands rest on his knees and he starts crying. The old man actually springs a leak.

"Aw sheesh, what happened to you, Joe? We tried to help

you. We really did. You could have stayed with us, Mama said you could stay. Why'd you leave again? Why'd you go with that awful man? Why?"

⤜↭⤚

Magnolia

Levy, 1929

The evil man is not dead. Ash told me he burned in the fire, but it's not true. I don't know how to feel about that.

It's Sunday morning, and I'm sitting in the church pew next to Joe. He's so close I can feel the heat through his shirt. Mama sent us here so we'd be out of the way while she and Daddy and Ash and the Jacobses go and meet with the magician. I wonder if he's doing tricks for them. He sure tricked us once, I reckon. Better than Houdini. Houdini never came out of a fire alive, far as I know.

'Course, I did, come to think of it. Maybe I'm magic. I was holding the wand. I did wave it and ask God to do something to stop all the fighting. And then the fire started. Oh no . . . I started the fire! I look around at the townspeople who are here worshipping, the ones who were trying to put out the house fire yesterday, the one I started with that evil man's magic wand. I feel it under my dress in the back. It pokes me and keeps me sitting up straight.

I'm bad. What kind of girl sets her own house on fire? Thank goodness nobody got hurt. Even that awful man, I'm glad he didn't die in that fire. I don't want to kill anybody. Don't want that on my head! They'll send me to jail, just like they did Mama. I don't want to go to jail! Don't ever want to be locked up!

Joe leans over to me and he's putting his hand in mine. I'm woozy. He smiles at me and I wonder what it might be like to stay here, in his sweaty palm forever. On this pew. Listening to the preacher talk about . . . well, something. I can barely hear him now. Joe is beside me. He's holding my hand. I forget all about Ash and Mama and Daddy and that awful man. Truth be told, I'm glad he came to town because he brought Joe.

All of a sudden, somebody pulls my pigtail. I turn around and see George sliding into the pew behind me. I scowl at him. Joe lets go of me, and I'll never forgive George for it as long as I live.

"I been listenin' through the door," George whispers. "Mama says you can stay with us, Joe." Stay with us? Joe is staying here in Levy? I clench my fists. If I could jump over this pew and hug George, I would do it. Kiss him, even. He's looking at his hands.

"Maggie, since your house is gone, you'll . . . you'll be takin' up in one of the empty colored houses."

"By Miss Maple? Well, maybe we can stay with her; she's got two rooms. Maybe me and Ash can sleep on that colored rug . . ."

"Miss Maple ain't—" George turns green. Looks like he might tip over. "Maggie, Ash—" George looks at me now. His eyes are sad as an old hound dog's. "Ash's leavin', Maggie. He's gonna leave us, and when he goes, he won't come back. Not ever. That's what I heard them say anyway."

George

"Listen, Joe, we're gonna go, we're gonna leave Harmony House, but then we'll come right back. Okay? Just a little day trip. A little drive down to Levy to pay our respects to Ash, Maggie's brother. So what do you say, old boy? You with me?"

Joe is working hard to process what I've said about Levy. His lips are moving. "Thirteen, five . . ." His eyes are going back and forth over my face. He looks off out the window.

"Maggie?" I go to my wife and pull a chair over next to hers. I touch her warm arm through her shirt. That softness above her elbow. My Maggie. "Honey, I don't want you to worry about anything. Okay? I know . . . I know you probably don't remember much, and it's better that way. Believe me. But I need you with me. I always need you with me." Maggie's eyes soften. She doesn't smile, but I can see it in her eyes, I think. I hope. I lean in and slowly kiss her cheek. She doesn't back away like she does sometimes. Being this close, smelling her powder, makes me forget about all the years. Makes me forget the distance between us. Makes me feel like we are young again, when my eyes are closed, and I smell her so close . . .

"Good. It's settled. I just wanted to make sure you all were on board. Joe, I'll jimmy your door so I can unlock it in the morning."

"Highly i-improbable," says Joe.

"What?"

"I knew a boy named George."

"I know, Joe. I've been trying to tell you. It's me. *I'm* George. I'm the very same one."

"Odds are too great."

"Joe." I stand and take my wife's wheelchair and push it to where it's directly in front of him. Their knees are almost touching. "Look here. This is Maggie. You remember her? In pigtails? She was only seven in Levy. She was Ash's little sister, Magnolia. Remember? Long, long time ago."

I watch as the two lock eyes. They're both in there, somewhere, trapped by the binds of age. A minute, a long minute goes by. Then Joe leans forward and puts his shaky hand on Maggie's. She clenches it and won't let go, and Joe looks at me, maybe more teary-eyed than normal and says, "My name is Joe. Joe S-Stackhouse."

THIRTY-NINE

Annie

THE NEXT MORNING . . .

I knock before I come in. Always do. You got to respect
people's privacy no matter what their situation. I firmly
believe that. Treat people like you would like to be treated.
"Mister George? Honey, listen. Not sure how to tell you
this—" The room is quiet. I can hear the air conditioner
humming around the made-up bed, the tidy drawers, the
reading chair beneath the window. "Mister George? Miss
Magnolia?" They can't be out to breakfast already.

Something's not right. They've been in bed this time of
morning since I can remember. No early risers, no sir. Great
God, did I miss something? I didn't see a note about them at
the front desk. Neither one of them's hurt. Somebody would
call me. Somebody had to help Miss Magnolia get up and
dressed though.

I dart around. The bathroom. No. The bag is gone. The bag I packed him is gone! Oh, Lawd have mercy, the letters! That stack of letters from Miss Magnolia's brother, they gone too! I grab my chest, think I might fall out. He knew it. He knew I couldn't get that outing to Levy. I should have known he'd check the board and see no sign-up sheet. His daughter? Did his daughter come and pick him up?

Joe. I run down the hall and knock on his door. "Mister Joe? You in here?" Open it up, not a trace of him. Old man's gone! I haul over to the breakfast room and see Jessica and Emmet Conlan in there. "You folks seen Mister George and Miss Magnolia today?"

"No. Why? Something wrong?"

"Oh . . . well, I'm sure there's not."

"Annie, please. You're scaring my wife. Tell us what's going on."

I plop down on the seat and rub the place mat. "Oh, Mister Emmet, I . . . I done lost 'em! They took off, I know it."

"Lost them? How?"

"Not lost, really. I know where they gone. I just prom-ised I'd help him. And now . . . oh, Lawd have mercy, gonna lose my job! Gone and lost my peoples!"

"Calm down now. Should we call the police?"

"Police? Oh no! Least, I don't think so . . ."

Then I spill it, tell them all about it, about the trip to Levy I was supposed to be driving, about the whos and whys and what-alls I know. And at the end of it, Mister Emmet says, "Annie, go check George's car. Man couldn't drive to save his life."

I light off toward the parking lot and all I can think of is he's trying to drive on an empty stomach! If his eyesight don't do him in, low blood sugar sure will.

FORTY

Joe

Joe can't remember what he ate for breakfast, and he hates forgetting things. He thinks he may have had eggs this morning, but he can't be sure. It may have been oatmeal. Or grits. No, eggs, he thinks. Or maybe he didn't eat at all. His stomach is grumbling. He looks out the window and sees cars down below. He is in a bus, a vehicle of some sort. He sees white-haired people sitting a couple rows in front of him. There is a black man driving.

Joe wonders if he's almost home. It seems as if he's been on this ride for quite a long time, but maybe it just started. Maybe he's missed his stop. Maybe he was sleeping when they stopped and he didn't know it. No one woke him up. Now, how long will he have to ride before they come back around to his station?

Joe can't remember anything he especially needed to do today, so perhaps it's all right. He looks down at his feet and sees a creature. A cat.

"Hello, kitty," he says, breaking into a smile. "How nice to see you on this bus."

The cat jumps up and purrs in the seat beside him. Joe puts a shaky palm on the soft tiger stripes, and the cat walks tenderly onto his lap. *Oh, it's a very nice cat*, he thinks. And so warm. The green eyes look into Joe and it nearly brings tears to his eyes. This cat seems to love him, seems to love what he sees in Joe.

Joe would like to be loved. He suddenly feels fiercely loyal to this cat. Yes, he will take care of it and never let it out of his sight. He will pet this warm, purring cat until his dying day. He vows it. He'll let nothing, *nothing* harm a single hair.

A teardrop falls on his button-down shirt. It leaves a wet spot, and Joe suddenly wonders if he remembered to bring an umbrella on this trip.

He wonders, in fact, where he's going. These days he can never be sure.

George

The driver gestures wildly and rolls down his window so air blows in my face. "Now if you look out da left," he says, "you see de ole slave quarter, barely standin'. Over right there you gwine find de massa's house—"

"I told you," I say, "we don't want the Gullah tour. We really just want peace and quiet on the way down."

"But the tour is included. You done paid for it."

"I know it. But look, we're just old people, needing some peace. I got some reading to do. How long you think before we get there?"

"Levy? Oh, 'bout hour, hour half now."

"Good. Thank you, uh—"

"Isaiah."

"Isaiah. Good man." The window rolls back up.

"I don't regular go down this way, jes stay in Charleston. Dis here not part o' de tour."

"I know it. But you were the only bus not booked already."

"Woulda been, sure 'nough. You sure is lucky caught me early, 'cause I figure coulda been a busy day what with the cruise ship comin' in and all."

"Mister Isaiah?"

"Yessir?" He turns around and glances at me for a second. Sees the look in my face. "Right. Quiet as can be. Not another word you gwine get outta me."

"Thank you. Good man."

We're riding south on Highway 17. I always liked this drive, except now, it's four lanes. They cut down the pretty trees. When did they do this? What a shame. Doesn't feel so quaint anymore. Time changes everything, doesn't it? It's the only true thing there is.

I can't believe we left Harmony House. Part of me wants to never go back to the oatmeal, to the rails on the hallway walls. The other part is scared like the dickens. I'm dying. I might never go back. Might never see Emmet and Jessica again. Might never see Miss Annie. Or Fantasia. Or the old ladies who watch the sunrise. Miss Betty with her pretty smile.

I look over at my wife. At least I have her here with me. I couldn't do this alone. I couldn't meet Maggie's nephew and not bring her along. I couldn't face my past head-on without her.

She's asleep, her head nodded forward a little. My bride. I wonder, when she sleeps, does she dream about the way things used to be? When she's in her subconscious, does she remember all the love we used to have between us? The little house we had at the farm, the chickens running around in the yard. The two of us giggling through the cornfields, hiding and seeking. The feather bed we slept in. It was next to heaven, I can still feel it. *Do you go there, dear, when you're alone in your head? Do you know me still, deep down inside?*

I reach over and touch Maggie's hand. It's limp. The only time her hands relax is when she's asleep. There's a tinfoil wand resting loose in her palm. As soon as she wakes, her hands will become possessed again and nervous, and she'll grab it and not let go. I brought some extra foil just in case. I can't have my Maggie biting her knuckles raw.

It's been so long since any of us have left the confines of Harmony House for anything more than a grocery store or doctor visit that my eyes turn and feast on everything outside the window—at the trees rolling by, at the telephone poles and wires, how the sky looks so large and wonderful even though it's covered gray. A sign says KEEP RIGHT EXCEPT TO PASS.

Maggie is stirring, her eyes flicker with the light of every passing car, every bus. I wonder, *What does she see, really? What is she thinking?* I reach over and hold her hand. She wakes and slowly opens her eyes to see who's touched her. Her fingers clutch the tinfoil again, and looking past me, she gazes out the window.

Can she remember? Is she thinking about the trips we used to take to Sullivan's Island when Gracie was little and we'd go down to the beach for a week at a time and do nothing but walk the waves, read, and make love when Gracie was finally sleeping? Does she remember any of it? Does she remember her own child, for goodness' sake? She gave her whole life for us, for her family, and now she's slipped away. What is life really about if, by the time we reach the end of it, we can't remember having lived it at all?

Age. Look at what it's done to her. To us. Makes me so furious at whoever's in charge. I turn to the glass and fog it up with what are surely some of my final breaths.

❧

Magnolia

LEVY, 1929

The air is steamy with mist from the heat and fallen rain. Daddy holds Mama in his arms, but she's flailing and trying to pull loose. "Charles, do somethin'!"

"There's nothin' we can do! Ash's right. If he stays here, he'll just come back for him. And next time, somebody could get hurt. Real hurt. The man won't stop. You heard him yourself!"

"But he's my son! And your son! You raised him! How

can you just let him go like this?" Mama is crying and melting. "How can you let him goooo . . ."

I don't know what to say. I'm having a hard time feeling anything. Seeing Mama this way, knowing Ash is leaving, I am not a person anymore. I might be a rock. Or a tree, maybe. No feelings at all. I want to go to Mama and hold her and tell her it's all right, but I can't move. Can't speak. I want to go find Ash and beg him to stay. Tell him to take me with him, but I'm frozen, and empty, and disappeared. I am growing roots out of the bottoms of my feet and branches out of my head. I will never move from this spot again. I can never, ever move . . .

I wake to a loud, awful sound. Snoring? I look over and see an old man—it's just George. He's bouncing up and down. Behind him, the world is flying by his window. Where are we?

"Hey, Maggie," he says, crinkles at the edges of his eyes.

I look down at my hands. There is a silver wand grasped in my fingers. They are pressing in tiny controlled movements, making the silver harder, straighter. I look in front of me and see the back of a dark head. We're driving somewhere.

"We'll be there soon," says George. He stretches his arm around me and lightly touches the back of my shoulders. His skin feels warm like sunshine. *Go ahead and hold me, George. Hold me tight. I promise not to squirm. I promise not to run away.* But he doesn't. I can't blame him. He has to tread lightly with this old body of mine. It's got a mind of its own, I tell you what.

In George's lap there are letters. *Read to me, honey, like you*

used to when we were younger and we lay in the fields, the sunshine on my eye-
lids, the tan on your skin, The Great Gatsby *in my ears. Oh, read to me*
and take me somewhere I want to go. With you. Always with you.

CHARLOTTE, 1939

I am a young woman now, my beauty at its peak, my figure full
and gracious with curves. There is warm sun on my shoulders, down the backs of my legs. I am relaxed, fully, forgetting
about the other bathers and sun-worshippers at this municipal pool. They can swim and laugh and chat all they want. I
will lie here and relax, and think about George.

My friend Queenie is silent, occasionally flipping through
the pages of Agatha Christie's *Death on the Nile.* I can tell by her
breathing when she's getting to the good parts. We haven't had
time to make too many friends since we've been in Charlotte,
but Queenie is becoming a good one. And she makes me
laugh. If we could only find her a husband.

With my head down on this sunning board, my arms
cradling my head, I think of George as I twist the band of
gold on my finger. He's away, working for his father's store,
buying grain and other whatnot in Atlanta. I know he has
to travel, but I miss him. We've only been married for six
months and I miss the way he holds me. I miss the way he
makes me his wife in the deep of the night. He's so much
more than the boy I knew in Levy. So much more, and yet,
still that boy. He's a man now, a man who knows me inside
and out. A man who shares my history and never, ever has to
speak a word of it.

My husband, George. *What are you doing now, dear? Do you miss me in Atlanta?*

"Maggie, look up," says Queenie.

"Hmm?"

"Look up."

I raise my head a couple inches and see the feet of a man, rather shabby shoes. My heart leaps, thinking maybe it's George. I follow the trousers to a belt. I'm raised up off the ground several feet on this platform, so I find myself nearly eye-level with a man, a stranger, holding a camera to his face. He clicks. I'm stunned and I blink.

"Excuse me, do I know you?"

The man pulls the camera down and smiles at me. He's a good many years older then me, maybe thirty or so. He has a twinkle in his eyes, one I've become accustomed to from men. It is the look Mama always told me about as a child. It's the look I recognize as a warning, bells ringing in my head with alarm. I touch my wedding band.

"Sorry to disturb you, ma'am. I saw you lying here, and thought I'd take a picture . . . for the newspaper. See, I work for the *Charlotte News and Record* and, well, may I take another? Now that I'm not sneaking up on you?"

"I don't think that—"

"Oh, come on, Maggie. Be a sport." Queenie has her book lying facedown on her stomach now. She's amused at this.

But what would George say? This is completely inappropriate.

"You'll be doing your part to spread cheer throughout all of Mecklenburg County, ma'am. After the past few years we could all use a little cheering up. What do you say? Just one smile."

"Oh." I look over at Queenie who is about to laugh. I would tell the man to take her picture, but Queenie has not been blessed or cursed with physical beauty. She has the ability to remain invisible when she likes. It's a luxury, I think. No, I can't ask him to take her photo. What if he says something to embarrass her?

The Depression. I think of the newspaper, photos of people waiting in lines, poor people who have no work. They need a little cheering up. I smile despite myself. "All right. But take it quick before I change my mind." I smile what I know to be my best smile. A girl always knows. She knows which smile makes her appear innocent. She knows the one that reveals too many teeth and turns glaring and dark. She knows the smile that is the most alluring, maintaining her dignity and her mystery. I choose that smile, and the man snaps my picture.

"Wasn't so bad was it?"

After tipping his hat, he's gone, and I am lying here in the sun, missing George, feeling as if that smile I gave him is really much larger than it seemed. If I could take it back I would! What will George say if he sees me front-page in a bathing suit like some trollop? It's as if I've changed history with that smile. I remember seeing Mama's face in black-and-white. Nothing good ever came of it. I'm going to have to hide the paper from George somehow. My heart is racing, and I can't put my head back down comfortably. I can't relax anymore.

Oh, George, hurry home. I need you here, holding me tight. You should never, ever leave me again. Always be by my side.

FORTY-ONE

Annie

"No, you cain't leave with me," I tell them. We're standing in
the parking lot by Mister George's Cadillac, thankful he ain't
tried to drive to Levy—but he's gone. Him and Miss Magnolia
and Mister Joe.

"But we need to go," says Miss Jessica, holding her skinny
white fists in front of her chest. "George needs us."

I look to Miss Jessica and hate to be this way, but I got
to. "I need you here. I need you actin' like nothin's wrong
a'tall. Hear? Can you do that for me? Can't be haulin' you
around, no offense . . ."

"None taken," says Mister Emmet. "She's right, Jess.
Miss Annie." He looks at me with wary eyes. "Go on. Find
them. Bring them home safe."

"Thank you," I say. "Lawd as my witness, I will." And off I go.

Never in all my life! Never in all God's creation . . . I hate to say it but Mama was right. *Nothin' but trouble.*

Mama.

Oh, I'm gonna regret this, I know I am, but look at this, the Lord's pulling my steering wheel to the left. He's a-driving me down her street, he's stopping my car right out in front of her house. And Mama . . . there she is out front. I pull in and roll my window down. "Mama?"

"Lawd have mercy, chile," she says, throwing her arms up and shaking her head. "Done talked to Isaiah."

"Isaiah who? Cousin Isaiah?"

"He done took the old folk on a Gullah tour to Levy."

"Ain't no Gullah tour to Levy!"

"Chile, there is now, mm, mm, mm. Heard him talkin' 'bout it on the ham radio. 'Bout lost my mind when I hear him say 'Harmony House' and 'old folks to Levy.'" Mama opens the door and squashes into the car right next to me. She's got her lipstick on and everything, purple warm-up suit and walking shoes on. She means business.

"How long you been waitin' out here?"

"Jes' a little while," she says, breathing hard as I press the gas pedal and she buckles in. "Good Lawd told me you was a-comin'. Told me, *Them old folks is gone and Annie needs you,* he did. I said, *Awright Lawd, yessir.* Let's go."

"I thought you ain't goin' to Levy no matter what. Thought you said it had the curse."

She clucks her tongue and says, "Shoot. Don't talk the fool, Annie. Jes' drive. Ain't gettin' no younger. Older every minute."

Mama reaches in her bag and hauls out this big black contraption with curly cords every-which-a-way.

"What in the world, Mama?"

She pulls out my cigarette lighter and sticks in this big CB radio.

"Big Mama to Cujo," she says into the receiver. "Come in Cujo."

"Cujo?" I say.

The machine crackles, then there's a man's deep voice. "Cujo here. How you be, Big Mama?"

"Fine, fine. In the car with Annie. Headin' yo way. Where you is now? Where the old folk?"

"Roger dat. Old folk sleepin'. I'm, uh, headin' south on 17 'bout twenty mile to Levy. Out."

"Oh Lawd. They almost there." I can feel Mama looking at the side of my face. My cheek grows hot.

"Let me talk to him, Mama." She hands me the receiver, and I press the button in on the side and put it up to my lips. "Isaiah Wright, you crazy?"

I let go of the button and there's quiet on the other end.

"I said, you outta your mind?"

"You got to press the button and give him your name," says Mama. "You can be . . . Sugah Spice."

"I ain't no Sugah Spice, Mama!" I squeeze that button so hard, think my finger might break. "Now listen here, Isaiah, I got somethin' to say. This is your cousin Annie, the one down over at Harmony House? You know I work there! How come you took them peoples on out the home and ain't told me? You crazy? You out your mind? Let me tell you some-thin' . . . you hurt one hair on them head and I'll personally haul your butt up out your ole Gullah-Geechee bus and your ole Gullah-Geechee ever-livin' mind, and you ain't be able to sit till Christmas. You got that? That a big ten-four?"

Static. Finally I hear, "Uh, roger dat, Lil Mama. Cujo out."

"Cujo out? Cujo outta your cotton-pickin' mind!"

"Leave him 'lone, Annie. Don't make it worse. Let's jes' get there quick." She takes the receiver from me and says, "Big Mama to Cujo. Roger that. We'll see ya when we see ya. Be good now. I'll make you some of my chicken when we get back, hear? You like Big Mama chicken or how 'bout some pork chop?"

I reach over and pull that little cord out the cigarette lighter, and Mama looks at me like I'm crazy but don't say a word. Just sits back, crosses her arms, and settles in for the longest hour and a half on earth.

FORTY-TWO

George

ON THE ROAD TO LEVY

April 4, 2009

Dear George,

I'm not sure I have much more life in this body. It's half the size it used to be. My bones are running hollow. To be honest I can't believe I've made it this long, but now my heart is breaking. I'm getting weaker.

I'm looking at my picture of Maggie over the fireplace. I think of all that must have happened for her photograph to make it to the World's Fair, for me to come all the way across the country in order to work there, in order to see Maggie beaming at me, the most amazing smile, saying, "It's okay, Ash. I turned out just fine. Everything turned out just fine." No, I can't comprehend all that had to go into that chance meeting. How could a man be so lucky as to find her picture and be able to look at her lovely face all his life? How could a man be so fortunate as to meet my sweet Rosie and have her love me all of her days? And I have a son. A good son. All in all, I've led a nice life. But I think it's almost time to go home. I think it's time Maggie's photograph went back to its rightful owner.

Surprisingly, I don't harbor any more resentment of you, old boy. Maybe that's why I've lived so darn long, I had to work it out of my system. Maybe that's what we're supposed to do in this life. To metamorphose into creatures far removed from the babes who entered this world, all selfish and desperate to survive. At the other end of things, it's quieter. We're desperate to give things away, knowing we can't take them with us, and survival, in our final hours, seems useless. Doesn't it? It seems I've been preparing for this trip all my life, and now I'm eager to go. I really am. When I get there, I'll see everyone I've ever loved. What could be better, I ask you? What, indeed.

No hard feelings, friend. You've done well by her. It was your purpose on this earth, I see that now.

Signing off,

Ash

Ash. My childhood friend. No other bond like it. Children are true to themselves, undefiled by the world. They don't worry about social graces or putting on a good face. They simply are who they are. Ash accepted me for exactly who I was—not that he had much choice, not like there were too many boys our age in Levy. Truth be told, I was a little pain in the rear and spent most of my time jealous of Ash for being so dad-blum close to Maggie. And for other reasons . . . he was always so sure of himself, so headstrong, so willing to do what was right in his eyes, come what may.

This Gullah bus is pretty comfortable, I have to say. Isaiah, our driver, has settled down and stayed quiet for a while. I wonder why we don't get out like this more often. I miss seeing cars and trees and houses tucked back in the woods on the side of the road. I miss seeing egrets flying high above and marsh grass and rivers flowing. I miss the blue sky and—

I'm choking up. I can't help but think I won't see too many more blue skies. I want to soak in everything. I want to carry the Lowcountry in my soul when I pass from this place. But I wonder if I can let go of Levy.

When I was a boy in Levy, we lived in a six-room house a stone's throw from the store, Jacobs Mercantile. To me, the store was an extension of the house, the place I played and worked, although at ten or eleven, even the chores felt like play to me. Unloading the co-colas and stacking up the jars of honey. I didn't mind sweeping the wood floor because I found a penny in the corner or under the shelves every now and again and Mama would let me keep it. I'd pocket that money and set it under a loose board in my bedroom. When Joe Stackhouse came to stay in my room that couple of weeks back in 1929, after a few days, I showed it to him.

"That's a-a-a lot of money," he told me, eyes wide. He was lying on the foot of the bed on his elbows, watching me on the floor as I held up the board and proudly showed off my treasure.

"Yep," I said. "Almost a dollar. Pretty soon I'll have more."

"What will you do with it?"

I looked at him then, fast and furious. I'd already showed him my stash and now he was wanting to know my biggest secret. I thought I could trust him with my money, but wasn't sure I could trust him with my heart. I wasn't sure I wanted anyone to know.

But he looked innocent enough. Dark hair in waves around his forehead, blue eyes like a puppy dog. That stutter.

"You know Maggie?"

"Yeah."

I lowered the board back into place and moved slowly to the edge of the bed. I sat down on it and listened to it creak. I thought better about telling him and then felt this tickle down inside my belly and thought I might burst with the thought of her.

"I'm gonna marry her someday," I told him. Just like that. I looked at my hands, the cracked skin, the dirty nails. "I'll use the money to take care of her. Buy her dresses. Maybe a farm of our own." My heart was pounding in my chest clear up to my head, and when I turned to look at Joe, I saw a flash of something in his eyes. Did he want to marry Maggie someday too? He did! Son of a gun, I shouldn't have told him! I started clenching my fists and feeling dizzy like I needed to run out and find her right then, ask her right then and there at the age of ten to marry me. But Joe just looked across the room at the wall and said, "That's a good idea—for the m-money."

I moved to the pillow and lay my head on it, arms folded

across my chest and ankles crossed. Joe and I stayed there, head to foot for I don't know how long then. We talked about Maggie and Ash and Levy. I asked him about New Orleans and about his pa. At the time I didn't think it was strange he got quiet whenever it came around to him, his side of the story, his family and whatnot. Joe was sort of a quiet fellow. When I asked him how long he and his father would be staying in Levy he said he didn't know. When I asked him if he thought Maggie was pretty, he started snoring and I wasn't sure if he was really asleep or if he just didn't want to answer me because he wanted to marry her after all.

Joe is snoring behind me. His head is back on the blue and red fabric of the seat of our chartered bus. His ears are as long as two pickles. His skin droops down like turkey wattle from his chin to his chest. How long has it been? Eighty years. Eighty years, old boy, and we're heading back to Levy. I wonder what it's like. I wonder if my daddy's store and our old house are still there. I think about that old floorboard and if some other little boy uses it now for a hiding spot. I turn around again and whisper to sleeping Joe, "I kept my word. I told you I'd marry her." Then I take Maggie's hand in mine and ignore her stranger's stare from the side. I close my eyes and pretend we are young again. We're in love and we have our whole lives ahead of us. Yes, our whole lives together.

I have never felt more alone.

There is a dark pool of water before me. I see a flicker of light and can make out the form of a great alligator under there, waiting for me. Then I see another, and another. They are laid out, long and lined up, covering every inch of the bottom, so there's no hope for me should I step in . . .

My heart jolts. "Comin' up on Levy," says the driver. I open my eyes and look to my left. I see houses lined up all the same in a row, manicured streets. Something's not right. Maybe I shouldn't have come back. Maybe this was all a terrible mistake!

"This can't be Levy," I say. "It doesn't look like this."

"It does now. Sign just said Levy. How long since you been here?"

I'm embarrassed to say it. "Quite a few years." I look, crestfallen, out the window. I'm lost. Nothing looks the same. This should all be woods. And over there, that should be a big field where the animals used to graze. I look ahead and see a flashing yellow light. It's the main intersection. My house used to be right there. The store used to be right there and we didn't need a dad-blum yellow flashing light to slow people down! We had signs for fresh corn and strawberries in the summertime! My heart is pounding and I grab my chest. I feel queasy. This isn't at all what I expected.

"Where you want me to go, exactly? Just drive around the neighborhoods?"

"No. No, just . . . pull in up here . . . on the right."

There's a gas station where our store used to be. A gas station! Where's my house? Where's my treasure and creaky floorboard?

I squeeze Maggie's hand a little too tight and she pulls away. I look at her face. Everything has changed, hasn't it?

Levy doesn't look the same or feel the same. And Maggie, well, she's the very same way. Is a town the same place if you tear down all the houses and put up rows of cookie cutters? If you tear down all the trees and take out the very heart and soul of a place? If no one remembers what it used to be like here, then is it the same place at all? Well, is it?

God, what am I forgetting?

FORTY-THREE

George

The train station is still intact. It's shifted to the left a little and the red paint is faded and peeling. I look at her and she groans with the weight of age and winces with pain from the effort of standing. How many people have come through her doors? How many travelers have sat on her benches, waiting for the next chapter of their lives to begin? The benches are gone, only their rusty metal stumps remain. Grass grows between the floorboards of the porches; weeds reach up and say there's still life here at the Levy depot.

I look to the rusted rails and my eyes follow the trestles until they get blurry and the track seems to disappear altogether into the clouds. I don't imagine they use this track anymore, the grass is too thick. Looking at it now, I can shed all these years I carry with me. They are gone in an instant and I am a boy again, barefoot in overalls, hands behind my back, balancing on the rail while Ash and Magnolia travel with me. Always at my side. Ash and Magnolia.

This is harder than I thought. Why is coming home so difficult? Do we not notice the changes brought on by each new year until one day, the distance from point A to B is miles upon miles? Why didn't I come back sooner? There are pieces of me on this track. There are pieces of me, that little boy I used to be—a boy that if I could have him here, I'd hug tight as I could. I'd tell him, "It's all right, son. You did the best you could. You're a brave boy. A brave, good, good boy." I wipe my face and look over at Maggie. She's sitting in her wheelchair on the worn gravel, elbows on her armrests, hands clutching tinfoil. It's just a big ball of mess right now, but just you wait. Soon it'll be something else entirely.

Maggie is looking far off into the distance, maybe at the gray clouds rolling in. The sun shines through a large flat dark one, sending beams of light from heaven. She always did love it when that would happen, as if God were reminding her he's still there. Still up there somewhere.

Magnolia

LEVY, 1929

We are standing by the train station, the Boll Weevil large and hungry behind Ash. "I'll still be with you," he says to me, "right here." He touches my chest and I melt into his arms.

"You cain't leave me! Take me with you! I'll be good. I won't be no trouble."

"You cain't come, Maggie. Maggie, look at me." He pulls my chin up and I see him all blurry through my tears. "It's got to be this way." A tear rolls down his face and he leans his head over and wipes it with his shoulder, never letting his hands off of me. "I know you don't understand, but that man, my real father, my flesh and blood, he's bad. Real bad. And he won't leave this family alone until I go with him."

"But you don't have to go!"

"Maggie, don't you see? Don't you get it? He's my father. Half of me. Half of me is pure rotten. Bad to the core. It's in my blood and I can feel it in there. Makes me want to—stop yore cryin', Maggie!"

"I cain't, I cain't, please don't go!"

He pushes me away and the look in his eyes changes. "You're so stupid, Maggie Black. Cain't you see? How dumb are you? Who do you think set that fire? Who do you think burned our house down? Don't you think I knew you were in there too? Do you even think I cared?"

I am shaking. I stop crying for half a second and see Ash standing there, twisted and breathing heavy like a mare in labor. "No."

"It's true, Maggie. You're better off without me. Now, go on. No more cryin'."

It's not true. Ash would never do that. He's not bad. He'd never set our house on fire knowing I was in it. He wouldn't do that! And he wouldn't leave me. He wouldn't! He can't. I'm so confused.

Mama gives him a hug, but her arms are limp. It seems unlikely she's even standing upright. He picks up a bag on a stick and puts it over his shoulder. The magician in the mustache is standing on the edge of the train. He tips his hat to us as Ash walks to him and I think I hear him say, "There, there, son. Hop on in." I remember sitting there with my brother the day the train pulled in and brought this evil. I wish I'd never seen him coming. Wish the train had just gone on by.

Now it's Joe's turn. He slinks right past us like a beat-up tomcat. He has no hope now, no family. He's just a slave to this man. At least he'll have Ash. I am jealous of Joe, to be honest. Joe and Ash will be together—

I run to the train and there is yelling from behind me and arms come grab me and twirl me away. I am screaming and reaching, all the while the Boll Weevil is belching smoke and growling louder. Ash slips into the doorway and his foot is the last part of him I'll ever see. I look for him in the window but he's not there. Joe turns to me then and I see something in his eyes. He's not crying. He stands straighter. He blows me a kiss, and I kick with all my might at whoever is holding me. I break free and tear through the dirt and get there, panting and crying in front of Joe. I reach up under my dress in the back. I pull out that silver wand of the evil magician and I hand it to him. "Watch over him, Joe. Take care of Ash!"

And then the forces that be have grabbed me again and I have no more fight left in me. No more words. No more tears. No more magic. I see George as they carry me away and he's torn up real good. If I could touch him and make it all better, I would, but I can't. My life is gone.

I watch as Mama crumbles to the ground and Daddy tries to comfort her. She lifts her face and with eyes closed, screams for Ash. Then she moans for Miss Maple. I wait, and I wait, but Miss Maple never comes.

FORTY-FOUR

Annie

*Lawd in heaven, take care of 'em. Watch over Miss Magnolia with them
stitches on her head and George, in his stubborn ways and dyin', and Mister
Joe, a sweet fella who got to be so confused by now . . .*

"There! Right there they are." I pull the car over real
slow on the gravel behind Isaiah's "We Be Gullah Tour of
Charleston" bus. My heart is wild and trying to break free of
me. "Mama, why don't you stay here?"

"You crazy? Come this far . . . Come on, let's go hep
these folks. Whatever haint gone get me done had its chance
already." Mama opens the door and rocks herself a couple
times until she pops out and stands upright on heavy hips. I
shut my door and feast my eyes on Mister George and Miss
Magnolia and . . .

"Where's Joe? Oh, great Gawd, tell me Mister Joe's here!"

"He's here, Miss Annie," says George. "He's still on the

bus. Seems the Harmony House cat somehow hitched a ride and Joe won't let it out of his sight. Little beast of a thing . . ." His eyes go soft and he smiles slightly. "Fancy running into you here, Annie."

"Fancy . . . I'll fancy you, I—oh, come here, you done scared me to death!" I go to him and squeeze the daylights out of him. He's skinny. I got to make sure he's eating more. "Miss Magnolia? Hey there, sweetie. Your husband done brought you all the way down here? How you doing, honey? You feelin' all right? Somebody got your old outfit on." I cut my eyes at George. "Why you ain't put her in her nice blue suit, George?"

"I did the best I could, Annie."

"Well . . ."

I hand them each a banana. I look up at Isaiah who seems to be trying to disappear into the background. I point to him and glare. "You. You and me, we gonna have a good long talk later, hear?"

He nods and don't say a word. Never have known Isaiah to be quiet on anything. Well, least he got them here safe.

"Oh. This is Mama," I say. Mama moves forward and takes Mister George's hand.

"Oh, bless ya. Done come a long way. You's a mighty brave man. Mighty brave. I woulda drove you myself, I would, even told Annie here—"

"Mama!"

"Well, I did."

"Pleased to meet you," says Mister George, crinkles in his eyes. "I can't tell you how much your daughter means to us. She's part of the family, really. Don't know what I'd do without her."

"All that sweet-talkin' cain't get you out this trouble, you know."

"I know it, but I thought I'd give it a try."

I turn around and lean up into the bus and look back. Mister Joe is asleep, snoring a little with that gray striped cat asleep on his lap. Well, I'll be. For a second it's sweet and for another I don't feel right. That cat is always there when somebody dies at Harmony House. How it knows, I'll never understand, but it sits there and meows outside their room for days. Finally we let it in, and it curls up on the bottom of the bed just as comfortable as can be. I wonder, I just wonder why it's so fond of Mister Joe all a sudden.

I climb down and go to Mister George's side. I hold on to his arm so he can lean on me a little. "You seen Miss Magnolia's nephew?"

Mister George shakes his head. "Not yet. I don't know what time he's coming though. What if he already came? What if we missed him?"

"Oooh, it's early yet. Before lunch. What say we grab you a bite to eat at that diner over yonder and watch for him? I know you ain't had breakfast. A banana ain't enough."

"We won't know what to look for." Mister George looks around him. "I don't know what I was expecting. I guess I figured I'd come down here and there he'd be, but I don't recognize much of this place anymore."

"Did he say where he was goin'?"

"No. Just said he was coming to scatter—"

"At the waterin' hole." I raise my eyebrows. "The waterin' hole."

"Togoodoo Creek." Mister George walks away from me and moves toward the street. He waits to make sure no cars are coming with the yellow light flashing overhead. I move toward him, but he waves me off. He walks into the filling station and a minute later comes back out, slow, small steps. The first wet drops of the day fall light on the ground though I can't feel them yet. The smell of washed hot asphalt fills the air, and I tell Miss Magnolia, "Come on, baby, let's get you out the rain. Miss Annie here. Everythin' gonna be all right now."

FORTY-FIVE

George

We drive all the way through this neighborhood called Sheridan Farms where the houses look the same except for a couple changes here and there, color, garage on the other side, that sort of thing. I don't know who Mr. Sheridan is, and I don't see a farm around here at all. Don't remember anybody by that name. I can't believe how many people are living here in Levy. What in the world brought them here? What kind of work could they have found?

"I 'magine most commute to Bluffton or Hilton Head, Beaufort, Savannah," says Isaiah, and he must be right. There are little colorful toys and Big Wheels and whatnot littering the yards. Maggie and I never had anything like these. We found mystery and magic in climbing a tree, walking the tracks, fishing in Togoodoo Creek.

"I don't recognize it at all," I say, head hanging, disoriented.

I pull out the map I got in the filling station and try to get my bearings. Nothing looks the same, but by the tracks, I can tell Togoodoo Road used to be around here and that means the creek must be . . .

"Here," I tell Isaiah. "Turn right here. Map shows there should be a pond over yonder. I think that must be it."

"You sho'?"

"No, sir, I'm not. But it's the best I can do."

The windshield wipers swipe one last time before he turns off the bus.

Miss Annie and her mother are following us and we all stop in a cul-de-sac. There are no other cars here, except for the ones in driveways. I was hoping Ash's son might have already found this place, but my heart sinks. There's no way he'll ever know where to go, is there? Maybe the man at the filling station might be able to give him a good idea . . . it's hard to keep hope. No matter, I'm going anyway.

"It's rainin'!" Annie hollers at me from behind. "You can't go traipsin' through the woods in the rain."

"It's barely a sprinkle, Annie. We'll be fine."

"But I ain't brought my umbrella! Oh gracious, why I ain't brought one—"

"We have a blanket you can keep on Maggie, all right?" I look at her and let her know I need to do this, rain or not. We all do. After lowering Maggie down on the lift and rousing Old Joe and talking him into coming with us and leaving that cat for a few minutes, we are all standing ankle deep in the damp, overgrown grass of an empty lot. I hold my map in one hand and Maggie's wheelchair in the other to keep me steady. Miss Annie is behind her, pushing and using all her might to get the wheels to go through the brush. She's breaking a sweat and I see the strain in her face. I would expect she'd complain about it any minute now, but for some small miracle, she stays quiet.

"You want me to push?" says Isaiah, moving in.

"Shoot. You done enough." She scowls at him. "Leave me 'lone."

Annie's mama is holding Joe up and they walk, tiny awkward steps over sticks and such. Good thing she's a hefty woman like her daughter. Looks like a great big caterpillar dragging a lame butterfly. "Doing all right, Joe?"

Joe looks at me a mite confused—nothing unusual there—but he also seems up to the adventure, like it's been missing from his life, from all our lives.

"Looks small," I say when we get to a clearing in the woods. There's a body of water in front of us, no bigger than a swimming pool. "Smaller than I remember."

"Maybe you got big," says Annie.

"Maybe."

"You sho' this is it?" asks Annie's mama, still holding up Joe. It looks like the walk wore him out. And her. I know it did me. I'm trembling all over.

"Yep. This is it, all right. You see that tree stump? That was our diving board."

Back here, this deep in the woods, not much has changed. The pine trees might be bigger, may be more scruff and

Nicole Seitz

palmetto fronds sprouting at our feet. I imagine kids don't
play back here anymore like we did. Mothers are too anxious
to let their children play in ponds with moccasins, drowning, all sorts of dangers. Ticks, chiggers in the woods . . .
kids have swimming pools these days with chlorine water and
lifeguards always at the ready, but long ago we had this reser-
voir at the trickle end of Togoodoo Creek.

Have all the fish died? I can see him—me—just a kid, sitting on the edge of that pond with my knees up, fishing pole
between them. Ash is on the other side. We're competing
to see who got the better spot today. Who will get the bigger
fish? Maggie, she's just a little girl. She's chasing butterflies
and trying to catch crickets for us to hook. I hold the pole
tight between my knees and watch, her blond hair flying up
with every leap, the tall grass on the edge of the pond rustling
as she moves by in her simple dress. I don't know how long
I've been in love with Maggie. Maybe since the time I was
three years old and got my first look at her soft, pale skin,
those long eyelashes. Maybe when I was five and she would
come into the store with her beautiful mama and Ash. Ash
and I would play with wooden trucks and Maggie would sit
there and laugh with blue eyes dancing, a stray tooth growing in her radiant smile. I have loved Maggie since before I
knew what love was. She is love to me. Without her, there is
nothing for me here.

I shake my head and see her as she is now. Miss Annie
has her wheelchair a few feet back from the watering hole,
careful not to get too close. Maggie's hands are pressing her
tinfoil, and her eyes are intent on the blackness of the water,

242

the lily pads covering a full third of the pond in a wide green blanket. Does she remember it?

"Do you remember this, dear?" Of course she stays silent. I'll never know if she does or if she doesn't.

I stare into the black glass and hear voices crying out into the night, water splashing, the crackling of fire off in the distance. I smell smoke. I hear my own breath as I scoop up two buckets of water and pull with all my might, trying not to spill any, desperate to get back to Maggie's house and douse the fire, to be her hero, to put everything right again.

But it's no use. I will fail at this.

There is a ringing sound in my ears and my head goes light. I picture Ash's son finding this place, all well-intentioned, with an urn full of soot. He'll want to open the urn and turn it over and let the wind scatter Ash's ashes over the water until they float like snow on top and finally get enveloped by the pond, sinking to rest after a long, hard haul.

FORTY-SIX

Magnolia

I am standing at the edge of darkness. It's hot here. The blackness moves and shifts and sparkles, and I see her again, Miss
Maple. "Why is your skin funny-colored, not black like those
others?" I ask her.

I'm sitting on her lap on the front porch steps. We watch
as two colored men help Daddy cut up a fallen tree in our
yard. Bad storm last night. Daddy says they can have all the
wood they can chop and haul.

Miss Maple looks at me and studies my face, so I study her
freckles, specks of tar across her cheeks and her wide nose.
She starts to say something, then stops. Finally, she watches
the men loading wood onto their cart and rocks me. Just
rocks me.

She whispers in my ear, "Gawd make a body in his image,
now, and nobody can nail down what-all color he be. He

got black, white, brown, yellow, red, even all kind like yore mama dress. What-all color he gone make a body like you an' me? Gawd a painter, Miss Maggie. Him de first artist there ever be." She holds out her arm and stretches her fingers, laces them with mine. "You see that color? Be the color of sunshine and honey. To Gawd? Be the color of beauty. Now look here."

She pulls my arm out long. "You see this? You ain't really white, now, is you? You got specks of red, yellow, brown. Look how purdy. Gawd give yore own special colorin' in his image. Yessir, colorin' of de Almighty. Dat's what we got, you an' me."

I seem to understand what she's saying, and when I look in her eyes, she's beautiful to me. I watch as her face fades away into that black sparkling before me, and my heart aches for her. I miss her. *Why did you leave me? Why does everybody have to leave . . . Miss Maple . . . my brother Ash?*

Joe

Joe's knees are getting tired. He shifts from one leg to the other. He is grateful to be held up by . . . he turns to look at the woman beside him. Her skin is dark and glistening in a shaft of light. She's perspiring around her temples, around the gray tufts of hair there. Joe thinks she looks like a kind woman and he's glad she is holding him up, though he doesn't remember how he got here, exactly. He looks at the people around him, an old woman in a chair with wheels, a light brown woman behind her, another man, and an old, old white man, standing at the water's edge. Joe wonders if he'll go swimming. Joe tries to remember what it is like to go swimming, for the body to have no weight at all, for the soft mud at the bottom to squish between his toes. He closes his eyes for a moment and yes, he can remember swimming, although he can't remember when.

"Hold up, now," says the woman on his arm. "Startin' to tip, don't want you to fall over."

Joe nods and smiles. He is grateful she didn't let him fall.

Joe feels something at his leg, something pressing him. He looks down, careful not to lose his balance, and what he sees warms his heart, sends a bolt of heat from his chest to his arms, his wrists, his fingers. There is a cat, a gray striped cat at his feet, looking up at Joe with glowing green eyes and a tail, wrapped lovingly around his calf. "Oh, kitty," he says. He wants to reach down and pet the cat, but when he tries, the woman beside him keeps him from it. *Oh, please let me pet this kitty.* Joe wants to with all his heart. The cat's eyes flicker and it walks to the edge of the pond, sniffing the grass. It chews on it a little and makes a gnawing sound with its head turned sideways.

"Look at that," says the old man across the way. "The cat followed us out here? What in tarnation? I have never. Go on, cat. Shoo! Go on back."

But the cat doesn't listen to him, and Joe is glad. Joe watches as the cat puts a paw on a lily pad and plays with a jumping bug. How sweet. How absolutely wonderful. The cat looks back at Joe just before it puts both paws in the edge of the water, teasing him, and then, simply walks in.

⤋

George

"Do cats swim?" I ask.

"Here, kitty, kitty," says Annie's mama. "Oh, now, come on back here. What'd you do that for?"

"This one sho' does," Isaiah says to me. "I ain't thought cats like to be wet."

"Well, this is no regular cat, sir. This is the Harmony House death-wish cat. The Grim Reaper's henchman. Go on, cat, see if I care. Drown all you want to."

"Mister George," Annie scolds me.

"Maybe it thinks it's a dog," offers Annie's mama, round face honest as she can be.

The little thing has its triangle of a head sticking up on top of the water, ears pointed back, and the lily pads move to the side as it goes through them. "Well, I'll be . . ."

"No . . ." I hear a deep moan. "No, kitty . . ."

I hear a splash and the water ripples, the lily pads rushing over to one side. Miss Annie's mother is screaming a high-pitched something, though I can't understand. I need to pinch myself to see if I'm awake. To see if this is really happening. Old Joe Stackhouse is stumbling down into the water!

"No, Mister Joe! Don't!" screams Annie's mama, reaching for him. "I can't swim!"

I look over at Annie and her eyes are big. Two white

poached eggs. "You can't swim either?" She shakes her head no. "Isaiah?"

"N-no, sir."

"How can you grow up in the Lowcountry and not know how to swim? Oh, dad-blum. Joe. Joe, come on out!" I holler. "The cat is fine, he's swimming—he likes it!" Aw, to heck with it. So this is how I'm gonna go. It won't be from the cancer at all, it'll be from drowning in this dad-blum pond trying to save Old Joe Stackhouse. My heart sinks, but there's some things a man's just got to do.

FORTY-SEVEN

George

It's not so bad. Comfortable, even. My wife is sitting in her wheelchair, eyeing me with interest from the edge of the pond. *It's not that cold in here, dear, and I can touch the ground.* I want to tell her that. I want to tell her, but I don't. I've got to get to Joe. I've got to get him out of the water.

But I can't take my eyes off Maggie. If I didn't know better, I'd say her hands are busy, doing something different. The long skinny silver wand she usually makes has been bent into a perfectly round circle. She watches as I move chest deep into black water. She turns and turns and turns her circle and then finally, a flick of the wrist, she throws it into the water. It lands beside me and disappears.

I can hear Miss Annie and her mama squealing *get 'em out*, and *we can't swim*, and *look what you done*, and this is all happening so fast but so slow.

The dark water around me begins to lighten. It turns nearly white, and then a glow comes up so bright, sort of like sunshine on water. It's all over the pond now. Little shards of light become color, all colors of the rainbow. I am wading in the pool of a prism. I pull my hands up out of the water and nearly fall over when I see them. They aren't old hands anymore, no more age spots or sores—my skin is thick and smooth and my fingers are much smaller, my veins hardly there. I look at my chest. The light shines off of me. It's bare and hairless and puny. "I'm young again!" I yell to the tree-tops. I just can't believe it! I must be dreaming. I look over at Joe who is now doing the backstroke. He spits some water out of his mouth. "Joe? Look at you!" Good heavens, he's a boy! This can't be happening.

I have never been one to subscribe to all that psychological mumbo jumbo you read in books, those near-death experiences people go on about, psychedelic drugs our ignorant youth used to do. But I have to wonder at this moment if I haven't crossed over to some other plane, some other realm as real as the one I've been living in.

I see glowing colors all around me. Our sacred watering hole has come alive. Maybe it's some portal into heaven? Am I dead? Is that what this is? I feel energy coursing through my body, not cancer. I feel youth and vigor and laughter, and I splash and holler, "Come on in, Maggie! Come in! Look at us!" I'm intoxicated. Through beams of light moving, pulsing, I watch as Maggie pulls her legs up in her wheelchair. She pushes and stands fully and I cannot believe my eyes. She is the most beautiful creature I've ever seen—long blond flowing hair, those sparkling blue eyes, creamy white skin with not a blemish on it. She is about seven years old, wearing a white pinafore, showing delicate knees, and she puts her arms up over her head and smiles at me before diving right in.

"Maggie!" I say, holding my arms out to her. To see her this way, alive and moving and young and smiling, it's more than I can bear.

"Maggie," says Joe, giving her his handsome grin.

For a second, I think I might be sick. We are young again, all of us, and she could choose him if she wants to. She could choose Joe Stackhouse over me! My heart is beating in my ears. My world would end. Maggie looks at Joe and grins and giggles. "Isn't this wonderful!" The sound of her voice is sweet Jesus music in my ears.

Maggie's watching me. I must be all goo-goo eyed. She swims to me and gets close, so close. Her hair is darker and slicked back smooth behind her head. There are beads of water on her long, thick eyelashes. She puts her arms around my neck until I can feel her warm breath on me, and she says softly, "You've always been the boy for me, George Jacobs." Oh, to hear her say my name again. To be this close. To see that sweet love shining in her eyes. Her lips on my cheek are a thousand butterflies, and I know I must be in heaven. When she pulls back from me, she says, "The ring, George. You got to give me a ring now."

I remember the silver one she threw in the water, and I search the surface. I can't see underneath, but I smile anyway and hold my breath. I will find that ring for Maggie. I go down and feel the murky softness of the mud floor, the sticks and ancient leaves. I come up empty-handed and take another breath. This time I swim toward the middle and grope blindly. I feel nothing, nothing, until . . .

My hand touches a rope. It's slimy and thin. I grab on and follow the rope deeper and deeper and find it tied around the handle of something large. I swim back up, gripping the rope in my hands, gasping for air.

"Joe, help me with this!" Joe rushes to me in a wave and I hand him part of the rope. We go down together and start pulling. We pull and struggle with this big box and for a second, I imagine we might have found treasure. Real treasure! Right here in Togoodoo Creek. It's not until we get it wedged out onto the edge of the pond that I see what it is. The dark, moldy, leather sides. The silver corners tarnished from years of submersion. Oh no . . .

"What is it?" asks Maggie, still smiling. I know it. I remember it now, but I'm afraid to tell her.

All the beauty and colors grow dark and eerie. Deep evergreens and putrid browns and black. I feel sick to my stomach. A sharp pain rips through the side of my head and all the way down the other, and I see it clearly—oh, God—I see something I've put aside my whole life, tucked inside synapses, wrapped in neurons so deep, it never had a chance to see the light of day. The alligators. I look at my sweet Maggie's face, and oh, it all comes rushing over me.

Did it actually happen? Can it really be? I'm holding the rope and I see my Maggie's innocent face. I don't want to tell her! I'm afraid she won't love me anymore. *God, why did you bring this back to me? My shame for you and all the world to see.*

"George? What is it? Are you all right? Say something."

I remember now.

Forgive me.

I fall to my knees and taste muddy black water, my belated, brackish baptism.

FORTY-EIGHT

Annie

"Mister George! Say somethin'. Anythin'!"

Jesus, help me! Give me something to haul them outta there! Give me a tree branch just long enough or use your angels to fly them up and out, oh dear God, just help me!

I am scurrying around, looking all over the dirt and pine straw. I grab a branch with pine needles still on it, but it's not long enough. I look over and see Mister Joe with his head and shoulders above the water, have mercy, his hands on either side of him, wading, keeping him upright.

But I don't see Mister George. "Sweet Jesus, help me!" I look at Isaiah and I swanny I'd throttle him if I could. "Get in there and get 'em, Isaiah!"

"But I cain't swim!"

"Boy, you gone swim today! Let me get my hands on you!" He runs from me and sets a foot close to the water.

"Okay, okay," he says. "Mister? Mister, come on over here."

"In there! Now! Lawd have mercy! Mister George, he's under the water!" I shriek.

Isaiah takes his sweet time, taking off his shoes and socks, and moseying down into the water. He goes under, all the way, then comes up spitting.

"Do you see him? Oh, get Mister George!"

Isaiah looks around, surprised he ain't drowned. "Don't worry, I can touch." He goes back under. This time he's gone a good long time. My heart's about to pound outta my chest! When he comes back up, there's another head with him. Mister George! I go and reach for him. *Oh, thank you, Lawd!* I get my feet wet and everything and pray Good God won't let me fall right in. Isaiah shoves George up to me and heaves, his face straining, to put him on the edge of the pond.

Mister George is soaking wet and lying in the tall grass. He spits and coughs, and I've never seen anything so lovely in all my life.

"Mister George? You all right? Speak to me!" I'm patting his face and listening to his chest. I can hear his heart beating, fast for him. He doesn't move. I turn his head to the side and reach in his mouth to see if I can pull anything out like I remember from the CPR class, but Mister George comes round and shakes his head back and forth. He opens his pale eyes and looks right through me.

"Did you see us?" he says, almost smiling. "We were young." Then his mouth falls. "She's still in there."

"Who? Who's in there?!" I check to make sure Miss

Magnolia is all right and she is, still sitting there in her chair, watching all this. What must she think? I see Mama, hunched over, straining to keep her eyes on Mister Joe. I hear her holler, "Joe's under! He under! Aw, sweet Jesus, hep that man! Hep him!"

Isaiah rushes back and pinches his nose shut, dips down under the blackness. He comes up, takes another breath, and goes back down. And when he rises again, he has Mister Joe in his arms, Joe's head resting on his shoulder.

"Over here, over here!" Mama screams.

But the more Isaiah tries to pull on Mister Joe, the more they don't move at all.

There's no sign of that trouble cat anywhere, but when I get ahold of him, I swanny . . .

"He stuck!" Isaiah pokes his head under the water one more time and how he can see under there I'll never know, but all of a sudden, he spits out water and says, "He holdin' somethin' in his hand, a rope, hooked on a trunk maybe. Won't let go. Let go, sir! Come on . . ."

"Yes," says Mister George, nodding slightly. "She's in there . . . I'm sorry, so sorry . . ."

I look to him and say, "Mister George, I hear you, baby. Let me help Mister Joe on up out the water, then we gonna find out what's down there, hear? You and me." He closes his eyes and nods and seems to drift off to sleep, right there in my grateful arms.

George

"Mister George? Mister George, honey, you all right? Say somethin'."

I feel wet, hot sunshine on my face and the warm, strong arms of Annie, a pillow beneath my head.

I open my eyes a little and see how bright it is with the sun come out, feel how heavy I am in soaked clothes. I lift my hand slowly to my face and see the sinews and long fingers, the blue veins and thin, mottled skin. I'm old again. Diddly.

There's a colored man sitting a few feet from us on the ground. It's our driver, wrapping Maggie's blanket around Joe. Joe is saying something over and over, mumbling, "Nineteen, fifteen, eighteen, eighteen, twenty-five . . ."

He's old, age dripping off his face, just like me, just like Maggie, and I have to wonder if I was just dreaming we were all young and swimming, but I know I wasn't. I know what happened and I can't explain it. I know what's under that water too now. Something holds me steady. "I'm okay, Annie, I—"

"Shhhhh . . . don't talk. Just rest."

"I thought you wanted me to say something."

"Gracious, you're your old self, ain't you? Whew! Mister George, that was a close one. Don't know what we woulda done if—"

"Nineteen, fifteen, eighteen . . ." says Joe.

"What's he sayin'?" asks Isaiah.

"I don't know," I say. "Haven't a clue. He did this back at the home too."

"Seems upset to me," says Annie's mother.

"'Course he's upset," snaps Annie. "He just come out the water!"

"No," I say. "No, I think it's more than that." Joe's eyes are blue clouds, drifting far away. There's something I have to say. "It's time to get it out in the open, Joe. Don't you think? It's why we had to come down here. I understand now. We had to come back . . . for her."

I take a long, deep breath and begin.

"It was the day Maggie's house burned down, 1929. That morning before it happened. This magician had come to town and brought Joe, here, with him, trying to pass him off as his son. Ash and me, we knew the man was hiding something." I crumple a parched leaf and turn it to dust in my fingers. It falls to the ground. "I'm not sure whose idea it was . . . no, it was my idea, I think, to go to Miss Maple's house and steal her moonshine."

"Who's Miss Maple?" asks Annie.

I look at the freckles across her wide nose. "She was always kind to us. Light-skinned colored woman. Sorta, well, sorta looked like you, Annie. Real name was Mabel, but we called her Miss Maple because of the color of her skin. That, and she was sweet. She was a preacher lady for the colored church. Well respected. Used to help Maggie's family quite a bit."

I try to take a breath, but my lungs are shallow, filling with water. My voice comes out sounding like someone else is saying the words. "The idea was for us to get the moonshine from Miss Maple and then get the man drunk enough that we could—well, whoever's idea it was, it worked. The magician drank it all and passed out cold while we rifled through his trunk . . ."

We all look over to the water, at the edge of the trunk sticking out.

"I don't know how to explain this, but I guess I'd forgotten it or put it all aside, I don't know. It's clear now. There were newspapers in the trunk. They said Maggie's mother had been . . . had known this man, this magician. At least he was posing as one. We knew now he'd come to town because of Mrs. Black, Maggie's mother, we just didn't know why.

"Ash and Maggie were torn up and ran home. Joe and me stayed behind and watched the man sleeping all day through the slats in the boarding room wall. We waited, like Ash told us, so we could come and tell him whenever he woke up. But he woke up madder than spit and then saw that empty mason jar. We watched him pull himself together long enough to ask my mother if there was anyone around who made moonshine. She said Miss Maple was the only moonshiner in town and then told him exactly how to find her."

"So he found her . . ." says Annie, mouth dropped.

I nod and try to take a deep breath. "My God, I haven't thought about this in so many years. I almost didn't believe it happened."

Joe is rocking in Annie's mother's arms, still spouting out his numbers.

"He was furious," I say. "Never seen anything like it. We ran ahead of him. Joe and me, we ran to Miss Maple's house and banged on her door. We tried to tell her she needed to get a gun or run away, but she wouldn't listen. She wouldn't! Said God would protect her from harm, and she almost had me believing it too. But then he came . . ." I close my eyes so I can't see Annie's. "And he struck her. Joe and me, we tried to get him to stop, but he was a devil, right there in front of us. It only took a minute. Then he turned on us."

"Aw, Lawd have mercy, have mercy," Miss Annie is whispering. "Yes, Jesus, have mercy . . ."

Her mother is holding Joe and crying softly, "Shhh, shh, it's okay, baby, okay."

"So de trunk in de watah," says Isaiah, spooked. "Dat dis man trunk?"

"It is."

Annie stops moving. "How'd the trunk get in the water, Mister George? What's in it, them newspapers?"

I stop breathing altogether. "No." I reach over and touch Joe's shoulder. He's shaking. "He made us help him carry it down here. We were just boys, scared to death. All Joe and I could do was pray she was already gone."

FORTY-NINE

George

There are some things I guess we bury so we can get on with living. I don't think it's wrong, necessarily, just what we do to survive. It's the remembering part that's hard. Some people remember and some never have to. The blessed and the cursed. Like Joe and me, here.

We bake in the hot sun and let our clothes begin to dry, water evaporating into the air as if it was never there. I can feel the age spots and basal cells forming under my skin. Joe and I sit on the edge of the pond, legs straight out, ancient and tired from the day. Long gone are the moments we were young in that water, but I remember the feeling. Maggie was there too, I swear it. I know it like I know my name, but I can't explain any of it. She's as dry as can be and doesn't seem to have moved a muscle. Maggie is in her chair, moved into the shade a little so she doesn't burn. I should have brought her hat. It's heating up pretty good out here.

We watch Isaiah and Annie pulling up the trunk, sloshing around in Miss Maple's watery grave, erasing the long mystery of her death. I fight to keep it together. I fight the memories coming at me in clear, loud blasts—the man yelling, his red face, the feel of his hand hitting my head, the weight of the trunk as we carried one end of it all the way down to Togoodoo Creek. The smell of Joe's fear mixed with mine as we panted and cried into the water.

How could I have buried this for so long? What does Joe really know about it? I look at his dopey old face, staring off into the water, and I realize I've been hard on him, been repulsed by him because of that trunk, because of what we had to do. I didn't want to face it and . . . now I'm just glad it's out in the open.

I lie back slowly on the ground and close my eyes against the sun. The backs of my eyelids are scarlet and veiny. My knees are warming up through my damp pants. It's time I told them everything, I guess. It's time I got all this off my chest. I'll be gone soon and no one will have to know, but I know. God knows, and what he chooses to do with me after this, well, he might be more lenient if I just say the words in the open. *Confess, George. Right here. No better place to do it.*

I open my eyes and shield them with my hand. I see Maggie's silver wheels next to me, the cotton of her hair blowing in the breeze, the shade of a tree dancing across her face. "Maggie?"

She doesn't move.

"Maggie, honey, look here."

Slowly she turns. I know she can hear me. What she'll understand, I'll never know. She may not love me after this. Or she may not care. I grab onto the wheel and slowly pull myself up to sitting. Her little blue eyes follow me up. We are two feet from one another. She's staring, not in my eyes, but at my big honker of a nose. My heart pounds in my old chest.

"I know how much you loved Miss Maple. I wish I'd been stronger or bigger somehow. I can't tell you what it was like. Nobody knew what had happened to her. I went on letting everyone think she'd been done unto by black magic. I was too afraid to tell the truth." I close my eyes. "And, Maggie, there's something else. I've always been a coward when it comes to you . . . but I love you, Maggie. Do you know how much?" Maggie puts her hand up to her mouth and starts chewing on her knuckle. She's looking over my shoulder. "Don't do that, honey." I try to move her hand, but it stays. Her tinfoil is gone.

"I can't ask you to love me no matter what. Can't ask you to forgive me." My voice catches. "Do you remember the great fire when we were children in Levy? You remember that big fire that destroyed your house? And how your brother Ash left after that? He left on the train, the Boll Weevil, and he told you he started that fire. He told you he did it." I look down at the trunk, now fully up out of the water, slimy green on the sides, black mud and decay along the bottom.

"I started that fire, Maggie. It was me. I knocked the lantern over when I was running out. I thought it was out, but . . . I promise I didn't know you were in there, I promise . . . but it was me. I've had to live with that all these years." I take a deep breath, fighting back emotion, the words falling to the ground around me. They're real now, solid like rocks. "I let your brother take all the blame. All this time I let you think it was Ash. I was just afraid . . . but I was wrong. I was wrong, Maggie. Can't see how you could ever forgive me—"

"'Course she forgives you."

I look over at Isaiah with his head on his knees, catching his breath. His eyes are closed.

"You say something?"

"I said of course she forgives you."

Isaiah's lips have not moved. I feel it then. Someone behind me.

I turn toward the trees and blink in the light. What I thought was a palmetto trunk is an elderly man, hunched over in brown trousers, suspenders, and a yellow shirt. Nary a hair on his head. He totes a twisted wooden cane. My blood drains.

"I see you folks started without me."

I close my eyes. It's just too much. "It can't be." The words drip and ooze like sap from my mouth.

"Mister George, honey, you all right?" says Miss Annie.

"It's been a long time, hasn't it, friend?" The gravelly voice crawls under my skin and makes me shiver. It's Ash's ghost! But no . . . Ash Black. Is it really him? The years are deceiving—look what they've done! He's old and stooped and . . . my God, I barely recognize him. So this is how we meet, after all these years. Here I am, sitting on the ground soaking wet, trying to hold myself up on shaky arms. Annie's mother comes to my side and helps me stay steady.

"I didn't expect to see you here," I say. "I expected . . . I thought you were—"

"Dead?" The old man locks my stare and inches his cane forward until he's just a few feet away from me. For an instant I imagine he'll strike me with it, and if so, it's how it must be. Yes, it may be exactly what this old reprobate deserves. Go ahead, old friend, let me have it. *I've been eighty years skirting justice. I'm ready as I'll ever be.*

FIFTY

Magnolia

"Maggie."

Someone is calling my name. It's faint, as my hearing isn't all it used to be. I turn but can't see anyone but George. *Hello, dear. What was it you were saying? About a fire? No, I don't think we need one; it's hot enough to dry linens out here.*

"Is it really you?"

I look to my other side and there, standing next to me, is a man, a very old man. It seems all the men around me these days are extremely old. Though very kind. I shouldn't complain. One should never complain about the company of kind men. It's something my mother taught me. She once told me that my father was the kindest man she'd ever met. She had no idea there were such creatures in the world until him. Mama told me how to use my beauty in this world, to use it to my advantage, but she said if I ever found a kind man, to use it for nothing but keeping him.

My George is a keeper.

"My goodness, you're just as beautiful as you ever were. Look at you. Is it really you?"

The man beside me is touching me. I look at the hand on my arm. It's old and gnarled. I follow the arm up to the face and a little closer now, I can see him more clearly. He's got a substantial nose, broader than George's. His face is a little rounder, penetrating eyes. He appears to be fond of me, quite fond, though this is not the look I am accustomed to. This is different. Is he crying?

"It's me, Maggie. It's your brother, Ash. Do you remember me? Do you remember when we were children living in Levy?"

Ash? My brother? I turn to George. *Is there news from Ash? Oh, please tell me he's all right. Please tell him I love him. Tell him I don't blame him a bit for anything and I just hope he'll come home and see me.* Yes, the old man has tears in his eyes. *Don't cry, old man. Is Ash all right? Tell me. Tell me he's happy and healthy. Don't cry, you're making me worry!*

"She doesn't remember," he says.

"She does, I'm sure," says George. "She just doesn't talk much these days."

"No. I can see it in her eyes. Those beautiful eyes. Aren't you still beautiful, my sweet, sweet girl? Oh, Maggie."

The man falters and nearly falls to the ground. My hand reaches for him and grabs him. That's better. He smiles at me and takes my hand in his. I let him hold it, it's the least I can do.

"If I had a penny for all the times I thought of you over these years, I'd be the wealthiest man alive," he says.

What a nice thing to say. *Don't you think it was nice, George?*

"I—well . . . you know, George, in all the times I've dreamed of our reunion, it never played out quite like this. I never once thought she might not even know who I was. I guess I look nothing like I used to. And eighty years is a long time. It's a lot to ask."

"I know it's hard," says George. "I know. Maggie, this is your brother, Ash. You remember Ash? It's been a long, long time. He's come back to see you. He's here, can you believe it?"

Ash is here? Oh, please tell me! Where are you hiding, Ash? Are you playing hide-and-seek again? Are you in one of our secret places? The hollowed-out tree out back, or maybe the attic? You're not hiding in Mama's dressmaker dummy, are you? Because I wouldn't advise it; it's not a safe place. Not safe at all. Oh, maybe he's hiding in that old trunk over there or down near the water . . .

I look beyond the pond and see a woman in a colored skirt and apron. She looks familiar. She's coming closer, closer, and smiling, her teeth glowing. Now all of her glows.

Miss Maggie, she says.

Miss Maple? Where have you been? We looked everywhere for you!

She smiles, and it melts me. The world goes dim around her.

Miss Maggie, open your eyes. Yore brother's back. It's Ash, Maggie. Melt the years away and look down deep. Look in his eyes. You're his life. His every-thin'. Look now.

I turn and stare at the old man holding my hand, and

scales seem to fall away from my eyes. Shackles fall from his body, his face. His eyes are teary and know me through and through. Can it be? *Is it really you, Ash?*

"Ash." The breath escapes my lips.

"Yes, honey, it's me. Oh, Maggie." He's crying now and something drips down my own cheeks.

"Ash."

Yes, it *is* him. Look at him. That chiseled chin, dark brow, scar on his left cheek from taunting Mr. Rachett's Doberman. It's him! My brother, Ash!

I push to get up and nothing is holding me. I'm light as air, floating. He wraps me in his arms, and I am home again. Safe again.

Is it really you? "Ash?"

"I won't ever leave you again, Maggie, I promise, I . . ." Just as he says it, his eyes start to quiver, lines begin to form and then more. Wrinkles take over him, his hair recedes. He's an old man. I fall back into my chair. Of course, he will leave me again. He's old. I'm old. But he's here now.

I close my eyes and thank God for answering my prayers. He's here now. After all these years. Ash has finally come home.

FIFTY-ONE

George

He's holding her. He's crying. I don't know what to do with
myself. I never thought I'd be happy if Ash came back, but I
am so much more. My wife just spoke his name, just spoke
her first word in I don't know how long. She's in there still.
She's not gone. I cover my face and press my eyes. It's almost
too much for me.

Ash has always been like the wood of his namesake tree—
hard, strong, unyielding—but he stands here now, gnarled and
bent, tearful. I can almost see the smoke coming off his skin,
smell the mesquite from long ago. Smells like home. I struggle
not to feel like the kid I used to be, living in the almighty Ash's
shadow. He was tougher than me. Stronger than me. Smarter
than me. The only thing I had going was my parents' store. We

had more money than Ash and Maggie's family, I reckon, but it's never been about money, has it? No. Not where Maggie is concerned.

"Ash," I say. He turns to me and we hold each other's gaze for a second. The words I wanted to say vanish. We don't need to speak. It's all there. I nod and he returns it. Nothing is left unspoken.

I can't watch anymore. A few more moving minutes of reunion with Maggie and then Ash stands tall. "What's in the trunk?" he asks, using his cane to point.

Annie, her mother, and Isaiah look down at their feet and stay quiet.

"Do you remember Miss Maple?" I say.

"'Course I do. She was almost like a mother to us."

I let the silence do my talking for me, but he doesn't seem to get it. "She's in there."

Ash puts his hand up to his face and covers his mouth. I watch his eyelids close as he grips his cane tighter. "What do you mean?"

"Everyone thought she disappeared when you left, Ash. There were rumors about magic . . . she was never found. He came after her."

"Why?"

"The moonshine." Ash looks like he might fall down. "Joe and me, we watched it happen. The man, your father, forced us to carry it down here."

"Don't call him my father." Ash's face squeezes, a sour lemon. "Tell me you're lying."

I am struck with the memory of Ash and Maggie and me,

Nicole Seitz

sitting in this very place at the edge of the watering hole, letting the sun dry us back to normal. How time turns circles.
It makes my body, my mind ache.

"I'm sorry you had to go through that," he says finally. "I
don't know what to say. You just don't know the regret . . ."

Joe is a couple feet away from him, legs straight out,
leaning against a tree stump. His mouth is moving.

Ash clears his throat. "These friends of yours, George?"

"That's Annie, the most wonderful woman on earth, aside
from Maggie. Over there is Annie's mama, and that's Isaiah,
our driver for today. He's got that Gullah bus out there."
Ash waves his hellos, but they keep their distance. They must
understand how personal, how difficult this is.

"Nineteen, fifteen . . . nineteen, fifteen, eighteen, eighteen, twenty-five . . ."

Ash stops and turns to look at Joe. He is quiet and studies him, the way his hands are tugging on the fabric of his
khaki pants, how his eyes flicker out over the water.

"You won't believe who that is, Ash. It's Joe. You remember Joe, don't you?"

"Joe . . . Joe Stackhouse? No. How in the world did Joe
find you?" Ash sounds as if he's accusing me of something.

I shake my head. "I don't know. It's a long story."

"Joe? Friend, is it really you?" Ash stretches his arm
toward him, and Joe watches as if it's a snake and may bite
him. "Nineteen, fifteen . . ." A bug flutters up and hops onto
taller grass.

"Can't figure out what in the world he's saying." I gesture
toward Joe.

"You can't? Well . . . didn't you read the letters my son sent you?"

"Yeah, but not all of them. I still have two or three left to read. Hey, where is your son, anyway?" I look around.

"He got tied up—"

"Nineteen, fifteen . . ."

"Goodness, I'm pretty sure I know what he's saying," says Ash. "He's trying . . . yes. He's trying to say he's sorry."

"Sorry. About Miss Maple?"

"No. Well, maybe."

"How in the world would you know he's saying he's sorry? He's talking numbers, just gibberish." Joe shivers. "Isaiah?" I say. "Be a good man and run on back and get some dry clothes for Joe." Isaiah nods and says, "Yes, sir," before heading back to the cul-de-sac.

"How you doin', Joe?" Joe looks at Ash, warily. Nothing registers.

"He's barely there," I say. "He's the lucky one, I guess. Just lives in oblivion. Doesn't have to remember all this."

"Then I won't be the one to bring it back up for him. Suffice it to say, he's speaking in code. Doing it for survival. He's braver than you'll ever know." Ash pulls back and puts both hands on his cane. He closes his eyes, turns his head toward heaven, then opens his mouth to speak. "You wonder how I know what Joe is saying? Well, I'll tell you. I was there that first day when Joe started speaking in numbers."

FIFTY-TWO

Ash

May 10, 2009

Dear George,

This is some hard stuff. It's time I wrote it all down, got it all out. Here goes.

It was the most awful day in my history and the hardest thing I'd ever had to do—saying good-bye to my parents, saying good-bye to you, George, and Maggie, and knowing I could never come back to Levy. A part of me hardened that day. The world has spent the last eighty years trying to soften me up. And now I'm here, fully pulverized, one foot in the grave.

After the fire, Joe didn't have to come with us, you know. He could have stayed in Levy. Your parents, the Jacobs, offered to take him in. He would have been like a brother to you, George. He would have taken my place. He would have had a family who loved him, a place to call his own, hard work to keep him busy. But instead, he chose to come with us, with me and that terrible, awful, hated man. I need you to understand this, George. I do believe it was Joe's choice.

It's just another thing I've felt guilty for my whole life, though—all the sacrifices that had to be made on my behalf. My family had to let me go because of my blood, because of who my father was. And Joe, he gave up everything for me. And he barely even knew who I was.

It was 1929 in Levy. June third, I'll never forget it. Maggie was screeching for me, I could hear her over the rumble and coughs of the train, and it crushed me. No one could see, but I was crying and hiding down between the seats, wishing all the noise would just stop. I'd just confessed to my little sister that I burned our house down, that I knew she was still in there. I wanted to make her okay with my leaving, glad about it, even. I thought it would be easier that way, but I felt like dying. I've never felt anything so terrible in all my life. When the train door closed, I sat up in my chair and peeked out at the very bottom of the window. I saw townsfolk standing there, handkerchiefs to noses, Maggie being hauled off, some folks turning to leave and others still standing, as shocked as me.

I was looking at you, George. Could you hear me? I was saying, "Take care of her! Take care of Maggie!"

Joe came and put his hand on my shoulder, and I sat there, half-dead, as we left Levy forever.

Where were we headed? We weren't sure. We knew we were going north, so we figured at least North Carolina. The man, my father, smiled at me in a victorious sort of way and rustled my hair. He licked his chops and his mustache quivered. "Now she'll see what it's like to lose a son. Now you'll see what it is to be a real man," he told me. "A boy needs a father to raise him up right. And you," he said to Joe, "well, I don't really give a flick where you go, really, but I figure I'll let you work to pay off my generosity somehow. Where we're going, it's so far away you'll forget there ever was a Levy or a New Orleans. And I'll forget that whore ever came into my life. Tore up a happy home. Yeah . . . who gets the last laugh now?" And then he laughed.

He had to lean over and hold his stomach to get it all out.

Neither one of us dared to ask a question, and when we did talk to one another, he yelled at us to separate. Said together we were trouble, and if either one of us tried anything funny, he'd throw us off the train. Just like that. And we believed him.

"Have you ever r-read 'The Gold Bug' by eh-eh-Edgar Allen Poe?" Joe whispered. I shook my head. He smiled. How he could smile at a time like this, I'll never know, but Joe had that way about him. Resilient. "There's a code in it, a secret code, a c-cryptogram." His eyes lit up. "You use a number in place of a letter. Say, 'A' is 'one,' 'B' is 'two.' 'Cat' would be 'three, one, twenty.' Got it?"

We talked that way for the next couple hours while the magician snored a few seats in front of us. When he woke up, we talked with hand motions, making our secret messages from across the car. We formulated a plan. If we were going so far away, we were bound to have to change trains. So at the next stop, when it was time to board again, we'd run in separate directions. He could only run after one of us, we figured. So one of us would get away scot-free. One of us would have a chance at a normal life.

The Hamlet, North Carolina, passenger depot was grand, much larger than anything in Levy. It was in a new style, Victorian, with all sorts of details around the windows and decorations on the railings. There was a round white roof in the corner that went up to a point like a witch's hat. Seeing it, I knew I wasn't home anymore, nowhere close—the thought of it fueled me like hot coal.

The tracks formed a crossroads in front of the depot. I stood there, listening to the rustle of feet behind me, people rushing here and there with bags in hand, workers wiping sweat from their brows, women in suits, holding children. Not a familiar face to be found. I'd never seen so many people, so many strangers, and my blood quickened. I was getting ready for fight or flight.

Joe and I nodded at each other when the magician shuffled us into the line to board. I could feel the heaviness of his han'd on my neck. It was a yoke, and I felt like I was choking. I looked down the length of one side of the train and then the other. I caught Joe's eyes. He jerked his head to the left a little to let me know which way he'd run when it was time. My heart jumped up into my throat and I swallowed. We were getting closer. Almost at the end of the line.

A man and his wife climbed up on the train right before us, and I'll never forget that lady's smile. She seemed excited to be getting on that train, excited about what lay ahead for her and her husband. I looked over at Joe, and he nodded three times. This was it. Now or never. One . . . two . . . three!

I took off, headed for the front of the train with the depot to my right and the train on my left. I could feel the heat of forty suns in my chest. I could hear the man yelling, cursing, off in the distance and then his voice began to get closer.

He was gaining on me.

I didn't hear cursing anymore, just the sound of my feet hitting the ground and his large and angry boots behind me. I looked up ahead. The train was beginning to roll. If I could just get up there fast enough, I could jump in front and cross to the other side of the tracks, putting the train between us and enough time for me to get away. I picked up speed, but my chest was burning, my throat closing. I could almost hear the sound of his breathing behind me. He was a dragon, breathing fire. I ran like I'd never run before, like alligators were chasing me. I knew I had to zig and zag because alligators can only run straight . . . I had to get to the front of that train and cross it. I was almost there, I was almost . . .

I felt his hand breeze the back of my shirt. His finger snagged it and it slowed me down a little, but I lit up again. He was after me, closer. I was almost in his hands. I couldn't stop to think what he'd do to me when he caught me. I was almost up to the front of the train, but the train was going faster and faster. I wasn't sure I could get there, not sure I could cross in time, but it was my only chance at freedom, my only chance at life, so I had to, I had to. I zigged, leaped headfirst, and seemed to be flying till a force hit my hands, my head, my elbows—and all of a sudden, there was a great commotion like hell had erupted up through the mud flaps of the crusted earth. The train was squealing, brakes were being pulled, the whistle was blowing loud in my ears. There was blood in my mouth and I thought for sure I was dying, but I opened my eyes and saw dirt on my arms, I felt my legs. I lifted my head to see how close my father was behind me, but I didn't see him anymore. He was gone. Instead, I looked over and saw Joe on the other side of the train.

Joe Stackhouse was on his knees, holding his stomach, panting. I saw the raw fear in his eyes, saw the smoke coming up from the train tracks, and then let my head fall back hard on the earth when I realized it was all over. When I realized what had happened. I'd crossed over.

Ash

FIFTY-THREE

George

What has he done? I'm so furious with Ash Black. After all these years apart, we make our peace, and the least he can do is come back home with us. "Look how much it'll mean to Maggie," I said. "She's talking again . . . and Miss Annie can look after you. You can finally be with your sister again, be a family again. Isn't that what you've always wanted?"

But no. Ash said he had his "reasons" for leaving. He's always Ash, isn't he? Always doing things his way. *Dangit, all you had to do was come home with us. I would've welcomed you. I would have!* I wipe my eyes. Well, at least we got to say our good-byes. Maybe Maggie won't remember him.

We're on the front porch, rocking in chairs like the old farts we've become. I don't care. I like it out here. I never realized how much I liked it at Harmony House with its crappy Jell-O and bingo and old biddies. But I do. I like it here. I like these rocking chairs painted Charleston green, a green so dark it's nearly black. I like the trees dressed in Spanish moss. I like the feel of the September breeze on my fuzzy head.

Joe is beside me. His rocking chair stops and he reaches up and scratches his ear. The Grim Reaper posing as the Harmony House cat is sitting on Joe's lap. He loves that thing. Won't let it out of its sight. The cat was waiting for us on the bus that day in Levy, lying there in Joe's seat as if it'd never gotten off. Strangest thing. What kind of a cat goes swimming, anyway? 'Course if it hadn't, we might not have ended up in the water. I might not have remembered Miss Maple being under there. Might not have been young again with Maggie.

I don't know, maybe the cat's not all that bad. We all gotta go sometime . . .

I still have no idea how much Joe knows or doesn't know about what's going on in the real world. If he knows who I am, who Maggie is. If he remembers Levy or any of it. I'll never know. I'd like to think he's blissfully ignorant. That after what he had to go through—being stolen by that evil man, watching him kill Miss Maple, and then winding up throwing him in front of a train—having to live with that, with those memories all his life, I'd like to think that God has grace enough to let him simply forget at this ripe old age. Otherwise, why let him live it out so long? He's nearly ninety-two.

"Emmet?" I speak up. Emmet's hard of hearing and he's two chairs down on the other side of Joe. "I'm feeling good today. Extra good. How 'bout you try to take my title again,

Shuffleboard King. You up to it? Joe, you can have in on this, too, if you want. I'm feeling hot."

"George," says Emmet, "I don't know what happened when you left here, but you're running circles around me. I can hardly keep up. Maybe you and Joe should go at it."

"Haven't felt this good in years," I exclaim, stretching my arms out and cracking my knuckles. I smile and remember my visit with Doc Casey two weeks ago. Just after we gave Miss Maple a proper burial. He was looking over my latest tests, taking his glasses off and putting them on again. Perplexed.

"So tell me the truth, doc. I can take it. I'm gonna die. Right? I'm gonna die."

"Oh, you'll die, all right, George. I'm sure of it. We all will." He puts the chart down and looks me square in the eyes. "I just don't know if you'll do it from cancer."

"What are you talking about?"

"I can't find a trace. Your blood levels," says Casey, spooked, "they're back to normal. Almost as if your tumor is gone."

"Gone?"

"Gone. Not there anymore. Darndest thing I've ever seen. How are you feeling? Are you feeling good? Any more nausea?"

"Better than ever, doc. Better than ever."

Doc Casey walks to the door, muttering, "Have you been taking any medications?"

"No. None."

"Maybe there's something wrong . . . we'll have to do more tests . . ." He turns back around, grinning. "Say, what did you do exactly when you went down to Levy?"

"Oh, nothing much." I rub my skinny legs with my hands. "Went swimming in the old fishing hole."

He raises his eyebrows. "Some sort of fountain of youth?"

I smile and remember the light. I remember the colors and my sweet Maggie, young and beautiful, the sound of her voice and the way her kiss felt on my cheek. "You could say that," I tell him. "Got kissed by a beautiful girl. Saw an old friend. Went to confession."

"That could do it."

Casey helps me off the crinkly paper and I stand, looking him eye to eye. He puts his hand on my shoulder and his eyebrows dance. "I have seen some things in my practice, George, learned everything there is to know and . . . you defy it all. You may very well be a walking miracle. But I don't want to get your hopes up. Not yet. I want to see you in another two weeks for more tests."

"Aye aye, doc. Say, listen, all this chitchat's been nice, but how 'bout it? Can I go now? Am I free, Casey? I got a life to live, you know, a wife to love on."

"Two weeks, all right? But . . . yeah," he says. "You can go now, friend. Go on home. Get outta here."

FIFTY-FOUR

Annie

It's early in the morning and most everybody's asleep. Sun's
not even up yet.

I use my key to open Mister George's door. It's dark and
cool and smells like Miss Magnolia's powder. I can see her
white hair glowing real faint as she sleeps toward the windows. Mister George is snoring, just barely. I go to him and
put my hand on his shoulder. "Wake up, Mister George," I
whisper. "It's me, Annie. We got to talk."

I turn on the fan in the bathroom so Miss Magnolia can
keep on sleeping while we chat. Mister George stands up shaky
on my arm and I walk him, slow to the game table. I set him
down easy, that beautiful portrait of his younger wife looking
over us.

Mister George rubs his face and folds his skinny arms

across his chest, his thin white T-shirt. "This better be good, Annie. I was having a pretty nice dream."

"Oh really? What about?"

He smiles, but I can barely tell in the darkness.

"It was me and Maggie when we were children. We were playing hide-and-seek by this great big tree. I wanted to impress her, I remember, and I didn't think there was any way I could climb that tree, but I started out and sure enough, up I went. It was the best feeling I can remember. I looked down on everything, on her, and when she called to me, I jumped."

"Lawd have mercy."

"But the best part is, I started flyin'. Swoopin' here and there. And I picked up Maggie and carried her with me."

"Sounds like a real nice dream."

"It was. So what's going on?"

I take a deep breath and pray for the words. I want to tell him so bad about what happened at the pond in Levy. I want to tell him about her, the woman I saw coming from behind the trees. How she looked at me. How she looked *like* me. Her skin was the very same color as mine. I want to tell Mister George how she smiled at me and didn't have to say a word. I just knew. Mama saw her too, but she doesn't like to talk about it. Says the curse is broken now, and that's all there is to it. Nothing more to say. But I can't get over it. Can't get over the fact that my great grandmother is in heaven with the Lord right this minute, smiling on me, watching all this—me, caring for the children she used to know, and leading us to Levy to set their spirits free.

It's what I want to say, but the Lord won't let me speak

it. Maybe Mister George won't be able to handle it. Instead I mutter, "I'm sorry. I know you wanted to pay your respects to Miss Magnolia's brother down there. I just . . . wanted you to know. I'm real sorry things didn't go like you hoped."

I look at Miss Annie and something in the pit of my stomach tells me I knew all along. Didn't I? Miss Annie didn't see him. Ash wasn't there for her. He only came for Maggie, and me, and Joe.

I fumble and reach for the lamp next to the table. I pull one of the chains and it clicks, but Maggie doesn't stir. I pull out a little drawer, push over a deck of cards, and bring up a stack of letters. My fingers shake as I open one and hold it, the truth unfolded, before my eyes.

July 16, 2010

Dear George,

I'm dying. For real this time. My left lung is half-full of fluid and they keep draining it off, but . . . I can feel it. It's not working anymore. Won't be long now.

It's hard to breathe. I hope when death comes, it takes me fast. I wonder what it will be like. Strangely I'm not afraid. But the other strange part is I keep seeing people in my head. People I've affected one way or another. It's too late to do anything about it now, but I wished I'd given it some thought when I was younger. Wished I realized . . .

I have to tell you something, George. I've suffered over the years, for sure, but realize you've suffered too. Imagine, never knowing when I might come home and expose your secret. Imagine, year after year, the closer you get to Maggie, the more life you've built together, to still think somewhere in the back of your mind that I might come home at any time and tell my sister about her husband's shameful truth. How you knocked that lantern over and started that fire. How you kept it from her too. You've suffered all right.

But this is the part where I have to come clean. With everything. You may not ever see this letter, but I got to get it out just the same.

Joe told me about you, George, when we were on the train. I already knew deep down, but he told me about the money you had saved up, about how you loved my sister, how you wanted to marry her someday. It hit me like a fist to the gut, but I knew it was true as soon as he said it. I knew how much you loved her. Even as kids it was obvious.

And I was always mixed about you. I loved you one minute and hated you the next. I knew I'd have to share my sister someday, that I would no longer be enough for her. A brother can only be so much. And there you were with your fancy store and clean clothes, your big double bed and all the food you wanted. You were never hungry. Yet you didn't have enough, did you? You had to have Maggie, the most beautiful thing in my life.

It all came clear to me as I tried to catch my breath that day at the Hamlet depot. My birth father lay before me, mangled on the railroad tracks. There are moments that change you, and that was one of mine. I thought about coming home, but I realized it would never be the same. I wasn't the same, and Maggie would never feel the same about me, no matter what I told her. I could see it in her eyes. Her pretty, sweet blue eyes.

I stayed away because it was my birthright. I was still my father's son. You had inherited my sister, my beauty, and me—I had inherited the ugly stain of darkness in my blood. If you were going to end up with my Maggie, with my charmed small-town life, with nothing better to do than grow watermelons and fresh corn in the Southern sun, I was dang-well sure you were going suffer for it.

And I know you have, George. I just hope you can forgive me. It's hard to forgive myself—I've made a mess of things.

I'm having a hard time breathing. I hope you never have to go through this. How I wish I could have Maggie by my side now. Even you. It would be a lot less lonely. 'Course, I imagine we'll all be reunited one of these days. It's what I look forward to. It is my hope. Imagine, at the end of an old man's life, to still have hope. Maybe I've led a blessed life too.

Always your friend,

Ash

FIFTY-FIVE

George

Got a letter in the mail today. I've been saving it for when I
got outside, sitting in my favorite rocker on the porch, smelling the Lowcountry air all around me. So there now. I lower
myself and get situated. That's better. I turn to my friends.

"Mornin', Emmet. Mornin', Joe."

"Good morning, George," says Emmet. "Nice day, I
tell you. Say, did you hear the one about the two old couples
walking along?"

"Not sure I have."

"Well, the wives were walking in front of the husbands,
and the one old guy tells the other guy about this new restaurant they ate at. 'So what's it called?' The first man
replies, 'Well, this is where you're going to have to help me
out a bit. What's that sweet-smelling flower, you know the
one that comes in all different colors and has thorns?' The

other guy says, 'What? Rose?' 'That's it,' says the fella. 'Say, Rose, honey, what's that restaurant we tried last night?'"

Emmet and I crack up, and Joe smiles, at what, we don't know. Maybe he got it. Maybe so.

I pull out my letter opener, and Emmet watches me tear open the envelope, but he doesn't ask me who it's from. Just minds his own business. He looks off into the trees while I take a deep breath and unfold the paper.

August 27, 2010

Dear Mr. Jacobs,

I'm writing to tell you what has happened since my last letter. I had every intention on coming down a month ago, to scatter Dad's ashes in Levy, but one thing happened after another with work, with my ex-wife . . .

Anyway, it took awhile to get moving again, so I traveled down to South Carolina the following week instead. It took some doing, finding the watering hole Daddy talked about so much, but the man at the general store was helpful and he led me to it. He told me there had been a body found there the weekend prior, and honestly, I wasn't sure how I felt about that. Tracks were everywhere, and the watering hole had been disturbed, I suppose from the investigation into the woman's death. As I stood there, surveying it all, I wondered if I should follow through with what Dad had asked me to do. Did he know this woman? The man said she'd been down there nearly eighty years in an old trunk. I would say that was around the time Dad was still in Levy.

Should I scatter my father's ashes in another's grave? I

wondered. Was the water now tainted? Should I find some other body of water, perhaps the beautiful marshes I passed on the drive to get there?

I bent down at the waterside and closed my eyes. I have to admit, I'm not much of the praying sort of man. I guess I got it from my father. I never saw him utter a word out loud to God, though what happens inside a man, no one really knows. So there I was, bent down, holding Dad's ashes in my hands and praying, when all of a sudden, my face felt hot. I opened my eyes and saw the sun brighter than I've ever seen it, but it didn't hurt my eyes. I watched as the light enveloped the pond and turned all sorts of colors. I was afraid at first, but then I heard something. Voices.

I looked through the mosaic and there, in front of me, as if watching through a crystal ball of some sort, were children playing and splashing in the water. I was so stunned, I couldn't blink my eyes. There were three boys and a pretty little girl with long blond hair. They laughed and swam and I just watched them for a while, transfixed. Then one of the boys rose up from out of the water, standing chest deep. He looked at me, really looked at me as if he could see me too. Mr. Jacobs, I realize all of this sounds crazy, but I tell you, it was my father's eyes looking back at me. My own father, Ash Black, was young and healthy and free, and I cannot explain the peace that washed over me. I've never felt anything like it before or since. It's the strangest thing that's ever happened to me. My ex-wife thinks I'm losing my mind.

It may have been minutes or seconds, I don't know. As soon as it started, it was over, but I know what I saw. Something happened that day. Something I truly can't explain and may never understand. At my feet, lying there in the grass was a shiny ring, perfectly round silver like a wedding band. I know it hadn't been there before. I picked it up and felt it—felt connected, truly connected to my father again. I still have that ring up on the mantel now, and I hold it every now and again and remember.

I scattered Dad's ashes that day over that hidden pond in Levy, and all the sadness I'd been feeling at losing him was cleared away and replaced with . . . something else. Anticipation? I guess I'm writing you this, Mr. Jacobs, because if my father's spirit was there that day, I'm led to believe yours was too. And my Aunt Magnolia's. Perhaps someday we will all be children again in young, strong bodies, with joy and abandon. Can you imagine such a thing? Can you even imagine?

I hold on to this hope. It's getting me through these tough days following Dad's passing. I pray you feel it too. Please give my love to Aunt Magnolia. I would have come up your way when I was in South Carolina, but I was pressed on time and had to get back. One of these days I'll come down specifically to see you two and we can spend some time.

Till then, your nephew,
James T. Black

❦

Magnolia

Time passes slowly these days. When I was raising a child, it flew by too fast. Now I am quite old. I do understand that, though I'm not sure how many years. There is a colored girl who takes care of me here. Her name is Annie, and her skin is the color of maple syrup. I knew a woman once the same color back in Levy. We called her Miss Maple because of her skin. Sometimes I get confused. Sometimes I think Miss Annie is Miss Maple. My eyes are bad, everything's foggy, but I can tell it's Annie by her teeth. Bad teeth, poor girl. That, and she doesn't preach like Miss Maple did. Annie might not be pretty and she may not preach, but she's good. Deep down good. There is light inside her. Light so bright it spills out of her eyes. Sometimes I just look at her and pray for that beautiful light to spill out on me, purge any darkness still in there.

I have learned much from Miss Annie. She works tirelessly with little to no thanks. Yes, my husband, George, thanks her occasionally, but I never do. I can't. I cannot imagine taking care of some old woman like me, her bodily needs, combing her hair, trying to make her beautiful, caring for her like your very own blood—yet this is what Annie does for me. Every day it's another selfless act. Right now she's wheeling me to the garden to get some fresh air.

I once thought, when God took away my voice with that last stroke, and my looks and ability to move around, that he was punishing me, that he was finally done with me, but I can see that by placing Annie in my life, and me in her care, he wasn't finished with me yet. I sit here, day after day, watching the light shine all over Miss Annie. In her arms I learn that there are no conditions when it comes to loving somebody. There's no trickery with her. I have no idea why a scallywag like me might live to be this old, while a sweet child dies somewhere else. But I've learned there is a reason for it. It's a season, like every living thing goes through. I've been planted here so I can soak up rays of sunshine. Even in my chair, from behind my veil, I'm getting closer to the light, closer and closer, and I bask in its warmth, waiting for it to swallow me up one day.

My hands have been busy. They no longer make straight wands for some reason, only round circles, like crowns, or maybe wedding bands. I reach up and place my silver pressed circle just so around the sun and look through it. When I was a child, my brother and I used to play this game where we'd stare at the sun and see who could do it the longest. Wasn't the smartest, I reckon, but we didn't know. There was much I didn't know back then—like never play with matches. Mama told me not to play with them and I never did—I wasn't playing, I promise, but it was just *so dark* in that dressmaker's dummy. And I was scared out of my mind. I had to have some light. I didn't mean for . . .

"Stop starin' at the sun, Maggie. It's stupid. Make you go blind."

My cheeks flush like flames all around. I turn to see a boy standing beside me. It's *him*. My brother. *Oh, Ash.* My hands, having a mind of their own, reach over and give the pressed circle to him. He takes it in his fingers and grins. Look at that. My gift created that smile like magic. Brought him back into my life! These days there seems to be even more magic in my bands of silver than there ever were in my stick-straight wands. I'm not sure what caused the change, but I feel it in my spirit like a rumbling train—oh yes, the magic is even stronger now. It's hot elixir in my soul. It's almost too much. Miss Annie grabs my hand and squeezes, singing:

"Gospel train's a-comin', I hear it just at hand, hear the car wheels rumblin' and rollin' through the land. Get on board little children . . ."

I stare again into the fading sun.

"Get on board little children . . ."

Ash puts his arm around me. *"Fireflies at dusk,"* he says. *"Bet I'll catch more than you."*

My legs and body are heavy and won't move. I can't get out of this chair, but I look him deep in the eyes and move my lips. *"Better watch out. Pretty soon, I'll run faster than you, Ash Black. Just you wait."*

"Yeah, you always could run fast . . . for a girl."

"Get on board little children, there's room for many more."

"Listen. The fire, Ash. I didn't mean to—"

"'Course you didn't, Maggie, it just happened. It was supposed to."

"But you spent so many years away!"

"Well, I'm back now. It's all that matters."

My face may not show it, but my spirit is all smiles inside.

"Bide your time, Maggie," Ash tells me as the wind carries him through my hair. *"I'll stay, and I'll wait, but you're needed here. George, for one, still needs you."*

"But can he see you, like I can?"

"He could, if'n he wanted," says Ash. *"But then again, why would he want to? Look at you."* Ash smiles and places his hands on either side of my face. I'm overcome with the smells of dried rainwater, fresh cut grass, and mud underneath fingernails. It's

like heaven to me. He presses his young lips to my forehead and holds them there a long, long second. Then he whispers, *"Something tells me he only has eyes for you."*

Annie

Mister George is looking our way, so I nod at him and the other men in rocking chairs. I'm sitting out here with Miss Magnolia in the sunshine where she likes it most, where the honeysuckle is sweet on the cool morning breeze. She's a Lowcountry gal through and through, and she don't say it in words, but I can tell this is where she likes to be. She closes her eyes and leans into the light like it might grow her another inch or two.

"Beautiful day, Miss Magnolia," I tell her. "The Lawd done give us a beautiful day." I squeeze her on the shoulder and give her a kiss on top of her soft whiteness, and we rest here in the waving shadows of a hundred-year oak, just a handful more years than Miss Magnolia.

You got to wonder about a woman who names her children after trees. Was she hoping to give them deep roots? Was she hoping they'd be strong and long-suffering like ancient Ash and Magnolia trees might be? I don't know.

I figure old trees give us shade and rest. Sometimes they fall in the forest and take on new lives so we can have a cozy chair or pages in a book. Some, like Miss Magnolia, bask in the sunshine and stay here for another day simply to share their beauty with passersby like me.

I been here at Harmony House 'most eight years now, and I love this job. I'm blessed to have it. I love the people, every last one, like Miss Magnolia here, and Mister George, and Mister Joe, my sweet genius. We're all the family he's got, though an old friend comes to visit every now and again, not like he can remember. I can't understand why some people live so long in this life, sometimes slipped away like him and Miss Magnolia, while others have to watch them go down. I don't rightly know the purpose in all that. But I do know the Lord has a plan for it. Look at what he done with us. He strung us all together, brought me here to look after Mister George and Miss Magnolia, Mister Joe even.

I get shaken sometimes. I remember pulling that trunk from the water, remember setting a pretty white casket under the ground at the Levy church where my great grandmama used to preach. No one in their right mind could have guessed how these old folks could all be so connected. When I think back on it, it gives me chills, all the stars that had to line up just right to bring them back together again. I know in my bones my great gran had something to do with it. Her long-ago prayers for those children she loved helped to order my steps, now, didn't they?

I wonder if our ancestors urge us through this life. I 'spect my call into the field of nursing was to right a wrong done long ago. Amazing, I played some part in laying her to rest, in breaking the curse of our family, that there might still be hope for me after all. Some families are cursed, it's logical, biblical, but it only takes one to break it. One folk who just won't have it no more. Why, look here at Miss Magnolia.

See how long she's been here, quiet, just to bring things full circle for the menfolk in her life? And even me?

Her sweet face blossoms in the sun, and her branches twist and twitch in the warming breeze. Even though she can't speak, every now and again I feel the spirit inside her come alive, like a dancing child. She touches me. Some may doubt what she understands at this stage, but there are blessings and curses with understanding, so it's fine by me, whatever the Good Lord decides.

"We've been privy to a miracle of sorts. Don't you think, Miss Magnolia? All of us here at Harmony House." She opens her pale blue eyes, and it's either the light or I think I see somebody in there, looking back at me. I smile for the both of us. "Oh yes. We've seen miracles. You just got to know what you're lookin' for." I wave at Mister George and he sends it right back. The striped house cat treads soft through the pine straw and comes to sit smack-dab between Miss Magnolia and me. But it don't bother me none. I don't worry no more about her leaving this place. If there's one thing I've learned, it's a body will rise up whenever the Good Lord calls it and not a second any sooner. Not one Southern second.

THE END

The River

And I behold once more
My old familiar haunts; here the blue river,
The same blue wonder that my infant eye
Admired, sage doubting whence the traveller came,—
Whence brought his sunny bubbles ere he washed
The fragrant flag-roots in my father's fields,
And where thereafter in the world he went.
Look, here he is, unaltered, save that now
He hath broke his banks and flooded all the vales
With his redundant waves.
Here is the rock where, yet a simple child,
I caught with bended pin my earliest fish,
Much triumphing,—and these the fields
Over whose flowers I chased the butterfly,
A blooming hunter of a fairy fine.
And hark! where overhead the ancient crows
Hold their sour conversation in the sky:—
These are the same, but I am not the same,
But wiser than I was, and wise enough
Not to regret the changes, tho' they cost
Me many a sigh. Oh, call not Nature dumb;
These trees and stones are audible to me,
These idle flowers, that tremble in the wind,
I understand their faery syllables,
And all their sad significance. The wind,
That rustles down the well-known forest road—
It hath a sound more eloquent than speech.

The stream, the trees, the grass, the sighing wind,
All of them utter sounds of 'monishment
And grave parental love.
They are not of our race, they seem to say,
And yet have knowledge of our moral race,
And somewhat of majestic sympathy,
Something of pity for the puny clay,
That holds and boasts the immeasurable mind.
I feel as I were welcome to these trees
After long months of weary wandering,
Acknowledged by their hospitable boughs;
They know me as their son, for side by side,
They were coeval with my ancestors,
Adorned with them my country's primitive times,
And soon may give my dust their funeral shade.

—Ralph Waldo Emerson, June 1827

Acknowledgments

For many reasons, it seems that each book I write becomes more difficult, whether the subject matter hits close to home or perhaps I know more about writing itself. *The Inheritance of Beauty* was two years in the making, and I can't express the joy and gratitude I have for those who helped it become a reality. First, thanks be to God who gave his only son, Jesus, so we might live abundantly, who gives me words to share, and weaves my life and art into a beautiful tapestry. I trust you with my life and thank you, Lord, for your patience and nudging to grow as a writer, artist, teacher, mother, and person in general.

Now to Thomas Nelson who did not give up on me, even when it looked like I was climbing the impossible mountain that was this manuscript. I appreciate your generous spirit, your prayers and encouragement, and your patience to work with me and make sure we got it right. To Amanda Bostic and Rachelle Gardner, my amazing editors, you two rock. We've had quite a journey already together, haven't we? To all the others on the Thomas Nelson fiction team who've made this book possible and touched it along the way—Allen Arnold, Becky Monds, Eric Mullett, Ami McConnell, Natalie Hanemann, Andrea Lucado, Ashley Schneider, Katie Bond,

Acknowledgments

Heather Cadenhead, and Kristen Vasgaard—God bless you all. I appreciate all that you do.

There are some folks who have gone above and beyond for me and my little ol' books in the past couple years—Jonathan Sanchez at Blue Bicycle Books in Charleston, SC, Jacquie Lee of Books-a-Million who is determined to get *The Spirit of Sweetgrass* turned into a movie, and the countless other booksellers in the Southeast I've been blessed to come visit in person. Also thanks to Kathy Patrick and the Pulpwood Queens, Phyllis Sippel and the Sun City crew, and my amazing readers. My books would not move if it weren't for passionate people like yourselves who get behind them and make sure they get into the right hands.

Lastly, to my sweet family who puts up with my itching to write, deadlines, travel, and all that comes with this life of being an author—to you, Brian, Olivia, and Cole, I say thank you for being alongside me in the trenches. You mean everything to me, and I cherish every single moment we have together. Thank you for understanding that my writing is part of my purpose here on Earth. May I always support you in the same way. To my mother and stepfather, Miriam and Hollis Lucas, thank you for being not only my parents but my friends. You make life fun for all who know you. Thanks for allowing me to fictionalize only the most important parts of your lives :) For my extended family, the Seitzes, the Furrs, the Bensches, and the Bells, I appreciate your unending support, and I love you all.

God bless all who read this novel. Hope it touches you in some good way.

Additional Author Note

All the characters in this novel are fictitious, though certain ones were loosely inspired by real persons or events. Maggie and Ash's mother, Juanita Black, was inspired by the beautiful blond inmate Juanita Weaver, who eloped with a prison guard in November 1920 from Milledgeville State Farm in Georgia. Grateful acknowledgment is made to Eileen Babb McAdams for transcribing headlines from the *Macon Daily Telegraph* and the *Columbus Enquirer-Sun* on the Baldwin County & Milledgeville, Ga. American History & Genealogy Project website. More information can be found at http://www.usgennet.org/usa/ga/county/baldwin/home.html.

My character Joe Stackhouse was given the occupation of the head of SIS code-breaking operations. In real life, the head of SIS was William Frederick Friedman (1891–1969), who was introduced to cryptography as a boy after reading the short story "The Gold Bug" by Edgar Allan Poe.

The town of Levy, South Carolina, is a real place, though greatly fictionalized in this book, both past and present. I once wrote an article for *The Island Packet* about a general store there and the lovely owner, Tillie Fender, who said she felt closer to God while working in her field. Sadly, Harmony House is a fictitious place, though there are many such homes in the Charleston area with spectacular people who've led long, meaningful lives. And oh, what stories they can tell. If you have older people in your life, what a blessing! Be sure to ask them about their lives. In the process, you might find that you learn much more about yourself.

Last, but not least, the Harmony House cat was inspired by real-life Oscar, a nursing home cat in Rhode Island. Now five years old, Oscar has successfully predicted the deaths of over fifty people on the third floor of Steere House's Safe Haven Advanced Care unit. As an "early warning system," Oscar the cat has provided comfort for the dying in their final hours and has even received a "Hospice Champion" award from a local RI hospice and had a book written about him, *Making Rounds with Oscar* by David Dosa MD. Read more about this amazing cat at the Steere House website (www.steerehouse.org/Mediarelations/oscar).

Reading Group Guide

1. Magnolia's thoughts tend to go back to her childhood, yet George only visits his in dreams. Why? Do you know an elderly person who now seems to live in the past, or conversely, one who never speaks of it?

2. Magnolia says, "Magic can either come from one of two places, up above or down below." Discuss the role of magic in this book. What does Maggie make with her hands? Does this change by the end of the book? If so, why?

3. Beauty plays a major role in this novel. Who is or was beautiful? Discuss the difference between inner beauty and outward beauty in these characters. What about the title *The Inheritance of Beauty*? Whose inheritance is it? What comes along with that inheritance, blessing or curse?

4. Miss Annie says, "Some families are cursed, it's logical, biblical, but it only takes one to break it. One folk who just won't have it no more." Have you ever felt you were carrying the burden that comes from a troubled family lineage or from unresolved issues?

5. Does race play a significant role in *The Inheritance of Beauty*? Why or why not?

6. Discuss George and Maggie's love relationship with regard to age and time. Do you think of their love as

being perfected at some point in time or evolving and multifaceted as they age? Do you know a relationship like theirs? Would you want a love relationship like this one?

7. Why did Ash leave Levy? Why did he stay away? Were his reasons valid? Were they noble?

8. No one in this novel is perfect—they each have a mixture of good and bad in them and decisions they've suffered over. Discuss the themes of guilt, grief, and redemption in this novel.

9. In writing this book, the author states that she set out to discover why some people live so long with seemingly little or no quality of life. Do you think she discovered some answers? Did you?

10. Joe's character seems to come in and out of George's, Maggie's, and Ash's lives like a moth to light. How have they each shaped each other's experience? Would their lives have been the same had they not come together? What about if they'd not gone their own separate ways?

11. Why do you think these children must come together again at the end of life? Is this realistic? Do you believe in the supernatural guiding the natural world? Do you believe in miracles?

12. Who is the true hero or heroine in this book? Why?

13. Discuss Harmony House. Is this a place you would want to live? Is Miss Annie someone you would want in your life? In the end of the book, how has Miss Annie's life changed, if at all?

14. Discuss the symbolic role of the Harmony House cat in *The Inheritance of Beauty*.

15. Who set the fire in Levy? Why does this matter?

16. Do you have a special, sacred place from your childhood like Togoodoo Creek? Have you ever been back? If so, how had it—or you—changed? Can one ever really go back home?

"Nicole Seitz joins a long line of distinguished novelists who celebrate the rich culture of the Lowcountry of South Carolina."

—PAT CONROY

"Nicole Seitz joins...Josephine Humphries, Anne Rivers Siddons, Sue Monk Kidd, and Dorothea Benton Frank in her fascination with the Gullah culture. Her character, Essie Mae Laveau Jenkins, is worth the price of admission to *The Spirit of Sweetgrass*."
—PAT CONROY, author of *THE PRINCE OF TIDES*

THE *Spirit* OF *Sweetgrass*

a Novel

NICOLE SEITZ

THOMAS NELSON
Since 1798

For other products and live events,
visit us at: **thomasnelson.com**